CULT OF THE
OBSIDIAN MOON

Also available from Titan Books

Conan: Blood of the Serpent
Conan the Barbarian: The Official Motion Picture Adaptation
Conan: City of the Dead

CULT OF THE
OBSIDIAN MOON

A Black Stone Novel

JAMES LOVEGROVE

TITAN BOOKS

CONAN: Cult of the Obsidian Moon
Print edition ISBN: 9781835411674
E-book edition ISBN: 9781835411896

Published by Titan Books
A division of Titan Publishing Group Ltd
144 Southwark Street, London SE1 0UP
www.titanbooks.com

First edition: November 2024
10 9 8 7 6 5 4 3 2 1

This is a work of fiction. All of the characters, organizations, and events portrayed in this novel are either products of the author's imagination or are used fictitiously. Any resemblance to actual persons, living or dead (except for satirical purposes), is entirely coincidental.

James Lovegrove asserts the moral right to be identified as the author of this work.

Cover illustration: Jeffrey Alan Love

A CIP catalogue record for this title is available from the British Library.

Printed and bound by CPI Group (UK) Ltd, Croydon CR0 4YY.

This book is dedicated to the memory of

Robert Ervin Howard

who dreamed up whole worlds
and peopled them with heroes

THE
HYBORIAN
AGE
· WHEN CONAN ·
· WALKED THE EARTH ·

James Allison
Lost Knob, Texas
August 1935

Halston Knox
Anomalous Adventures
Chicago, Illinois

Dear Mr. Knox,

Enclosed is my latest submission to Anomalous Adventures, for your kind attention. I trust you will, upon reading it, find it suitable for inclusion in "The Monthly Cornucopia of Weirdery and Wonder," to use your magazine's very own slogan.

You'll note that the manuscript, entitled Cult of the Obsidian Moon, is of some considerable size. Indeed, it runs to the length of a novel, and I am well aware that your guidelines stipulate stories should be no more than 20,000 words. Might I suggest you could break the text down into three or four sections and publish it across that many issues in serialized format. There are several places where partitions may be safely made at a chapter's end, in each instance presenting readers with a moment of excitement and uncertainty that will encourage them to come back next month for more.

From my own perspective, this tale feels very… how shall I put it? "Personal" seems too weak a word. There are stories which stem only from the mind, feats of mere imagination reinforced by the thrill of creation and the satisfaction of a work well wrought. I do not denigrate those. Rather, they are the bread and butter of any self-respecting author, including me. But then there are stories which emerge from the heart, the gut, the very essence of oneself. They feel

torn from one's own lifestuff, brought out
into the world bawling and blood-covered like
a newborn baby.

I have, as you know, previously written
short tales based on adventures experienced
by my past incarnations, which you have been
good enough to publish in your periodical.
"The Valley of the Worm" is one such, another
being "Marchers of Valhalla."

You may be minded to think that claiming
these tales are no mere fictions, as I do, is
sheer delusion, perhaps even madness. After
all, what sane man reckons he has lived other
lives and can recall them as though they were
his own memories? (Or I should say what sane
Western man, for a belief in reincarnation is
common among certain peoples of the near and
far Orient.)

Yet I am firmly convinced that I have walked
in other ages, in different guises, throughout
history, going back to the earliest days of
human civilization, when our race was still
in its brutal infancy and the world was a
crude, primordial seed of that which it has
blossomed into. I have been Hialmar, flaxen-
haired denizen of an antediluvian era known
to scholars as the Hyborian Age. I have been
a Viking, name of Niord Worm's-Bane. I have
similarly been a Roman legionary, a Visigoth,
an Ancient Briton, a Crusader, a Tatar, a
samurai, and more besides, every time a warrior
or wild man of some description. I have dreamed
of these bygone existences both while asleep
and in intense, dazzling visions that visit me
during my waking hours and leave me enervated
and reeling, and I do not for one moment doubt
them to be true.

Cult of the Obsidian Moon takes place in the
aforementioned Hyborian Age and features that
past self of mine called Hunwulf, about whom
I hitherto wrote in a story called "The Garden
of Fear."

This Hunwulf, sometimes styling himself "the

Wanderer," belongs to a race of hardy Nordic types, the Æsir. Looming in the foreground in Cult of the Obsidian Moon, too, and indeed occupying greater narrative significance, is a barbarian of remarkable vigor and splendor, namely Conan of Cimmeria, who shares in Hunwulf's escapades.

Both figures, and the deeds they undertake and the challenges they face, came to me during one of those trance states I have referred to. The vision struck me as violently as a hammer blow. In intense, concentrated form, I saw it all unfurl through Hunwulf's eyes, felt everything he felt, suffered everything he suffered. His triumphs were mine, and his agonies likewise. I, as it were, remembered the whole account from beginning to end, as I might remember an episode from my youth or young manhood; and no sooner had the vision abated and my mind was once more my own than I sat down at my trusty No. 5 Underwood and began setting events down on paper.

I wrote in a fury of activity, churning out the pages as fast as I could type, all but bruising my fingertips on the keys. I scarcely paused, other than to eat, drink and take snatches of sleep, for ten days straight.

This story, Mr. Knox, is without question the most vivid of any I have produced, and at the same time feels the most freighted with significance, although somehow I cannot quite fathom why. Maybe in due course the answer will come to me.

At any rate, I have prattled on long enough, and doubtless tried your patience. Please let me know at the earliest opportunity whether this offering of mine passes muster and will see print in the hallowed pages of Anomalous Adventures. I eagerly await your response.

Yours faithfully,
James Allison

Thieves of Eruk

Night fell fast in Eruk, dusk drawing its purple shadows swiftly over the domed roofs and spire-capped minarets of that Shemitish desert city and bringing some relief from the stifling heat of daytime. A bright crescent moon rose, beaming down from the star-flecked heavens, but in the mazy streets below, despite the onset of darkness, the bustling flow of people barely subsided.

Eruk, standing at the confluence of several major trading routes, with Koth and Khoraja just to the north, Argos due east and Stygia not far south, welcomed in countless visitors to swell the ranks of its full-time residents. Caravans halted outside its walls, and their drivers, merchants, guards, and sundry dependents and hangers-on found refuge within, to replenish their stocks of food and water and patronize the many taverns, brothels and other sources of comfort and entertainment on offer. Desert nomads called by, seeking respite from their wearying, footsore travels, and itinerants in need of casual employment haunted its marketplaces, touting for work.

It was a city perpetually in flux, the composition of its inhabitants changing from day to day but always a polyglot mix of all races and types; and as torches were lit in its busier quarters and lamps flickered into life in many a window, the widespread urban hubbub persisted. Peace, even at nighttime, was hard to come by in Eruk.

Yet there were certain parts where the streets were less frequented and a relative hush held sway, and one of these was the residential area known locally and colloquially as the Golden Arbor.

The Golden Arbor earned this nickname by simple virtue of playing host to the city's wealthier denizens and being blessed throughout with an abundance of trees, shrubbery and other foliage. Its houses stood spaced well apart from one another, rather than neighbor crowding against neighbor as elsewhere, and were famed for their size and grandeur, the majority arranged in squares around central courtyards whose colonnaded cloisters and splashing marble fountains afforded coolness and shade all day long.

At one of these noble, luxurious residences, two men stood stationary in the spacious, palm-fringed garden.

One of them was a wiry little Nemedian, clad in the fashion of his people: a toga fastened at the waist with a belt of rope, and knee-high leather boots.

The other, a whole head taller than his companion and twice as broad in the chest, had his origins in the far north, in the bleak, mountainous land of Cimmeria. Jerkin, girdle, loincloth and sandals were his attire, all of which items of apparel were somewhat worn and tattered, betokening a certain impoverishment or else a lack of regard for appearance, perhaps both.

The sword he brandished, however, was a long-bladed weapon of fearsome sharpness and gleaming brightness, suggesting great care went into its honing and upkeep. The Nemedian's shorter sword, though no less well-maintained, seemed a paltry thing indeed by comparison.

The twain were rooted to the spot side by side, both staring ahead with wide-eyed fixity at the beast stalking towards them across the garden's lush, shadow-dappled lawn, its footsteps unhurried, its demeanor that of a predator utterly assured of its own powerfulness and its superiority to the humans before it.

The animal was a big cat, but of a kind rarely seen outside its natural habitat, which was the forests of the Pictish Wilderness and the benighted jungles of the Black Kingdoms far to the south. It was, in fact, a species widely believed extinct and considered the stuff of legend, a sabretooth tiger.

Higher at the shoulder and stockier in frame than a common tiger, the sabretooth had a pelt that was a uniform russet-brown rather than striped like its cousin's, while the elongated twin fangs that earned it its name extended a full handspan downwards either side of its bewhiskered maw, culminating in a pair of wickedly sharp points which shone white in the moonlight.

Lambent amber eyes studied the two men as it approached them, assessing just how much of a threat they posed, or by its lights how little. Everything about the sabretooth suggested it was confident it could easily dispose of them—and, for that matter, would relish doing so.

"Drusus," growled the Cimmerian softly to the man beside him, "you never said anything about a tiger. Let alone a sabretooth."

"I... I heard they might keep a guard dog in the grounds of the house," the Nemedian falteringly replied. "But since there was no clamor of barking when we climbed over the wall, I presumed it merely a rumor."

"You could still have mentioned it."

"Forgive me, Conan," said Drusus, with a twinge of chagrin and more than a little timorousness. "If we get out of this alive, I will offer you a fulsome apology and buy you several drinks to make up for my oversight."

"If we get out of this alive…" Conan drawled, his gaze never deviating from the sabretooth tiger, which was now only a few yards away, easy leaping distance for a feline of such proportions.

His muscles tensed, rippling beneath sun-seared, scar-crossed skin. He was gauging when and how the animal would attack. Would it rush them at a sprint, or would it pounce?

He spied a thick leather collar around its neck fitted with a horseshoe-shaped staple, and took this to indicate that the tiger was trained, if not domesticated. The staple allowed the creature to be fastened by a chain during those times it wasn't roaming loose in the garden. It had been taught to deal with unwanted interlopers, and doubtless was given free rein to indulge in its primal hunting instincts when doing so.

The beast came to a halt, setting four huge paws square on the ground.

Conan, who had drawn his sword the moment he espied the tiger emerging from the shadows of a nearby bower, inspiring Drusus to follow suit, readied the weapon. When the sabretooth moved again, he knew he would have but a split second to respond. A fraction too slow, and he would meet a grisly end.

"Drusus," he said under his breath as an idea came to him, "you must edge slowly to the left."

The Nemedian answered in a similar low tone. "Why?"

"Do as I say. I shall edge to the right. But keep your movements steady and even. No sudden lurches."

"We split up," said Drusus, "and then the tiger will have to choose which one of us to attack, thus giving the other the opportunity to get away. Is that your plan? One dies so that the other might live, and it is the tiger's decision which."

"No," Conan replied, although he could not deny that such a prospect had crossed his mind, nor that it was undesirable. Better a fifty-fifty chance at survival than none at all. "Close together as we are, we are a single target. Separated, we are two, and this may give it pause—a pause we can use to our advantage."

"Very well." Drusus did as bidden, tiptoeing carefully sideways, while Conan mirrored him in the opposite direction.

The sabretooth cast its gaze one way then the other, and its expression evinced a certain quizzicality. Its intended prey were behaving curiously. It clearly had expected them to run away, as humans were wont to upon encountering it, not creep apart. It swayed its shaggy, bearlike head towards Conan, then towards Drusus, and back again, weighing its options. Which to kill now, and which later?

Finally the tiger made its pick. Conan saw the sabretooth set its eyes resolutely on Drusus. "Stop!" he hissed to his companion. "Stand your ground. This is our chance."

Drusus shot a panicked look Conan's way. "Stop?"

"Trust me. Face the beast, keep still, and hold its attention."

"While you turn tail and flee?"

"Do as I say, if you would live."

The Nemedian remained unconvinced but obeyed Conan anyway. He froze, his sword held tremblingly forwards. His lip quivered and his face was a mask of abject dread, save for the faint, wavering glint of hope in his eyes, born from a fervent desire to believe the Cimmerian would be as good as his word and serve as savior.

The tiger settled back on its haunches, its claws digging into the lawn for purchase, its whole body coiling like a spring.

Conan took three swift steps until he was alongside the animal's flank. He knew he must time his assault to perfection. If he went too soon, the tiger would round on him instead of going for Drusus.

"Steady," he cautioned the Nemedian. "Steady. Hold."

Drusus offered a clipped nod in return. The tremors of fear that were visibly passing through him, however, were growing more violent, as though he were in the grip of the palsy. His eyes began to dart this way and that, as a desperate man's will when he is seeking an escape route from a dire quandary.

"I said hold," Conan urged, but even as he uttered the words, Drusus's nerve broke. He flung his sword aside, spun on his heel and began to run.

The sabretooth did not hesitate. It launched itself after the Nemedian, hurtling through the air like a bolt loosed from a ballista.

At the same time Conan lunged, darting across the gap between him and the tiger, broadsword lancing forward. With fighting reflexes developed in the harsh terrain of Cimmeria and honed thereafter in innumerable battles, he was as quick off the mark as anyone could be.

Yet Drusus had bolted just when he should not have, and the tiger was no longer where it had been. Conan's blade missed by a hair's breadth.

Next thing he knew, there were frantic screams and the wet, awful sound of flesh being torn.

He pivoted towards the tiger, which now straddled the prone, hapless Drusus, weighing him down with its rear paws and rending his back with its front claws. Drusus writhed and yelled in agony as the beast gouged bloody strips of meat off him.

"Ho, foul thing!" Conan cried, throwing himself at the sabretooth.

His cry drew its notice, as he meant it to, and the tiger abandoned the mauling of Drusus and about-faced to meet the Cimmerian.

Conan's sword thrust was augmented by the speed of his attack, and the blade sank deep into the tiger's breast.

It should have been an instant deathblow, but the sabretooth was evidently hard to kill, for it let out a yowl of distress but at the same time retaliated with a forepaw swipe that caught Conan on the arm and raked a row of parallel slashes across his biceps.

"Crom damn you!" Conan cursed, yanking his sword out of the creature and plunging it in again.

This time he went for the throat, skewering the tiger just below the points of its wickedly curved fangs. As the sword came out, blood jetted from a severed artery, and the sabretooth staggered and went rigid. It drew back its upper lip, its mouth adopting a queer, sneering look, then shook its head, as though, arrogant to the last, it refused to believe that a mere human could have delivered a mortal wound such as this.

Then the beast sagged to the ground, blood spurting from the gash in its neck. The light in its eyes dwindled, and with a series of convulsive spasms the tiger died.

Conan, crimsoned sword in hand, hastened over to Drusus.

The Nemedian lay moaning and shuddering, his entire back a gory, shredded mess. Conan had seen enough injuries in his time to know there was no hope for the fellow. It would be only a matter of moments before he expired.

Sure enough, Drusus fell silent and his pain-wracked body ceased its shaking. A sigh escaped him, which to Conan spoke of soul departing mortal shell. There was nothing more that could be done for him other than to offer up a brief prayer to whichever gods Drusus believed in, entrusting his spirit into their care.

Conan cleaned his sword on the grass, sheathed it in its shagreen scabbard, and took stock. A dead man, a dead guard animal, a nasty set of cuts on his own arm—and naught else to show for the night's handiwork.

With a grimace and a disgruntled oath, he made for the spot on the garden wall where hung the rope Drusus had used to clamber up it on one side and lower himself down on the other. Conan eschewed this as he had before, instead ascending using hands and feet only in the manner of a hillman born and bred, fingers and toes finding holds in the tiniest crevices in the stonework. He climbed down the other side similarly, dropping into the deserted street.

The whole affair had been a waste of time, and for that Drusus bore the bulk—if not the whole—of the responsibility.

The Nemedian had approached Conan the previous day with a proposal which seemed too good to be true and would, as it turned out, be exactly that. Drusus had said he knew of an empty house, home of a very rich merchant, filled to the brim with gold, jewels and other treasures, all ripe for the taking. The merchant, one Sakhimael, routinely decamped to the hills outside Eruk at the height of summer, taking family, servants and slaves with him. He had a villa there, up where the air was fresher and the heat less stifling, with a vineyard and farmland attached, and would stay for at least a month. He had left just last week, and his city home was simply begging to be plundered.

"You are Conan of Cimmeria, lately a pirate of the Black Coast going by the name of Amra," Drusus had said. "I know of your reputation, and I know that you have fallen on lean times. Why not join me in this endeavor? I could do with the assistance of a strong, experienced hand. Sakhimael's house promises more loot than one man alone may carry, and from a couple of hours' work we could find ourselves sitting very pretty indeed. What say you?"

Conan had assented to Drusus's suggestion, not because he felt any great urge to participate in larceny just then, but mainly because he had been looking for something interesting to do, and raiding a rich man's home seemed as good a solution as any to that problem. His life in recent weeks had been directionless, lacking meaning and purpose, a drift from tavern to tavern and lackluster, low-paying job to lackluster, low-paying job.

And his purse was getting perilously empty.

There had been no sign of the sabretooth as he and Drusus, having surmounted the wall, crossed the garden lawn the first time. The great feline must have been loitering somewhere in the dark, biding its time, waiting for the intruders to return so that it could confront them at its leisure.

Entering the house itself had likewise posed no challenge, for the back door was unsecured.

Conan's suspicion that the whole thing was proving a little too straightforward was confirmed as he and Drusus went from room to room inside the property. The place had been cleared out. Furniture remained, and a few personal belongings, but otherwise it was bereft of objects, and certainly of treasure.

"This Sakhimael," Conan said, after they had fruitlessly inspected the house from top to bottom, "does he take all his valuables with him when he goes to his place in the country?"

"I don't know," Drusus admitted. "He goes with a large wagon train, that is for sure, but I assumed it was for people and supplies only."

"Yet here is a shelf where ornaments once were on display. See the marks in the dust? The ornaments have been removed. Same with that alcove, where some form of statuary lay. And unless I am wrong, a strongbox was stored in the cupboard we found upstairs and is there no more. Aye, Sakhimael is a canny sort. He leaves his house in the city unlocked and unprotected when he stays in the country, and that is because he leaves nothing worth stealing on the premises. You have led me on a wild goose chase, Drusus. I am not happy."

"I had no idea," Drusus said. "I assumed—"

Conan cut him off abruptly. "Again that word 'assumed!' A good thief does not assume. A good thief does his homework and makes sure of his information. By Crom, I should have known better than to throw in my lot with you. I've a good mind to bury my poniard in your gut."

Drusus, eyeing the burly barbarian and seeing the grim expression on his face, blanched. "I'd rather you did not."

Conan shrugged. "Why waste the effort? Besides, I am in part to blame, putting my faith in the claims of a stranger. I once met another Nemedian thief, Taurus by name. He was a master of his art. I made the mistake of thinking you, his fellow countryman, were as talented as he. I regret that now. Well, the night is young. There is still time to find a tavern where I can spend my last few coins, drinking to forget our paths ever crossed."

Sullenly Conan exited the house, with Drusus traipsing disconsolately behind.

They had gone no more than a dozen paces when they found themselves confronted by the sabretooth tiger, with the results already recounted.

Now Conan, not one jot richer and minus some blood from the lacerations in his arm, wended his way out of the Golden Arbor, firmly resolved not to set foot in that enclave of the well-to-do ever again.

2

The Difference Between Wench and Woman

The tavern Conan repaired to, the Oasis in a Sandstorm, was one he had taken to frequenting since his arrival in Eruk two months earlier.

It was far from being the city's best-appointed watering hole, and moreover was situated in one of Eruk's shadiest, seediest districts; but the ale was cheap, the atmosphere raucous, and one could reliably depend on a fight breaking out at some stage during the course of the evening. Watching a drunken bar brawl and, should he feel so inclined, joining in, was, in Conan's view, perhaps life's most pleasurable recreation. Unless you counted instigating such a brawl oneself.

In a gloom-hung, musty corner of the tavern, elbows on the table, foaming flagon before him, Conan brooded.

Great were the Cimmerian's moods, whether high or low. When joyous, he was hearty, ribald company, ever ready with a back-slap and a bawdy quip. When melancholy, as now, he cut a glum figure, a human thundercloud, best left alone.

Beneath his square-cut fringe, his piercing, glacially blue eyes stared into the distance. He was musing mournfully on events just gone by: the bootless burglary, Drusus's demise, the altercation with the sabretooth. The wound the tiger had inflicted on his arm, now swathed in a linen bandage, smarted terribly, but this did not bother him overmuch; soon it would heal and become just a few more scars on a body already liberally garlanded with them.

What did bother him was the circumstances he found himself in and how they had come about.

His mind could not help straying back to Bêlit. She of the flashing eyes, richly black hair and slender yet voluptuous figure. She who robbed without compunction, slew without mercy and boasted the fearsome, imperious bearing of a true-born queen. And a queen Bêlit had surely been, if only of her pirate band. A ruler, too, of Conan's heart, in that she had stirred passions within him as torrential as a tempest, as mighty and irresistible as an erupting volcano, before which he could do nothing but submit.

The time he had spent crewing with Bêlit and her brigands aboard the *Tigress*, and serving as her consort and second-in-command, was among the happiest he had known. Life had been plain and untroubled, as suited the deepest needs of a Cimmerian's elemental nature. The future was narrowed down to the ocean horizon, the next raiding party, that night's fierce, fervent lovemaking—these things and naught else.

He had hoped it might last forever, and perhaps it would have, but for the ill-fated expedition up the River Zarkheba, which culminated in destruction and slaughter, not least the death of Bêlit herself, hanged from her own ship's yardarm by a devilish winged monstrosity.

Bêlit came from Shem, and so it was to Shem that Conan took himself in the wake of her death, a kind of pilgrimage to the land of her birth, a way of obliquely honoring his lost love. Here, he thought, among her people, he might perhaps catch glimpses of her, recapturing her through the faces, complexions and accents of her race, and thereby mitigate his grief.

But the opposite, alas, proved the case, and the longer he spent among Shemites, the more he was reminded of Bêlit and the more painful his memories of her became.

He wandered to and fro between the nation's towns and cities, from Asgalun to Akkharia, Shumir to Sabatea, in the forlorn hope that this wretched state of affairs might change and he might achieve some form of ease and contentment. Eventually he fetched up in Eruk, where, increasingly, he had been coming to the conclusion that his time in Shem was at an end and he should move on, journeying to some other land, any, to start anew.

Tonight had done nothing but reaffirm this conviction.

The Oasis in a Sandstorm was full, throbbing with clientele and noise. In one corner a pair of mustachioed Zingarans were arm-wrestling, with various onlookers cheering them on and betting upon the outcome of the contest. In another, some Aquilonians were warbling a filthy drinking song. In yet another, a quartet of very inebriated Turanians—tawny-eyed and goateed to a man—flirted aggressively with a barmaid, who had to slap away their groping paws as she laid their drinks in front of them. An Afghuli and a Kothian were arguing over something, probably a deal, although neither was well-versed in the other's language, so that the dispute was conducted largely by means of angry hand gestures and exaggerated facial expressions. A Corinthian lutanist was employed by the tavernkeeper to provide background music and thereby bring an element of sophistication to the place; it was a vain struggle. He plucked the strings of his instrument listlessly, playing some slow, sweetly plaintive melody that was probably lovely but had not a hope of being heard above the din of voices.

Conan observed the proceedings with detachment, finding little in this cacophonous mundane tumult to lift him from his despondency. He was about to order a fresh flagon of ale with the very last of the copper coins in his possession, when all at once his gaze was caught by a tall and exceedingly lovely woman.

She was Æsir, if he did not miss his guess, blue-eyed and snowy-skinned, of statuesque build, her long golden hair bound in a complicated braid, her features fine and sharp. She strode across the tavern with confident grace, a short leather skirt revealing lean, shapely, well-muscled legs shod in fur boots.

Here, at last, was something to rouse Conan's interest, for not only was the woman remarkably alluring but the presence of an Æsir this far south, even in so cosmopolitan a city as Eruk, was a curiosity. He wondered what had brought her hither from the icy climes of Nordheim. He wondered, too, whether he should attract her attention somehow and invite her to accompany him at his table.

There had been women in his life since Bêlit: a dancing girl here, a courtesan there, on one occasion an actress from a troupe of traveling players; nothing long-lasting. A night's tumble followed by a hasty goodbye, with no regrets on either side.

The Æsir woman, however, seemed an entirely different prospect. She held herself with clear self-possession and intelligence, qualities Conan prized highly in the opposite sex, higher even than a fulsome bosom and curvaceous hips. A fine feminine figure was all very well, but better still when complemented with brains. That was the difference, in his opinion, between wench and woman.

Just as he was about to rise and approach her, the Æsir woman came to the notice of the four Turanians.

As one, the swarthy-complexioned men's heads turned, tracking her progress. As one, their lips drew back in lustful grins. A couple of them nudged each other. Meanwhile the barmaid they had been harassing took advantage of their distraction and skipped smartly away from their table.

"Hey!" one of the Turanians yelled at the Æsir woman in guttural tones. "Northwoman! Over here."

The Æsir woman turned in his direction. "Me?" she said, hand flying to breastbone as though in modest disbelief.

"Yes, you, my pretty! I am Yahsun, and I invite you to come sit with me and my friends."

The other Turanians gave tongue to leering agreement. One gesticulated in an obscene manner.

"Thank you, but no," the Æsir woman said, with an affectation of great politeness. "I appreciate the offer, but apart from anything else there are four of you and I see only four chairs at your table. Where am I to sit?"

Yahsun patted his lap. "Here would be a good place, my blonde beauty. A fine and bountiful place indeed."

The Æsir woman looked puzzled. "I am not small in frame, and you are not large. Would that be comfortable for you?"

"Oh, very much! And for you too, let me assure you. I could make you *very* comfortable."

Conan could tell that the woman was toying with these four sots, even if they themselves couldn't see it. Yahsun stood and made a grab for the Æsir woman's arm. She snatched it out of his reach, but he, undeterred, lurched towards her with a view to taking hold of her and making her do forcibly that which she would not voluntarily.

This time the Æsir woman allowed him to lay a hand upon her. She peered down at the hairy-backed extremity now clutching her elbow, her face showing as much revulsion as though it had been a crawling tarantula.

"Let go of me," she said coolly to Yahsun. Gone was any playfulness from her tone and expression, replaced by disdain and a thinly disguised anger.

Yahsun did not let go. On the contrary, he firmed his grip. "Sit with us," he hissed, "or by Tarim and Erlik, I swear I shall mar that perfect face of yours so that no man will ever look favoringly upon you again."

"No."

"I am Yahsun, son of Arrakhan, a noble of Sultanapur on the shores of the Vilayet Sea—and no one refuses me."

Conan half-rose from his seat.

That was when a hand came to rest on his shoulder and a voice whispered in his ear, "No need, my friend." The accent, with its slurred sibilants and rolled R's, was Æsir, and the pressure of the hand was firm enough to restrain but not threaten. "Gudrun can more than take care of herself."

Conan glanced at the man who had appeared beside him.

The fellow was a match for the woman in looks, being no less pale of skin and flaxen of hair. A broad smile peeked through his beard, which was so long and luxuriant he was able to tie plaits in it. Intricate blue tattoos adorned one cheek, curling up around the eye.

"It would be safer, frankly," the Æsir man continued, "to stay out of her way."

Turning back, Conan saw the Æsir woman—Gudrun—staring down Yahsun, son of Arrakhan, whose hand remained clasped about her elbow.

"Listen to me well, sir," said she. "I shall say this only once. Remove your hand, or lose the use of it, perhaps permanently."

Yahsun, chortling, replied, "For a woman from a cold country, you have plenty of fire. I like that."

"I warned you," Gudrun said, and next instant, Yahsun was on his knees, cradling his wrist and howling in agony.

Conan had scarcely seen her move. In the blink of an eye, and with strength to match that tremendous speed, she had managed to twist the Turanian's hand round through almost a full rotation, practically snapping it off his forearm. It hung limp and useless, and Yahsun's face had gone sallow from shock and pain.

The other three Turanians shot to their feet, making furious remonstrations. One threw himself at the Æsir woman. She ducked under his outstretched arms and sent a solid punch into his midriff. As the breath whooshed out of him, she struck a sidelong hammering blow to his temple, and down he went like a felled oak.

The two remaining Turanians exchanged looks. Then, by mutual accord, each drew a crescent-bladed dagger from beneath his cloak. It seemed the woman must pay with her life for defending herself from their compatriots.

Conan looked again at the Æsir man, seeking his assurance that still no intervention was required. The other nodded comfortingly.

"Why should Gudrun Ingensdóttir be scared of two ale-sodden louts with knives?" said he, as if the notion was too absurd to contemplate.

For certain, Gudrun Ingensdóttir did not look scared. Deftly she snatched up one of the flagons on the Turanians' table and, just as deftly, she cracked it over the head of the nearer of the two assailants. Blood and ale flowed freely as the man's eyes rolled up in their sockets and he sagged to the floor, the dagger slipping from nerveless fingers.

The other knife-wielding Turanian swung his weapon in a sweeping arc that would have slit open Gudrun's throat, had she not leaned nimbly back outside his range.

Before he could bring the dagger round to strike again, she seized his arm double-handed and wrenched it downward and round as though breaking a branch off a tree. The Turanian looked down to find his own dagger sunk deep into his groin, all the way to the hilt. He gasped in dismay as blood gushed out, darkening the front of his silken breeks, and try though he might to stem the flow with both hands, it was hopeless.

He slumped into the nearest chair and began to weep as his life ebbed away before his very eyes. His head nodded forwards, chin settling on collarbone, and soon his face slackened, his mouth fell open and his eyelids closed, and he was gone.

In all, the fight had lasted less than a minute, and Gudrun, having rendered the four Turanians either unconscious, incapacitated or dead, was hardly even out of breath. Around her, the Oasis in a Sandstorm had fallen quiet, all eyes fixed on the scene of violence and its aftermath.

During this lull the Corinthian lutanist spied his opportunity and struck up a new tune, with the thought that now at least his audience might hear his efforts. He managed only a few notes when, unfortunately for him, a great gale of laughter broke out among the customers as they showed their unanimous, full-throated appreciation for the manner in which Gudrun had dealt with the Turanians. Huzzahs and cheers resounded deafeningly to the roof beams, for if there was anything the clientele of this particular tavern enjoyed, it was a fight well conducted and convincingly won.

Gudrun offered her congratulators a wry curtsey, and it was at that moment that Yahsun slipped his good hand inside his cloak and out came another of those crescent-bladed daggers.

The act was unseen by all—all save Conan, whose keen eyes spied the glint of lamplight reflecting off the blade and the surreptitious raising of the weapon by the crippled but still physically capable Turanian.

He did not pause. His poniard whipped from his girdle and flashed across the room like a silver dart. Even as the still-kneeling Yahsun brought his dagger up to stab Gudrun in the thigh, the Cimmerian's overarm pitch found its mark, his knife embedding itself hilt-deep in the other man's eye. Yahsun's other eye registered astonishment, and then he pitched sideways, dying with a long, dwindling gurgle.

There was a moment of startled hush, and then applause erupted again, this time directed at the Cimmerian.

Ignoring the acclaim, Conan went to retrieve his poniard, which he wiped clean on the late Yahsun's cloak, removing all traces of blood, eye jelly and brain matter.

Gudrun favored him with a look of gratitude and followed him as he returned to his table. The Æsir man was waiting for him there, and he, too, looked grateful.

"An amazing throw, by Ymir," he declared, grasping Conan's hand and shaking it hard. "You have my admiration as well as my thanks. I did not even notice the Turanian going for his blade. The sneaky dog! Well, he got what he deserved. And you, Gudrun." He addressed the woman, his voice turning tender. "Let me look at you. You are safe and unhurt?"

"Of course, Hunwulf," she answered with a dismissive wave of the hand. "Don't make a fuss."

"Can I help it? I was not at all concerned during the fight, but after... To think, that cowardly Turanian cur might have laid open your flesh, might even have killed you, were it not for the quick actions of this fellow here."

"I did only what any man might," Conan said. Already, the tavernkeeper was arranging for the spilled blood to be swabbed from the floor and the four Turanians, dead and insensate alike, to be dragged from the premises and dumped outside.

"Please, don't be so modest," said the Æsir man, Hunwulf. "You may very well have just saved my wife's life."

"Your wife." Conan nodded to himself. It made sense that the two Æsir were married. They were of the same age as each other— just shy of their thirtieth year if he didn't miss his guess, the age he himself was—and moreover, it would be a strange coincidence for a man and a woman hailing from the same distant country to be here in Eruk together if they were not kindred in some way. He had entertained the vague notion that they might be brother and sister, meaning Gudrun was free to be courted. He now acknowledged, with some sorrow, that that was not on the cards.

"And the absolute least I can do in return," Hunwulf continued, "is buy you a drink. Nay, several drinks."

"That is something," Conan averred, "that only a fool would refuse."

Talk of Winged Monsters and Man-eating Plants

In Hunwulf Ivarson and Gudrun Ingensdóttir, Conan found a pair of doughty drinking companions. Hours passed with the three of them quaffing flagon after flagon together and swapping anecdotes and tales of their exploits.

They compared their experiences as northerners in Shem: how one had to adjust to the relentless searing heat, the dust, and the aridity; how the country's desert vistas and bare rose-red mountains, though beautiful, seemed also the most inhospitable terrain one could imagine, utterly inimical to life; how, above all else, Shem was a far cry from the damp, chilly, often fog-shrouded landscapes that were a northerner's birthright.

The Æsir couple, it transpired, were strangers to their own motherland, having never set foot in snowy Asgard, but rather having been born into a nomadic tribe that had abandoned Nordheim years earlier for the more temperate and fertile regions just to the south in Brythunia and the Border Kingdom.

Conan, in turn, spoke with little nostalgia about rugged, barren Cimmeria, all drab gray skies, rocky hillsides and rain-sodden pine forests, a place he felt little affection for and even less inclination to return to.

"Why are you not with your tribesmen anymore?" he asked the couple at one point in the evening, to which query Hunwulf responded with a wary grimace, as of a man loath to admit a guilty truth.

"I suppose it can do no harm to tell you, Conan," Gudrun said eventually. "You seem trustworthy, and I feel you and we share a kinship as displaced people of the north—not forgetting, too, that I am greatly in your debt. It would be safe to say that Hunwulf and I did not leave our tribe so much as flee. We had no choice. To stay would have been to die."

"How so?"

Husband and wife shared a look, one that contained evident mutual love but also a certain furtiveness. A brief, unvoiced discussion was had in that glance, and an agreement reached.

They then began relating their history, dividing the narration between them, with each occasionally correcting the other on some point of detail or elaborating where elaboration seemed called for.

Although Hunwulf and Gudrun had grown up together, she was actually the daughter of another tribe. She had been found as a lost waif, barely older than a babe, starving and alone in a dark forest, having either wandered away from her own people or been the sole survivor of some massacre about which she had no recollection; Hunwulf's tribe, recognizing that she was of the same race as they, had taken her to their bosom and adopted her as their own. Not knowing who the foundling's father was, they gave her the patronymic Ingensdóttir, "Nobody's Daughter."

She and Hunwulf had grown close in their youth and a flame of ardor had been kindled between them.

However, once Gudrun achieved full womanhood she was promised to another man, Heimdul Leifson, for he, known to all as Heimdul the Strong, was the tribe's mightiest hunter and so deserved to take as his wife her who was by far the most beautiful, bold and accomplished among her peers.

But the burning love Hunwulf harbored for Gudrun—and she for him—could not be snuffed out as easily as that, and one night Hunwulf, overcome by jealous madness and seeing no other solution to their quandary, crept into Heimdul's horse-hide tent as he slept and slew him with his axe.

That same night, Hunwulf and Gudrun stole away under cover of darkness, forsaking the security of tribal life for the unknown. They took flight into the wilderness, and the rest of their people were soon hot on their heels, full of rage and seeking vengeance for Hunwulf's brutal act of murder.

For a day and a night the eloping couple stayed one step ahead of their pursuers, but the chase was hard and fraught, and in the end they escaped capture only by dint of entering a rising river and swimming across.

It was a desperate and dangerous measure, as they could easily have been swept away to their deaths by the torrent; but then that was the depth of their passion, that was the recklessness their love engendered in them, so great they would risk drowning rather than be denied a life together.

Nor were their travails over when they gained the safety of the opposite bank, for although their fellow tribesmen did not dare cross the river and gave up the pursuit, Hunwulf and Gudrun had to endure endless hardship and deprivation over the next few weeks as they roamed the unfamiliar territory they found themselves in. They were assailed by tigers, leopards and giant condors, and traversed a mountain range of surpassing precipitousness.

By luck, they came upon a village of mud huts nestled among the crags, where they were greeted warmly by the inhabitants, a peaceful lot who took pity on the tired, bedraggled pair and fed them meat, barley-bread and fermented milk.

Although these people did not speak the Æsir language, nor could Hunwulf and Gudrun understand them, it was made clear that the couple were welcome to stay.

There was an accompanying warning, however, imparted through the violent beating of tom-toms and much extravagant shaking of heads and miming. Some menace lay not far from the village, that was the clear import of all this dumbshow, and the Æsir guests must heed it and be on their guard.

Dusk fell. As Hunwulf was doing his best to comprehend what the supposed menace might be, there came a sudden beating of wings and a large, silhouetted shape swooped out of the twilight. He took a heavy blow to the head and was sent sprawling, and next instant heard Gudrun scream.

Staggering to his feet, he saw his lover being borne aloft in the talons of some hideous winged creature, carried away into the gathering night, while all around him the villagers milled about in fright and sought refuge in their huts.

At Hunwulf's behest, the village's headman explained what had happened. By means of images painted in black pigment on a strip of cured hide, he indicated that Gudrun had been abducted by a monstrous winged man, who had stolen away others from the village previously. Hunwulf made it known that he wished to follow the creature and bring his beloved back, at which the headman reluctantly drew a map for him.

Following this crudely drawn chart, Hunwulf traveled to a distant valley at the heart of which stood a tower, some seventy feet high and made of strange green stone. Around its base spread a field of tall, fleshy flowers, which proved to be carnivorous.

Hunwulf watched as an imposing, ebony-black figure, the winged man, emerged onto a parapet at the tower's summit and hurled a body down into these blossoms. Hunwulf had the heart-stopping thought that this was Gudrun, but then to his relief realized it was a man, presumably one of the villagers the winged creature had taken earlier.

He looked on in horror as the flowers writhed frenziedly around the fallen fellow's broken yet still living form. They wreathed him in their petals, dug hollow spines into him, and then, like vegetal vampires, drained him of blood, leaving him a pallid, lifeless husk.

The winged man, spying Hunwulf below, hauled Gudrun out onto the parapet and yelled mockingly at him. She fought in vain against his clutches but did not let out so much as a shriek as the winged man, far larger and stronger than she, lifted her up above his head and threatened to send her to her doom as he had his other victim.

Then, with contemptuous laughter, he dragged her back indoors where, in spite of her strenuous resistance, he thrust her into a windowless inner chamber and locked the door.

Hunwulf racked his brains to work out how he might pass through that field of deadly flowers to reach the tower, until at last he recollected that on his way into the valley he had encountered—and taken pains to avoid—a herd of mammoths.

It was a simple matter to spark a fire in the underbrush with a pair of flints, and the spreading blaze drove the huge, woolly beasts into a panic and sent them stampeding straight into the midst of the lethal blooms. They crushed them beneath their massive feet and thus carved a safe path Hunwulf might follow.

At the foot of the tower, he tossed up a rawhide rope with a loop that caught on the crenellations of the parapet and commenced hauling himself hand over hand to the top.

Just as he neared the parapet, the ebony winged man came out and attempted to cut the rope. The monster's gloating laughter, emanating from a savagely fanged maw, alerted Gudrun to Hunwulf's plight and, with a burst of extra strength born of terror and fury, she broke down the chamber door and charged out, hell-bent on saving her lover.

The winged man wheeled to face her, allowing Hunwulf the opportunity to scramble over the parapet and, with a devastating downward strike of his axe, cleave the monster's head in twain.

Together, reunited, Hunwulf Ivarson and Gudrun Ingensdóttir shinned down the tower and put that dismal place behind them as quickly as they could.

"Mayhap it sounds outlandish to you, preposterous even," Hunwulf said by way of conclusion, "this talk of winged monsters and man-eating plants. All I can tell you is that every word is true, and Gudrun will back me on that."

His wife nodded soberly.

"Outlandish?" Conan said with a shrug. "Hardly. I have met my fair share of such horrors in my time. I have fought a giant spider and a man-ape dressed as a priest. I have spoken with a being who was both elephant and god and more besides, and chased after an ivory-skinned siren who vanished into thin air amid the snows of Vanaheim. I have battled huge, venomous serpents like something out of legend. I have, indeed, faced a winged monster not unlike the one you describe."

Here, as he spoke these words, there was a slight catch in the Cimmerian's voice, for he was referring to the selfsame fiend that killed his cherished Bêlit and her crew.

"It was primate and demon both," he continued, "and it was gripped with a mad lust for slaughter. I ended its foul existence and was glad to."

"As was I in our case," Hunwulf said. "So we have that in common, Conan, we slayers of winged horrors. That makes me like you all the more."

"And I," Gudrun said. "Let us drink to that."

They all three clashed flagons, spilling some of their ale.

"Aye," Hunwulf went on, "there are abominations walking the world which no man should suffer to live. The gods alone know why they were ever created. At any rate, all of this that we have just related occurred nearly a decade ago. Not long after, Gudrun and I plighted our troth. Beneath the night sky, with the moon and stars as our witnesses, we made our vows in a ceremony that was no less solemn and binding for comprising just the two of us. Ever since, we have roamed hither and yon, moving from one place to the next, seldom staying anywhere long."

"Is there a reason for that?"

"There is, Conan of Cimmeria," said Gudrun, "and it is a simple one."

"Your tribe. They trail you still. They have neither forgiven nor forgotten."

"How did you know?"

"It is the northern way," Conan replied matter-of-factly. "It is our nature. A feud, once begun, festers until it is satisfied. It can no more be ignored than a weeping sore can. That goes double for a blood feud. No doubt this Heimdul has close kin who won't rest until his murderer is brought to justice."

"His brother," said Hunwulf, nodding. "Ragnar Leifson, also known as Ragnar the Relentless. Once he was my friend too, as close as a brother to me, but no longer. The last ever words I heard anyone of our tribe say issued from his lips. He shouted at the top of his lungs across the raging torrent that had allowed Gudrun and me to escape. 'You shall die, Hunwulf Ivarson!' he cried. 'You and your whore! No matter where you go, no matter how long it takes, I will find you, and I will make the blood eagle of you both!'"

Conan knew of the blood eagle, the ritual execution method favored by the people of Nordheim: the carving open of the victim's back, the wrenching out of the ribcage to form a pair of "wings," the extraction of the lungs to bring about death by slow suffocation. He was cognizant of most forms of torture and thought himself fairly sanguine in that regard, but even he blanched at the thought of such a gruesome practice.

"Thrice now," Hunwulf said, "Ragnar and his small band of followers have come close to catching up with us—once in Iranistan, once in mountainous Punt, and the third time in Kush. We were always able to get away in time before they found us."

"The one advantage of being displaced Æsir," said Gudrun, "is that outside Nordheim we are an unusual and distinctive sight. Thus when more Æsir are sighted nearby, it is reported to us by the locals, on the assumption that these others and we are kinfolk and would wish to meet."

"It may not be the most reliable system of warning," said her husband, "but it has served us well so far. At the same time, though, our Æsir looks do make us easier to track down. It is the proverbial double-edged sword."

"But ten years," said Conan wonderingly. "Ten years you have been on the run, and ten years this Ragnar has pursued you."

"You sound almost as though you admire him."

"I admire his dedication to his cause, and that of the men he has brought with him. Who would not? It speaks to a strong, determined character. He lives up to his nickname, 'the Relentless.' But admiring a man's actions is not the same as approving of them. I have only just met you two, but you strike me as good people who do not deserve such a vendetta. Or perhaps that is the ale talking."

Conan regarded his empty flagon, the latest of a long line—so many, he had lost count. Possessed of a hard head though he was, he had drunk more than his fill, and his vision was starting to swim.

"On that note," said he, "I shall make my way to bed. Hunwulf Ivarson. Gudrun Ingensdóttir." He shook both their hands. "I thank you for your generosity. May your gods watch over you."

"Yours too, Conan of Cimmeria," said Gudrun.

"Oh, Crom does not watch over me or anyone," Conan answered. "Crom could not care less what I do. That is why I respect him so."

"Perhaps we shall run into you again sometime soon," Hunwulf offered. "We have enjoyed your company this evening."

"Perhaps," Conan said vaguely. "Who knows."

With that, he tottered out of the Oasis in a Sandstorm and wended his way waywardly towards the inn where he was staying. There, he collapsed into his meager cot and was soon fast asleep and snoring like a goat.

4

An Adventurer-in-Waiting

The sun glared blindingly bright through the thin curtains of Conan's room, and the cot he lay on pitched and yawed like a skiff in heavy seas.

It was not until a good hour after waking that he felt capable of standing up, and for a further half hour his stomach churned and his gorge rose every time he moved. He gulped down a gallon of fresh water straight from a pitcher, and doused yet more water over himself. This sobered him up somewhat, but his head still throbbed and seemed to creak whenever he turned it, like a wheel on a rusty axle.

Was the pleasure of an evening's heavy drinking worth the suffering that followed the next morning? Yes.

Downstairs, the innkeeper helpfully reminded Conan that the coming week's payment for his lodgings was due, saying he would like to see some coin by day's end, otherwise he would have no choice but to let the room to someone else.

Conan snarled at the greedy, grasping toad, telling him he would get his damned money when he was good and ready to give it to him, and only then. The innkeeper—a soft, fat fellow—flinched, then nodded gamely, his jowls wobbling.

In truth, Conan had made up his mind to leave Eruk. To that end, he needed a horse, and since he lacked funds of any sort, that meant appropriating one.

There was a stables not far from the inn, towards which he now headed, with a view to browbeating the owner, threatening him at swordpoint if need be, until a steed with full riding tack was his. He would rather have paid fair and square for a horse, and would willingly have done so if the circumstances had been otherwise. Mayhap one day money would be no object for Conan of Cimmeria, but that day was not today.

He had cut down a narrow, zigzagging back alley, and halfway along he spied a lad of about eight or nine, with hair so palely blond it was almost the color of snow. The youth was accompanied by a dog which stood a couple of paces from him, or so the bleary-eyed Conan thought.

It took him a moment or two to realize that the dog did not actually belong to the boy. The opposite, in fact, seemed the case: animal and child were strangers, and the former—some sort of stray cur, judging by the shabby, flea-ridden look of it—was endangering the latter. Its tail was low, its ears were flattened, and its lips were drawn back, exposing two sets of wicked interlocking fangs, while the whites of its eyes showed around the edges and a deep, menacing growl emanated from its throat.

The boy was tall for his age, but the mangy canine was large—large enough that their faces were almost level, and certainly large enough to do the lad a great mischief if it so desired, which it very much seemed to.

For all that, the boy did not appear intimidated. He stood squarely in front of the dog, head up, spine erect. He gave no sign of wanting to flee, or even of cowering. Conan halted, hand going to the hilt of his broadsword, poised to leap in and stave off the dog's attack.

Then the boy started talking to the dog, his voice soft and mellifluous.

Conan could not make out the words but the tone of them was gentle and, to his mind, quite soothing. Certainly they were having a positive effect upon the dog, for its growling diminished and its ears lifted a little.

The more the boy spoke, the less aggressive the animal became. Soon the fangs had disappeared from view and the tail had pricked up. The lad raised a hand towards the dog's muzzle, and Conan wondered whether he might not get it bitten off, because to his way of thinking the canine was not completely subdued and could still lash out.

Yet, the dog sniffed the boy's fingers and next moment wagged its tail. The boy made a gesture, and the dog promptly sat down on its hindquarters. He reached out and patted its head, to which the dog responded like some cossetted, lap-loving pet, closing its eyes and letting its tongue loll out. Its tail wagged ever harder, thumping the earth as though beating a drum.

"Devil take me, lad," Conan said, impressed. "I thought that thing was going to tear you to pieces."

At the sound of his voice, boy and dog turned as one, and the dog sprang bolt upright, immediately resuming its hostile stance.

"Steady, steady," the boy said to it. "There's no need for that. This man means you no harm."

"I wouldn't be so certain," Conan said, preparing to draw his sword.

"Wolfblood here is just frightened. All his life, all he's known is cruelty and abuse from humans. He's been kicked from doorway to doorway. Had things thrown at him. He has learned that it's bite first or be bitten."

"You know this creature?"

"No, we've only just met."

"But you seem to know his history and you have given him a name."

"Yes. Wolfblood."

"Well, he certainly looks as though there is some wolf in him," Conan opined. "Along with a dozen other breeds. Quite the mongrel."

The dog, as though taking offence at the remark, started barking gruffly.

"Wolfblood, shush!" said the boy, and the animal, as though long accustomed to taking instruction from this person, obediently fell silent.

"Tell me, lad," said Conan, bemused, "do you go around making friends with every stray dog you meet?"

"Oh no," came the reply. "Sometimes it's cats, or birds. Once it was a salamander. Another time, a scorpion. Oh, and a crocodile."

Conan's eyebrows rose almost to his fringe. "A crocodile?"

"A young one," said the boy. "It crawled out of a river in Vendhya and it wanted to drag me off the bank and eat me. I told it not to, so it didn't."

"Really?" Conan said with a chuckle. His experience of children was limited but he knew they were apt to fabricate stories—the more incredible the better, as far as they were concerned—if not tell downright lies.

Then again, he had seen with his own eyes how this stripling had placated the dog and made it his ally, so he did not altogether dismiss his statements as mere juvenile fantasy. The boy evidently had a great affinity with animals and a talent for mastering them.

"I should have been cross with the crocodile for trying to make me its dinner," the boy said, "but it was very hungry, so I forgave it. The same with Wolfblood. Not many animals are actually bad. They just live by rules we humans don't always understand."

Conan surveyed the youth and arrived at a conclusion about him. "You are Æsir, are you not? Your looks betoken it."

"My parents are Æsir," the boy replied. "I don't belong to any nation or tribe myself. I am from nowhere and everywhere."

"I would hazard a guess that your father and mother are Hunwulf Ivarson and Gudrun Ingensdóttir."

The boy, a touch surprised, nodded in acknowledgment. "You know them?"

"I met them last night."

"Ah yes. They made a lot of noise when they came home, bumping into furniture and such. It woke me up. I heard them talk about a friend they made at the tavern. You are Conan of Cimmeria."

"At your service."

"They drank with you. A lot. They're feeling a bit unwell today, groaning and moaning."

"They are not alone in that," quoth Conan, rubbing his head.

"They are still in bed," the boy said. "I had to make my own breakfast, and now I've gone out, because I don't have anything better to do."

"What is your name, lad?"

"Bjørn."

"Pleased to meet you, Bjørn Hunwulfson."

"Same to you, Conan of Cimmeria." Bjørn canted his head to one side. "One thing I heard my father mention. He was saying how good you are with a dagger. You threw it at a man who was about to stab my mother and killed him stone dead."

"That is true enow."

"Show me how you did it."

Conan looked askance at the boy.

"My parents have been teaching me how to be a warrior," Bjørn continued. "I can wield a sword pretty well. I'm not so good with bow and arrow, definitely not as good as my mother is, but I'm getting better. And I know how to land a blow." He clenched his fist and punched the air, as though striking some invisible opponent. "See? And also how to take one. But I'd love to see your dagger-throwing and copy it. Please show me."

The Cimmerian shook his head. "I am no tutor. Besides, would your parents approve?"

"Why not?" said Bjørn. "All my life, they've told me I should know how to defend myself. They go on and on about how important it is. Our family has enemies, you see, dangerous men who want to do us harm. So I need to gain all the fighting skills I can. Don't you agree, Wolfblood?"

The dog gazed adoringly up at him—the same dog that mere moments ago had looked set to tear his throat out.

"Well," said Conan, "you are eager to learn, young Bjørn. No question about it. But as I just told you, I am no tutor. Now, I have places to be. It was good meeting you. Give your mother and father my regards."

He made to push past the boy, but Bjørn waylaid him with a hand. "Please," he said with a beseeching look.

Conan brushed him aside. "No."

"Just for an hour or two. I am a quick study."

"No," Conan repeated.

A slyness entered the lad's eyes. "I will tell my parents that you struck me."

The Cimmerian frowned. "What?"

"I'll bash my face against a wall, to raise bruises. Then I'll tell Mother and Father that their new barbarian friend hit me. I didn't do anything to deserve it. He took against me for no good reason and beat me black and blue."

Conan laughed mirthlessly. "Oh ho! That's how it is, is it?"

"Don't think I wouldn't."

"I don't doubt it for a second."

"Well?" Bjørn Hunwulfson said. "Do we have a deal?"

"A deal is no deal when it involves extortion," Conan said. "But," he added with a sigh, "you have me over a barrel. I don't want your parents thinking I am the kind who beats children. Nor do I want them coming after me in anger, for they are a formidable pair." He essayed a reluctant nod. "Very well, you insolent whelp. You have an hour of my time. An hour and no more."

Bjørn clapped his hands with glee. "Thank you, Conan. Where shall we go?"

"I have an idea. This way."

Bjørn addressed the dog. "You can't come with us, Wolfblood, so don't follow. I wish you well. Always beware humans, but remember, not all of us are mean."

Wolfblood whimpered piteously as he watched Conan and Bjørn walk away. Then, facing about, the dog trotted off in the opposite direction.

The foregoing was witnessed by someone on a rooftop overlooking the alley.

This person was clad in a full-length cloak with the kind of voluminous hood that hid the face entirely in shadow. Though manlike, there was something unusual about the figure's shape. Its back seemed larger and bulkier than it ought to be, as if afflicted with a sizeable hump which the cloak's material strained to contain.

Intently the lurking figure had observed Bjørn's interaction with the dog, and then Conan's interaction with Bjørn, unbeknownst to them. In particular the manner in which Bjørn talked to and about the dog had been of great interest, and now, as barbarian and boy exited the alley, the figure nodded to itself approvingly. What it had just seen merited further investigation and reconnaissance.

If its intuition was correct, then the boy was going to be of use. Of great use indeed.

Presently, the Cimmerian and the Æsir boy arrived at the stables that had been Conan's destination all along.

Conan put it to the owner of the stables, a man with little hair and far from the full complement of teeth, that he should permit them to use a corner of the yard for dagger-throwing practice.

The stables owner objected on the grounds that he had a business to run and it hardly gave customers a good impression if there were miscreants tossing knives around on the premises.

Conan grabbed him by the collar and pulled him close, so that their noses were almost touching. He suggested to the fellow that if he wished to keep the few teeth left in his mouth, he should rethink his decision.

The stables owner acknowledged the strength of this argument, coming as it did from a giant of a man with knuckles like wood knots and eyes that blazed pure balefire.

Conan gathered together several bundles of hay and, binding them together with leather thongs, fashioned them into a rough, man-shaped effigy. He rested this upright against a wall, then took out his poniard and gave a few demonstration throws. Each time he announced which part of the figure he was aiming at, and each time he hit it unerringly.

Bjørn marveled at how the dagger flew straight and true and how it thudded into the effigy with a satisfying smack. He begged to have a turn, and Conan let him try, but his initial attempts were not successful. Either the poniard missed its target altogether or struck the effigy hilt-first and bounced off.

"Your grip is wrong," Conan said. "You're cautious holding the blade. Yet when a dagger's handle is heavier than its blade, as with this poniard, hold it by the blade you must. Pinch it with your thumb along the flat of it, like so. That's the way. A dagger so thrown must turn one and a half times in flight. To make sure that happens, bend your wrist. The angle of the bend depends on the range—the farther you have to throw, the straighter your wrist should be. Now to your stance. Dominant leg back, other leg forward. Keep the weight on the back leg, none on the front. Then shift your weight from back to front as you throw, to create momentum. Your arm should be straight and parallel with the ground as you release the dagger, and your body slightly forward of vertical. Have you got all that?"

"I think so," said Bjørn.

"Remember, it isn't about throwing hard, it's about throwing smoothly. The force comes from neatness of action, not from sheer strength."

For the next hour Bjørn hurled the poniard repeatedly. Sometimes it missed, sometimes it fell short, but more and more often he was able to get the weapon to land point-first in the hay effigy.

He worked tirelessly: throwing, scurrying to retrieve the poniard, scurrying back to Conan's side and throwing again. His arm started cramping up, but he kept at it uncomplainingly. He cut his fingers several times on the poniard's edge and blood flowed, but even this did not daunt him.

Conan had to confess to a grudging admiration for the lad. Bjørn applied himself to the task, he paid attention to Conan's advice and tuition, and he strove for perfection.

Another hour passed, without Conan noticing it go by. It was pleasing to see Bjørn's facility with the poniard improve. The effigy was becoming quite ragged from all the intrusions of the dagger. A couple of the stable hands paused from their labors to watch Bjørn's progress, and started cheering the boy whenever he executed a particularly good throw. Their master came out to see what was happening, and even he seemed grudgingly impressed.

Exhaustion at last took its toll and Bjørn could carry on no longer. "I can hardly move my arm anymore, Conan," he gasped, dripping with sweat.

Conan tousled the boy's thatch of snowy hair. "You've done well. Let us call a halt."

"No! Just a few minutes' rest, and then I can start again."

"No, that's enough, Bjørn. *You* may not have anything else to do, but I do." Conan remained firm in his intent to depart from Eruk, and had his eye on a piebald mare he'd earlier seen being re-shod by one of the stable hands. He adjudged the horse to be sturdy and vigorous, and he could not foresee the stables' owner or his employees presenting much opposition were he to mount her boldly and ride her out of the yard, broadsword drawn. He did not think any of them prized his life so low that he would be willing to lose it over a horse.

He decided he would come back later in the day to purloin the mare. To do it in front of Bjørn would hardly be setting a good example to the lad.

As the two of them were leaving the stables, they encountered Gudrun moving with some haste along the crowded street. Her eye fell upon Bjørn and she greeted him with both relief and irritation.

"Where have you been?" she demanded. "Your father and I have been looking all over for you."

"With Conan here," Bjørn replied simply. "The Conan you and Father were talking about last night. The one you both liked so much."

"I can see that, but what have you been up to?"

"Learning how to throw a dagger. Conan has been showing me. I'm not bad at it now, Conan, am I?"

Conan gave Bjørn's mother a sheepish grin.

"Bjørn can be very persuasive," Gudrun allowed, with some feeling. "Sometimes I fear he gets his way too often, which isn't healthy in a nine-year-old. Throwing a dagger, you say,

Bjørn? Well, I suppose you could not have found yourself a better teacher."

"He is good," Conan said. "He has a knack for weaponry. He's persistent, too. You should be proud of him."

"I am." Gudrun clipped Bjørn round the ear, forcefully. "I am also angry with him for wandering off with a complete stranger."

"He wasn't a stranger," Bjørn protested, wincing and rubbing his ear. "He was someone you know."

"And what if he was not Conan of Cimmeria at all?" she rebuked him. "What if he was someone who had seen Conan with your father and me and pretended to be him in order to gain your trust? What if he was luring you away for some nefarious end? What then, boy?"

"Then I'd have killed him and run away."

Conan guffawed. "Say what you will, Gudrun Ingensdóttir, but the lad has spirit."

"I know," was her rueful response. "Mayhap too much of it. How many times have I told you, Bjørn?" she said sternly to her son. "Be careful whom you consort with. Notwithstanding that we have personal foes, everywhere you go there are people who prey upon youths like you, who would harm you in ways you cannot possibly imagine. Do you hear me?"

"Yes, Mother."

"Then, in future, heed me."

"I will, Mother."

Gudrun reinforced the edict with another blow to Bjørn's head. "And as for you, Cimmerian..."

Conan braced himself for vituperation from the Æsir woman. He wondered whether she might too clip him round the ear. He would not have put it past her.

"You are currently short on money," she said. "You said as much last night."

"What of it?" Conan said, taken aback.

"I wish to employ you. Bjørn obviously likes you."

"I do!" the boy exclaimed.

"And I have a strong suspicion," she continued, "that daggers are not the only armaments whose use you are proficient in; and moreover, if your physique is any indication, that you are highly capable when it comes to hand-to-hand combat."

"Aye," Conan said.

"I'd like you to train him. Teach him all that you know."

"Oh, Ymir's bones!" Bjørn cried, thrilled. "Yes, Conan, I should want that very much."

"I would pay you well," Gudrun said. "Name a price, and I will do my best to meet it. What say you, Cimmerian? Do you like the idea?"

"I shall have to think about it."

"Don't think about it," said Bjørn, latching on to Conan's forearm with both hands. "Just say yes."

Conan looked down at the boy, who in turn gazed imploringly up at him. Bjørn Hunwulfson reminded him very much of himself at that age: eager, physically strong, with a thirst to acquire the martial skills needed to survive in a harsh world—an adventurer-in-waiting. And he was being offered money to develop the youngster's talents and help build him into a fighting man.

Really, all said and done, how could he refuse?

5

Fortune's Precipice

"Slash! Swing! Thrust! Parry! Feint! And again! Slash! Swing! Thrust! Parry! Feint!"

The drill went on and on, Conan barking out instructions, Bjørn following them. The boy was practicing with Conan's own broadsword, far too heavy for him but he persevered. He repeated the sequence of strokes countless times until his lungs were heaving and his pale hair was darkened and matted with sweat, sweat also making damp rags of his clothes. Conan allowed him the occasional break to catch his breath and take some water, then had him back on his feet and wielding the blade once more.

"You're making me work very hard," Bjørn said during one of these pauses. He spoke without rancor.

"Life is very hard work," Conan replied plainly. "If you learn anything from these lessons, let it be that. Life will give you no quarter and show you no mercy. You must treat it the same way, as though it is your direst foe. Now, on your feet again, boy, and this time concentrate on your balance. Feet flat on the ground. Remember what I told you about sliding steps. Hips facing your opponent, torso at an angle to him so as to present a narrower target..."

When swordplay was done, they turned to hand-to-hand combat. They were at the stables, as they had been every day for the past ten days, the owner now receiving a small payment for the use of a portion of his property and much preferring this arrangement to the intimidation tactic the Cimmerian barbarian had employed the first time around. Conan had scattered hay liberally across a small area of the yard, which served as an arena for coaching Bjørn in the finer points of close-quarters, unarmed battle.

More often than not this culminated in the Æsir boy lying sprawled and groaning on the ground, having been knocked there, or had his legs swept from under him, or been thrown bodily, with the hay cushioning his fall but only somewhat. Invariably he would get back up and face Conan once more, merely to endure yet another toppling.

A bloodied nose, a split lip, a black eye, grazes, and contusions were the penalties he suffered routinely under his instructor's strict and uncompromising tutelage, and he bore them proudly like medals.

"An adversary will do anything to win a fight," Conan told him. "He will bite, he will scratch, he will kick, he will attempt to crush your male parts. There's nothing noble about combat. Your goal is to end it as swiftly as possible, any way you can, with the least damage to yourself and the most damage to your foe."

He said this after he had sent Bjørn hurtling to the ground for what felt to the boy like the hundredth time in a row and may well have been. Bjørn staggered upright, looking battered and hollowed-out. He ventured a couple of steps towards Conan before collapsing to his knees.

"Just a moment or two," he said wanly, waving a hand, "that's all I need. Then I shall be fit to go again."

"Nay, lad," Conan said, fists on hips. "Today's schooling is at an end. You've done well. It's time to go home and rest, so as to be good and ready for tomorrow's mauling."

"If you say so."

"I do."

Conan reached out a hand to help Bjørn up. Bjørn took it gratefully, but then as he began to rise he suddenly pulled hard on Conan's arm, at the same time hooking a foot around the Cimmerian's ankle. Conan crashed headlong into the hay, with bone-jarring force.

He lay stunned for a split second, before pouncing catlike back to his feet. He rounded on Bjørn, who said, with devilish glint in his eye, "An adversary will stoop to anything to win a fight—including trickery."

Conan burst into gales of laughter. "Well played, you young fiend!" He clapped Bjørn on the back, hard enough to make the boy totter. "I shall have to keep a closer eye on you in future."

"The pupil turns the tables on the master, eh?" This was from Gudrun Ingensdóttir, who had been observing Conan and Bjørn for the last few minutes from across the yard, unnoticed by either of them, for they had been too intent on their business. Hunwulf was with her. "Who would have thought one as tall, broad and mighty as you, Cimmerian, could be humbled by a mere child?" Gudrun added with a sly grin, as she and her husband approached the pair.

"That's how good a teacher I am," Conan replied, removing an errant piece of hay from his hair. "Speaking of which, my latest payment is due."

"Of course," said Hunwulf, and dug into a purse and handed over some silver, which disappeared into a pocket of Conan's jerkin.

The four of them then departed the stables together, Hunwulf tossing a coin to the owner as they passed him.

Out in the street, Gudrun and Bjørn drew ahead, the boy regaling his mother with a breathless account of the day's learnings, while Hunwulf strolled side by side with Conan.

"Every afternoon our son comes home covered in fresh bruises and aching all over," the Æsir man stated, nodding towards Bjørn, "yet giddy with excitement too, saying he cannot wait to begin his lessons anew on the morrow. He has also, incidentally, become a lot blunter in his speech and mannerisms since being around you. Yesterday Gudrun even heard him say, 'By Crom!'"

Conan laughed. "That," he said, "I did not teach him."

"But clearly your habits are rubbing off on him."

"Is that so bad?"

"No," said Hunwulf. "Gudrun and I have done everything we can to ensure that Bjørn is able to look after himself, not least in case we should not be around to protect him. But ever since you have taken on his training, his competence and self-assurance have grown immeasurably, and I can see for myself that he is becoming all the more adept at combat. Life has not been easy for him, what with us as a family having to keep on the move, unable to put down roots for long. He has known little stability and had scant opportunity to make friends. I believe, however, that he has come to look on you as one such."

"I like the lad," Conan vouchsafed, "and like sharing my knowledge with him. But something I must ask, Hunwulf. Whence this prosperity? My salary, the nice boarding house you're staying in—they do not come cheap. Do you come by your money dishonestly? I will not condemn you for it. I have oftentimes thieved for a living and have few scruples on that front. I am simply curious."

"It's no crime to be curious," Hunwulf replied, "and yours is a reasonable enough query. As it happens, rather than just tell you, I am in a position to show you, this very day. If you are interested, meet me tonight at our lodgings, say a couple of hours after sunset?"

Conan arrived at the appointed time, to find Hunwulf and Gudrun awaiting him at the main entrance to the spacious, three-story mudbrick building they shared with two other families, each in their own set of rooms.

"Normally I accompany Hunwulf on these excursions," Gudrun said, "to watch over him and make sure he returns safe and sound. That, Conan, will be your role tonight. Discharge it well, or you'll have me to answer to." There was a smile on her face as she spoke these words but also a note of admonition in her voice.

"*Watch over him*," Conan echoed as he and Hunwulf set off. "Sounds like this could be a hazardous undertaking."

"Not necessarily," the Æsir man replied. "The risks are minimal, but there is a chance I may overtax myself and need a steadying presence on the way home. Besides, Gudrun is over-cautious. She mothers me sometimes as much as she does Bjørn."

They crossed half of Eruk to reach a basement gambling den, entry to which was gained by reciting a certain predetermined phrase—somewhat like an incantation—to the massive Zembabweian guarding the door: "In Ishtar's name, be bountiful. In Bel's name, be wily. In Nergal's name, be ruthless." The Zembabweian nodded his enormous spherical head and stepped aside, directing a look at Conan as the Cimmerian strode by: a glare conveying the clear implication that disorderliness was not welcome at this venue and that Conan, in the Zembabweian's opinion, had the air of a troublemaker. Perhaps it was how the fellow treated all comers, but Conan felt singled out for special scrutiny.

Inside, the air was perfumed, heavy with incense and the smell of hookah pipes. Lamps glowed sulfur-yellow through a haze of fumes to shed light over a large central table around which sat a handful of people.

They belonged to disparate races but were unified by a certain shared demeanor, one which Conan recognized: the hungry, acquisitive look of those in thrall to games of chance.

A man from Khitai was there, sallow-complexioned, pensive-lipped, swathed head-to-toe in patterned silks held together by a jade pendant brooch carved in the semblance of Yun, the Khitan god of the underworld.

Next to him sat a thickset Zamoran whose bushy eyebrows merged at the middle and who was accompanied by a delicately beautiful young man with long fingernails and painted cheeks—his catamite, Conan assumed.

A woman whom Conan reckoned to be Ophirian looked about her with an imperious, no-nonsense gaze, her fingers laden with rings and yet more jewelry dripping extravagantly from her wrists, neck and ears.

A curly-haired Shemite had a jovial grin fixed on his face but it did not extend to his eyes, which were shrewd and calculating.

Various other individuals were ranged throughout the room, some lying athwart cushions, others lounging indolently on couches, all of them with eye-whites pinkened by the hashish they were smoking and the wine they were drinking.

Conan noted, too, a half-dozen men who showed no sign of intoxication; rather, each was standing crisply to attention and maintaining a watchful attitude, viewing the scene as a hovering hawk views a field full of mice below. Bodyguards, he surmised, doubtless brought along by the people at the table to mind their backs and see that fair play was observed.

"Come, Æsir, you are late," snapped the woman from Ophir.

"Only by a small margin," said Hunwulf.

"I despise unpunctuality. It shows disrespect. I hope you are a better dice-thrower than you are a timekeeper."

"You were not here a couple of months ago, Lady Maravina," said the Shemite, "when Hunwulf took me and our two companions here for everything we had. A dice-thrower of some caliber he is. Now then, sit, sit, Hunwulf. We are ready."

"Thank you, Baron Caliphar," Hunwulf said, taking the last seat at the table. "Greetings to you, and to you, too, Chang Hoh, and you, Bazaruun. It's nice to see you all again."

The Zamoran—Bazaruun—inclined his head. "And who is this brawny hulk you have brought with you tonight, Hunwulf?" he said, bestowing a lascivious look upon Conan.

"This is Conan of Cimmeria, a friend."

"Friend, eh?" Tongue-tip flicked over lips, snakelike. "Has he perchance supplanted that redoubtable wife of yours, who came last time?"

"Only as my confederate. Just as you four each have someone to guarantee your security and enforce adherence to the rules"—Hunwulf made a gesture that took in the assorted bodyguards—"so, in place of Gudrun, and for this evening alone, I have Conan."

"A pity your Gudrun is absent," said Caliphar. "I like her. She scares and fascinates me in equal measure, and that I find inordinately exciting."

"Are we playing," hissed Chang Hoh, the Khitan, with a hint of exasperation, "or are we indulging in small talk for the rest of the night?"

"Impatient as always, my Far Eastern friend," said Bazaruun, "but nonetheless I echo the sentiment. I do not pass through Eruk often, and neither do you, while Lady Maravina has traveled all the way from Ophir especially to join us tonight. Getting the four of us together in one place at the same time has required considerable organization, messengers riding constantly to and fro. Let us not waste the effort and expense we have all gone to."

"I have been promised an excellent evening's wagering," said Lady Maravina tersely, "against opponents who are of means and willing to countenance high stakes. I know that three of you here fit that description, but this Æsir stranger looks to me to be neither of those things."

"I admit, milady," said Hunwulf, "I do not present myself as elegantly as the rest of you. I am cruder in my speech and mannerisms, and far from affluent. But I can give you good sport, as these gentlemen will attest, particularly Baron Caliphar, whom I have played against thrice now. Or is it four times?"

The Shemite rolled his eyes. "Indeed. And each time you have cost me dear, northman. Yet, a glutton for punishment, I keep coming back for more."

"Enough!" interjected Chang Hoh. "The dice! Let's get on with it!"

Caliphar produced a set of six ivory dice, their faces engraved with symbols. He handed them to each gambler in turn for inspection.

"Perfectly balanced," he said. "Not weighted at all. Test them if you will. Try a few rolls. See? No fraudulence here. Nothing but plain dealing."

And so the game commenced. The dice were rolled into a flat-bottomed wooden bowl, scooped up and rolled again, with bets being placed on the outcome and play passing clockwise round the table. Coins were stacked, parceled out, won and lost, while the assembled onlookers upon their cushions and couches drowsily followed the action and made side bets among themselves.

Conan sidled to a corner of the room where he had a commanding view of the entire venue and everyone in it. One of the bodyguards looked him up and down and gave a tilt of the head, which the Cimmerian returned. Another seemed to stare straight through him.

The game, known by many names across the world but most commonly Fortune's Precipice, was a matter of pushing your luck. You rolled the six dice and rerolled as many of them as you wished, a maximum of three times in total. Each roll had to yield a better result than the previous, otherwise your turn was over and you forfeited your stake, as did any of the other players who had wagered on an improved combination of symbols; they handed their money over to the successful bidder or bidders at the table or else, if there was none, put it into a pot which was added to the winnings on the next round. The potential valid results on the dice ranged in order from a single pair, through various permutations of matching symbols, all the way up to six of a kind, the last trumped only by all the dice showing different faces.

Conan soon lost interest in the goings-on at the table, beyond registering how remarkably well Hunwulf was doing. Whereas the piles of coins in front of the other players diminished, the Æsir's steadily increased. He was amassing a tidy sum for himself at his rivals' expense, and he had started out with far less than any of them. He seemed to know exactly when to keep rolling and when to stay his hand, and he made sometimes ridiculously risky gambits that paid off.

Conan assumed that either Hunwulf was inordinately lucky or he had developed a system, long sought after by devotees of Fortune's Precipice, which enabled him to calculate the odds to his advantage.

After a good two hours of play, Lady Maravina was losing her cool, as well as her money. Every time another player triumphed, she clucked irritably and cursed under her breath, most of all when it was Hunwulf. For someone high-born, as she so patently was, she resented being outmatched by a relative pauper, and a commoner to boot.

Finally, as she resentfully shoved yet another stack of coins the Æsir's way, her agitation spilled over into outright anger.

"I cannot believe one person can have such luck," she spat. "It is absurd."

"You were warned about him, milady," Baron Caliphar chided wryly. "But does it not add spice to the occasion, having someone so seemingly unbeatable among us?"

"Spice! Bah!" the Ophirian aristocrat snorted. "I did not travel hundreds of miles to be fleeced like this." She pointed a heavily beringed forefinger at Hunwulf. "I say to you, man of the Æsir, that you are cheating."

There was a collective gasp from the spectators, while Bazaruun raised an unhappy eyebrow and Chang Hoh shook his head ruefully.

"Lady Maravina," said Caliphar in a mollifying tone, "you surely do not mean that. It is one of our rules, as we all know, that we refrain from accusations of cheating, for the simple reason that among members of our exclusive gambling coterie, cheating at the table would be beyond the pale. I pray you, apologize to Hunwulf for your intemperate outburst, and let us get on with the game, all forgiven. Who knows, mayhap things are about to change and the dice will start falling your way."

"I shall not apologize," Maravina said stiffly, "nor will I retract my comment. There is no way he can be winning so much except by underhand means."

"But we are all rolling the same dice," Caliphar pointed out. "We all play the same odds. Somehow, Hunwulf is simply better at Fortune's Precipice than the rest of us."

"Perhaps so—unless this is all some elaborate deceit. I know not how he is doing it, but the northerner is swindling us, and I would go so far as to say that you are in on it with him, Baron."

The affable Shemite fought to maintain his composure. "There are some, madam, who would be mortally affronted when spoken to like that."

"You and the Æsir are in cahoots," Lady Maravina insisted. "You have lured me here so that the pair of you can bilk me. Bazaruun, Chang Hoh, I put it to you that Baron Caliphar and

Hunwulf defrauded you the last time you played them, and they are doing so again tonight. All this talk from Caliphar about how the Æsir beat him prior to that—pfah! A lie!"

"But two months ago I saw, with my own eyes, Hunwulf exacting a king's ransom from Caliphar, no less than he did from Chang Hoh and me," Bazaruun said. His catamite, who it seemed had been there too on that occasion, nodded in agreement. "Caliphar laughed it off, but I could tell he was hardly best pleased."

"Hunwulf surely repaid him his money straight afterwards," said Maravina, "and they divided the profits between them. It was all a sham, and you and Bazaruun the butt of it, as the three of us are now this time."

The mounting tension at the table was spreading through the room. The onlookers, roused from their drug-induced torpor, were murmuring excitably among themselves, while the bodyguards were, to a man, straightening their spines and clenching their fists. Conan sensed the place was moments away from lapsing into chaos and perhaps violence.

"An appalling calumny!" Caliphar protested, all his previous good-naturedness falling away. "Lady Maravina, you are behaving outrageously."

"Is it possible?" Chang Hoh said, looking to Bazaruun. "Do you think we could be the victims of a pair of confidence tricksters, not just once but twice now?"

"I don't know," replied the Zamoran. "I should not like it to be true. But now that I think about it, Caliphar and Hunwulf did seem a little too close when we last met, a little too cozy. Perhaps sharp-eyed Lady Maravina has simply spotted something tonight that you and I have failed to. And let us not forget that Caliphar is a moneylender, famed for his usurious rates of interest. Moneylending is a profession not known for its trustworthiness."

"Oh, but a slave trader such as yourself is a paragon of virtue," Caliphar retorted. "Or an owner of gold mines, for that matter, eh, Chang Hoh? One notorious for cutting corners and treating his workers abysmally."

Hunwulf himself had remained silent throughout this increasingly heated exchange. Conan assumed he was just trying to be discreet and not cause further dissent by accidentally saying the wrong thing.

That was until he noticed that the Æsir man had a vague, distracted air about him and seemed oblivious to the adverse turn that events were taking. It was time, the Cimmerian decided, to become involved.

"Hunwulf," said he, stepping towards the table, "let us call it a night. What do you say?"

Hunwulf's head snapped round. "What's that? What is happening?"

Conan took him by the arm. "We should go. Gather up your winnings and bid everyone goodnight."

The bodyguards were on tenterhooks now, and general consternation was breaking out in the room. Baron Caliphar called for calm but was not heeded. Lady Maravina, meanwhile, was shrieking in rage. "Someone stop them! They're trying to get away with their ill-gotten gains!"

Two of the bodyguards converged on Conan. One he sent instantly to sleep with a straight uppercut to the jaw. The other grappled with him, shoving him against the gaming table hard enough to send coins and dice flying.

Conan drove a fist into the man's gut, and then, as he bent double, rammed an elbow upward into his neck. The bodyguard reeled away, choking and spluttering, trying desperately to draw air in through a crushed windpipe.

Conan grabbed Hunwulf and hoisted him bodily from his chair. "We leave!" he growled. "Now!"

He hauled the Æsir towards the doorway. Another of the bodyguards barred his way. This was a wiry, droopy-mustached

Khitan, presumably in Chang Hoh's employ, and he brandished a curved sword not unlike a scimitar, its blade broader at tip than base.

Conan let go of Hunwulf and whipped his broadsword from its scabbard. He drove at the Khitan, pounding down hard with his weapon. The other man managed to deflect the strike, steel clanging against steel, and riposted swiftly. Conan ducked aside, and the Khitan's sword slashed thin air.

The Cimmerian's next swing was devastating, his blade shimmering bluely in a waist-high arc to open up the bodyguard's abdomen. The Khitan sank down, his innards spewing out in a purple-crimson jumble. Conan seized Hunwulf once more and resumed the journey to the door.

Baron Caliphar jumped up and tried to grab hold of the Æsir. "Please, Hunwulf, you must stay. Tell everyone that you are no cheat and that you and I are not colluding together. My good name is in jeopardy."

Conan batted him aside. "Not now, man. Her Ophirian majesty has set the hounds running, and I must wrest Hunwulf from their jaws."

Caliphar backed away miserably while Conan lunged for the exit, towing Hunwulf behind him.

At the door, the enormous Zembabweian blocked their path, all but filling the frame with his bulk. In one hand he bore some sort of war club, whose knotty, fist-sized tip he smacked into the palm of the other hand.

"Move," Conan rumbled at him. "Your club is no match for my sword."

The Zembabweian debated inwardly, then stepped aside.

"The right choice," Conan said, thrusting past him.

With the hue and cry from the gambling den ringing in his ears, and there being a distinct possibility that the remaining bodyguards might be giving chase, he half carried, half dragged

Hunwulf at speed through the still-thronged nighttime labyrinth of Eruk.

He could not think why his Æsir friend was so listless and seemingly apathetic. Had Hunwulf been drinking, this might have made sense, but Conan had not seen him touch a drop of liquor the whole evening; and while one might suppose that success such as Hunwulf had had at the gaming table would have left him invigorated, it clearly had not. If anything, the contrary.

At last Conan was convinced he had given any pursuers the slip. By now Hunwulf was all but insensible, just so much dead weight, mumbling nonsensical words to himself as he stumbled along.

Conan swept him up in both arms and thus, like a parent with an exhausted infant, carried him the rest of the way home.

6

Hunwulf's Myriad of Different Lives

Hunwulf lay in bed, tossing and turning, breathing stertorously as though in a fever. Gudrun sat beside him, caressing his brow and cheek in a vain effort at soothing. Conan stood looking on, arms folded across the bulging expanse of his chest. Bjørn slumbered in an adjoining room.

"I don't understand," said Conan. "Hunwulf was fine for most of the evening, and doing unusually well at the table. Then, at once, he lost all focus. This was around the time one of the other gamblers—that haughty noblewoman from Ophir—accused him of cheating. I got him out before he was torn apart, but during our flight he fell unconscious. Is he prone to fainting spells? Or might he have been drugged somehow?"

"No," said Gudrun. "No, this is something else. There are certain facts about my Hunwulf that I am loath to share with another, and yet I feel, Conan, that I am able to entrust you with them, and that you are owed an explanation." She paused a moment, collecting her thoughts, before continuing. "My husband—how to put this?—is privy to knowledge denied the rest of us. Tell me, do you believe a person may lead other lives before and after the life they currently lead?"

"One life should be enough for any soul. To have more is greedy."

"I thought you might say something like that. You are a most practical sort, Conan."

"I trust in naught save that which is in front of me and which I can grasp with my five senses. All else is illusion, and I have no truck with illusions."

"Nonetheless, whatever your views may be on the subject, Hunwulf knows he has been other men in the past and will be other men in the future. He knows this because he is able to commune with these past and future incarnations."

Conan gave a dubious snort.

"Do not be so quick to dismiss the notion," Gudrun said. "Just listen. From an early age Hunwulf would be afflicted by sudden, unexpected visions in which he experienced events from times gone by and times yet to come, seeing them in his mind's eye as though they were his own memories. Voices would whisper to him unbidden, in languages he did not know but nonetheless could understand. He would receive fleeting glimpses of ages similar enough to ours to be recognizable and likewise ages so alien and unfamiliar as to almost defy comprehension. He would see himself battling enemies of all kinds, some using weapons he could identify easily enough such as swords, spears and axes, others carrying ungainly, exotic armaments—steel crossbows, for instance, that spat small, fiery projectiles and could slay from a great distance, or metal balls that, when thrown, exploded like small volcanoes. Always, always, he seemed to be someone who was born for warfare and conflict, fighting his way through life from cradle to grave. The older he got, the more intense these mental visitations became, and once passed they would leave him dazed and enfeebled, uncertain of his surroundings and the people around him."

"As now."

"Just so. His father Ivar Erikson called it a gift from the gods, but Hunwulf himself was not so sure. His father, I should tell you, was our tribe's shaman, and for all Hunwulf's protestations, he held firm in his view that his son had been divinely exalted. 'It is granted to precious few of us,' Ivar would say to Hunwulf, 'to see beyond the material plane into realms unknown. My boy, you owe it to yourself and all of us to develop this ability of yours.' Hunwulf did his best, and over the years, with his father's aid and encouragement, he managed to gain some control over the visions. It got to the point where he could commune with his incarnations, who might reveal to him forthcoming events in his own life and alert him to potential dangers he might face. This was never an easy or comfortable process, and I daresay he never grew fully accustomed to it."

"Hunwulf uses this access to future knowledge at the gaming table," said Conan.

Gudrun favored him with a smile and a nod. "Well reasoned, Cimmerian, and your supposition is almost correct. What has happened is that, over the years, Hunwulf's grasp of the passage of time has become..." She searched for the right word. "Distorted. You and I perceive time as a straight line, a journey in a single direction like an arrow in flight, from past to present to future. Hunwulf, thanks to his interactions with his myriad of different lives, has evolved a looser, less subjective sense of time's flow. You and I are, as it were, borne along by the river's current, helpless to change that, whereas Hunwulf is able to step out and stand on the bank and view the water coming towards him and moving away from him."

"So he can foresee the outcome of a roll of the dice before they are even thrown."

"Exactly that," said Gudrun Ingensdóttir.

"Little wonder he felt safe making those bold wagers of his."

"You are sounding far less skeptical now, Cimmerian."

"Aye, clairvoyance," Conan allowed. "There are any number of wizards and necromancers who possess such a power. But as for these forebears and successors who supposedly speak with Hunwulf... I say he only imagines them. The gift of second sight is known to addle the mind. Hunwulf's other selves are mere delusions, phantoms of a disordered brain."

"A pretty piece of sophistry," Gudrun said. "Would not the simpler explanation be that my husband has actually lived and will live other lives, and so do we all, but that he is exceptional in as much as he is aware of them and the vast majority of us are not? At any rate, Hunwulf deploys that time-bending talent of his at the gaming table, and it accrues us a tidy sum of money. The main problem is that, by winning consistently, he sooner or later makes himself an unwelcome presence. In Baron Caliphar, for instance, whom you met tonight, Hunwulf found a useful mark, for the man has more money than sense and seems to derive a perverse satisfaction from losing some of it. Yet there is only so much losing someone can take before resentment sets in."

"Were Hunwulf and Caliphar working together?"

"Not at all. Friendship, of a sort, has evolved between the pair of them, but as I said, Caliphar has a streak of self-sabotage in him. He would seem to have deemed Hunwulf a necessary evil, a corrective to the obscene wealth he has accumulated through his moneylending. A kind of self-imposed taxation, if you will. I believe, too, that he had come to regard Hunwulf as a challenge, and looked forward to a day when his luck would turn and he would recoup much—if not all—of the money Hunwulf had taken from him. That, as you can imagine, would be unlikely, and once Caliphar realized it, he would surely have started making life very difficult for us in this city and we would have had to pack up our belongings and go elsewhere. It has happened to us in other places, so why not again here in

Eruk? In fact, it would seem, from what you have told me of the night's events, that Caliphar's tolerance for Hunwulf will now have reached its limit. The baron carries a great deal of influence around these parts, and if Hunwulf has earned his enmity, then all hands, not least those of the authorities, will be turned against us."

"But what has brought about Hunwulf's current state?" Conan asked, indicating the prostrate, restless figure on the bed. "You said he'd gained control over his visions."

"He has, to a degree," Gudrun replied. "However, the visions can still strike unpredictably and with considerable force. I wonder whether repeated use of his clairvoyance at the gaming table has left him more susceptible to them than he once was, and thus less able to cope with their impact."

"If you pick repeatedly at a callus," quoth Conan, "you shouldn't be surprised if the skin starts to bleed."

"A fair analogy. His visions usually take the form of premonitions, and I'll warrant this one may have been just that."

"Premonitions?"

"Hunwulf told you, the night we met, that because we are Æsir, we are apt to be given notice if other Æsir are seen in the vicinity."

"It's how you stay ahead of Ragnar and his cronies."

"That, however, is not entirely the truth. It is just an excuse we have concocted. We do sometimes receive word that kinfolk are nearby, and by the same token our distinctiveness as Æsir has doubtless made it easier for Ragnar to keep finding us, but..."

"But," Conan finished, "the truth is that Hunwulf's clairvoyance warns him about Ragnar."

Gudrun shook her head pityingly. "You persist in your skepticism. Often have I heard it said that there is none so stubborn as a Cimmerian, and you, Conan, could give a mule lessons in obstinacy."

Conan smiled to himself. This woman teased him with just the right mixture of impertinence and affection, and he liked her all the more for it.

"Well, regardless," Gudrun continued, "Hunwulf tends to know when trouble is imminent, and said knowledge is imparted thus, by means of a vision." She smoothed down her husband's long, rumpled locks. "All we have to do now is wait for him to return to his senses, which he should do in short order. Then he can share whatever insights his incarnations have conveyed to him and we may lay our plans accordingly. In all likelihood, he will confirm what I fear: that Ragnar has sniffed out our whereabouts yet again. Regrettably, Conan, this will mean farewell, and that is a shame. It has been a pleasure to make your acquaintance, and Bjørn shall certainly miss you."

Before Conan could answer, Hunwulf jerked awake. He sat up with shocking suddenness, his eyes flying wide open. "They come!" he cried, hands clutching the air. His gaze seemed to be fixed in the middle distance. "Oh, they come! Even now, they ride west from Shumir. They have crossed the Zuagir Desert and the Mountains of Fire, suffering thirst and heatstroke and sunburn, but their anger is undimmed. They will be upon us soon. Soon!"

He collapsed back onto the bed, as though drained by the effort of these proclamations.

"Ragnar?" said Gudrun to him. "Is it Ragnar Leifson you speak of, husband?"

"Ragnar..." Hunwulf murmured. "Yes, that is what they tell me, they who are also me but not me, they whom I once used to be and one day shall become. It is Ragnar the Relentless, and with him, as ever, Halfdan, his cousin, and Sten who is like unto stone, and the twins Njal and Knut. They come... They come..."

His voice trailed away as he lapsed back into his erstwhile stupor, his eyelids fluttering shut.

"That settles it," said Gudrun. "We are quitting Eruk. I shall leave Hunwulf to rest and regain his strength, and then, at first light, we ride."

"Or," said Conan gravely, "you do something else."

Gudrun cocked an eyebrow at him. "What do you mean?"

"How long have you been pursued by Ragnar? A decade now? It is high time that that state of affairs was brought to an end."

"What would you suggest?" Gudrun said sardonically. "That we give Ragnar what he seeks? Let him and his men overtake us and slaughter us at long last?"

"You've allowed Ragnar to make the running, all these years. He comes, and you drop whatever you are doing and flee. He has power over you. You three are the hare, he the hound, and while he lives, you will never know peace."

"Such is the choice Hunwulf and I have made, and we are resigned to it. We have Bjørn to consider. He is our focus. Were it just the two of us, perhaps we might act differently, but our son's safety is our foremost priority."

"Suppose one day your luck runs out. What if Hunwulf's powers should fail him and your pursuers catch you at last?"

"Then we shall fight them—fight them to our very last breath—and if we die doing so, such is the gods' will."

"Damn the gods!" Conan ejaculated. "Damn them and their whims! Has it not occurred to you, Gudrun, that Hunwulf's warning visions are a blessing?"

"In as much as they have so far kept us from harm, then yes, Conan, obviously they are a blessing."

"I mean that, rather than telling you when to run, they could allow you to meet your pursuers head-on. You have the advantage."

"You're suggesting we ambush them?" Gudrun asked.

"Just so. It's what I would do, were I you. I have never fled from a foe when I can stand my ground. Now you can do just that."

Gudrun, intrigued, pondered his words.

"You speak a lot of sense," she said at last. "If I am honest, I'm tired of all this running. Ten years is a long time. Perhaps, if we were able to settle down somewhere, we could start to make an honest living. Hunwulf could pursue a less ephemeral and precarious profession than gambling. We could live as ordinary folk do." A somber look overcame her. "But no. It is not possible. For one thing, Ragnar and his accomplices outnumber us."

"If numbers won battles, I'd be long dead. Find the right spot for your ambush, and you can kill most of them before they can mount resistance. Higher ground, a few well-aimed arrows, and you'll knock the heart out of them. Better yet, kill Ragnar himself first. His cronies will turn tail."

Gudrun showed every indication that she was giving his counsel serious thought. "If Hunwulf will agree to the idea, then perhaps it would be a wise course of action, albeit not without its risks."

"I, naturally, will join you."

"It would undoubtedly tilt the odds firmly in our favor, having you at our side, Conan."

"I wouldn't even ask to be paid."

"Your sense of honor does you credit," said Gudrun. "But this is our business, Æsir business. It is up to us, Hunwulf and myself alone, to resolve it."

"If you insist."

"Besides, I can think of a better use for you."

"Indeed?"

"We can hardly take Bjørn with us on this expedition, can we?"

"Of course not." Instantly Conan saw where the conversation was headed. "You wish me to act as his chaperone while you are gone?"

"Someone needs to keep an eye on him, and who better than you? You can continue his martial education, too. What say you to that, Conan?"

Conan thought long and hard. "Very well. I accept."

"There is, though, one condition."

"Namely?"

"Should Hunwulf and I fail to return, you look after the boy from then onwards as though he were your own."

Conan scowled. "Adopt him?"

"Take him under your wing, make him your ward," said Gudrun. "Whatever name you care to give it, you become his guardian and have full responsibility for him."

"You are asking a lot."

"I would require your word on it, your solemn vow."

"No," Conan said. "My vow is not something I give freely, and besides, there's no reason to think that you and Hunwulf will not be successful. You yourself are a capable and resourceful fighter, and so is he, if his story about that winged man is anything to go by. I don't doubt that, having set your minds to the task, the two of you will defeat Ragnar and his cohort."

Gudrun eyed him levelly. "Well," she said after a moment, "even if you won't give me your vow, I strongly suspect that your sense of honor will compel you to do the right thing, if the occasion calls for it."

Conan was left with the impression that, notwithstanding the lack of a formal pledge, he had somehow committed himself to being Bjørn's surrogate parent should the lad wind up being orphaned. Gudrun Ingensdóttir had her wiles, and she had used them adroitly upon him.

He ruminated wryly on the fact that, in the right woman's hands, Conan of Cimmeria could be quite the plaything.

7

Derketa Dust

At dawn, the three of them—Conan, Hunwulf and Gudrun—breakfasted. Bjørn slept on, in that profound, serene state of slumber that seems the sole preserve of the young.

"Ragnar Leifson and his companions are some thirty miles east of the city," Hunwulf said. He looked wan and haggard, clearly still suffering the aftereffects of his vision from the night before.

"A hard day's ride away," said Conan. "Can you be any more specific about their location?"

"Not very. My visions are not, alas, always very precise."

"Yet you can predict the outcome of a roll of the dice, time after time."

"What I do at the gaming table comes from within me, Conan. It is a knack I have acquired, a by-product of my inborn gift. My visions are different. They come from without, from my future incarnations, who are remembering events that occurred not in their own lives but in lives past. My other selves recall, at best, dim fragments, and these they convey to me piecemeal. It is then up to me to fit them together somehow so that they make sense, like assembling a mosaic."

"More than a dozen roads run eastward from Eruk," Conan said. "Did your vision show you any landmarks?"

Hunwulf reflected frowningly. "I remember there being a ruin, an old, disused fort that has fallen into decay. Do you know of it?"

"There are several such derelict forts in the region, dating back to the era when Shem was in turmoil, the cities of the desert at war with the cities of the meadows," said Conan. "If Ragnar is coming from the direction of Shumir, the fort in your vision could well be the one overlooking the Tabaarak Valley. The principal trade route between Eruk and Shumir passes hard by it."

"How far hence does it lie?"

"Ten or eleven miles, no more."

"As a place of ambush, it sounds more than suitable," said Gudrun. "A high vantage point, with plenty of cover for us to shoot from."

"But it could be some other fort," Hunwulf said. "Dare we stake everything on it being the one in the Tabaarak Valley when Ragnar and his men may not be coming that way at all?"

"I don't see that we have a choice, Hunwulf," said his wife. "We shall hire horses and ride out thither, and if it transpires that we are wrong, we can be back before nightfall."

"By which time, Ragnar and company could have reached Eruk."

"Reaching Eruk and finding us are not the same thing. This is a big, busy city. It could take them a whole further day, maybe two, to pin down where we live. That leaves plenty of time for us to gather up Bjørn and go."

"Gather me up and go where?" said a sleepy voice. Bjørn had just wandered in. His snowy hair was a disheveled mop and he was rubbing his eyes and yawning. He took in the grim faces around the breakfast table. "Mother, Father, are we leaving?"

He looked crestfallen and bitter. "Is that what you and Conan are talking about? Are you telling him my lessons are at an end and we're moving on?"

"Not as such," said Gudrun. "You remember, Bjørn, how our enemies keep finding us?"

"I know, I know. Ragnar the Relentless and friends."

"Well, your father and I have decided enough is enough. We are putting a stop to it once and for all."

"Oh. But they are dangerous men. You've always said that."

Gudrun rose and went over to the boy, going down on one knee beside him so that their eyelines were level. "One can only keep running for so long," said she, "and there comes a time when one must call a halt. Now is that time. Your father and I are going to confront Ragnar and convince him to leave us be."

"You've told me Ragnar would not stop unless he was dead. Are you going to kill him?"

"I fear we have to."

"We do have to," said Hunwulf. "Him and the rest."

Bjørn digested this information. "Could you get killed trying to kill them?"

"It's possible," said Gudrun, "although we shall try our hardest not to."

Conan was quietly impressed. She and Hunwulf were not sparing the child's sensibilities. They were being as open and honest with him as they could. Most parents, he had observed, when breaking bad news to their offspring, elected to honey it up or downright lie; but children were shrewd, resilient creatures, by and large, and preferred to be treated with candor, however unwelcome. Looking back on his own boyhood in Cimmeria, Conan could not think of an occasion when an adult would tell him aught but the pure, unvarnished truth, and he had been grateful for it.

The world was savage and arbitrary, full of perils and pitfalls. Why pretend otherwise?

"But," the Æsir woman added, "if we are careful and handle things right, we will prevail. And then, no more running. Does that not sound good?"

Bjørn nodded. "I like that idea a lot," said he. "And you, Conan? Are you going with my parents to slay Ragnar?"

"Nay, lad, I'm staying put to watch over you."

At this, Bjørn's face brightened somewhat. "I like that idea a lot, too."

Thus the matter was settled, and soon Hunwulf and Gudrun were collecting together their weapons and making preparations to depart. Each hugged Bjørn tight and kissed him goodbye, and Bjørn, for his part, put on a brave face, although anyone could tell he was struggling to keep his fears in check and his tears at bay.

Outside the boarding house, Conan stood on the front doorstep to see the Æsir couple off.

"Cimmerian," said Gudrun with a tense smile, "you know what is expected of you. Do not disappoint."

"I could say much the same to you, Gudrun Ingensdóttir," replied Conan.

"Just remember that if you fail to uphold your end of our bargain, I will come back as a ghost and haunt you for the rest of your days."

"A terrifying prospect."

She patted his cheek. "Good. Then we understand each other."

Conan watched the pair walk off down the street, laden with armaments. He did not envy them the task ahead, and he prayed they would return victorious.

No sooner had the Æsir couple rounded the corner than a man came hobbling up from the opposite direction and accosted Conan.

"Cimmerian."

The hoarse voice, more croak than speech, emanated from a face that was etched with lines of pain. The owner of voice and face was bent forward, as though laboring under an invisible heavy burden.

It took Conan a moment to realize who this was in front of him, and his scalp crawled in startlement.

"Drusus?" he exclaimed.

"None other," said Drusus of Nemedia, with a loose, crooked grin. "You seem surprised to see me."

"But..."

"But I am dead, no?" said the thief. "Torn to shreds by that sabretooth tiger."

"The breath had left your body," Conan said. "I was sure of it."

"I live, as you can see. Injured, in agony, but I live." Drusus turned and drew aside his toga to reveal his back. From shoulder blades to waist it was a mass of crisscrossing gouges, like a quarry face in flesh form. Some of the wounds appeared to be mending but others were clearly infected, suppurating greenish-yellow pus. "Nemedians are perhaps harder to kill than you thought."

"By Crom! How are you able to walk? Or for that matter stand?"

"With difficulty, I admit," said Drusus. "I have availed myself of an apothecary's services. Certain curative unguents are aiding the healing process, while drops of a tincture derived from the golden lotus serve to lessen the pain. I still do not know whether I shall survive. If infection takes a firm hold, it will inevitably kill me. I would put my chances at three to one. I thought I would come to see you anyway."

"To settle scores?" Conan's hand went instinctively to his sword.

"Nay, nay, not at all. Why would you think that?"

"I left you for dead in Sakhimael's garden. That would give cause for rancor."

Drusus laughed, then winced. "I must remind myself not to do that. Anything that jars my back doubles the pain. Rancor, Conan? Not in the least. Were the roles reversed, I would have done as you did. Obviously you assumed I had perished, and who can blame you? But in fact I had merely lost consciousness, and I came to perhaps an hour later, to find the corpse of the sabretooth beside me and my companion-in-thievery long gone. Body wracked with searing agony, I was nonetheless able to muster sufficient strength to clamber over the garden wall. I sought refuge at a friend's house, and there I have been residing since. It wasn't until the day before yesterday that I felt well enough even to think about rising from my sickbed, and then last night word reached me of a fracas at a gambling den that involved a large and lethal Cimmerian. Tracking you down to this house was child's play for one like me who has contacts and informants throughout Eruk."

"If not revenge," Conan said, "what do you want from me?"

"Nothing, nothing," said Drusus airily. "I came only to inquire whether you might care to join me for a drink."

"A drink? The sun has barely risen!"

"Since when has that deterred one like you from imbibing?"

"True enough. Yet still I must say no. I have certain duties." Conan cast a brief glance towards the house, wherein lay Bjørn, his charge. "Another time, Drusus."

"I feel, Cimmerian, that the least you can do for the man whom you abandoned to his fate would be to have a drink with him. If only to show that bygones are bygones."

"You would have met a different fate, had you not lost your nerve."

Conan turned to re-enter the boarding house, but Drusus stayed him with an insistent hand. "I beg you, Conan." Bloodshot, red-rimmed eyes bored into the Cimmerian's. "I may not have long on this earth, and if I am shortly to leave it, I would like to do so on amicable terms with everyone I know, with no ill will felt by either party. You owe me that, if nothing else."

Conan thought on it. He had, in hindsight, been rather quick to forsake Sakhimael's garden, and perhaps he ought to have examined Drusus's senseless form more closely before concluding he was dead. If he had known the Nemedian was still alive, would it have altered things in any way? Probably not. Even if he had hoisted Drusus onto his back and carried him out of the merchant's property with a view to finding him a physician, the man would be no less severely damaged than he was now, and at no less risk of dying.

Nevertheless, he felt he bore some responsibility for Drusus's plight. Would it hurt to share a drink with him?

"One moment." Conan went indoors and found Bjørn. "I have to go out for a while," he told him. "I will not be long. Keep the door to these rooms locked, and on no account open it to anyone. Have you got that? Not to anyone, unless, of course, it is me."

The Æsir boy nodded assent. "Where are you going?" he asked.

"To catch up with an old acquaintance."

"Why can't I come?"

It was a good question, but Conan had a good answer. "I would rather you remain here, where I know you are safe, than go somewhere with me where your safety can't be guaranteed. Besides, I do not wholly trust the fellow I am consorting with."

"Then why consort with him at all?"

"If he intends some villainy, I would rather deal with it now than later. Danger is best weeded out at the earliest opportunity, before it can take too firm a root."

"I understand," said Bjørn.

"Good lad. I shall return soon. Remember what I said: let no one in but me."

Outside again, Conan experienced a pang of misgiving. He really should not be leaving Bjørn alone. Gudrun, if she knew, would have excoriated him for it.

Yet he reasoned that Ragnar the Relentless was still far from Eruk and thus posed no immediate threat to the boy, while in the city itself there was nobody who wished Bjørn harm. He would be absent for an hour, no more. Nothing dire could happen in the space of an hour, surely.

"This way," said Drusus, indicating. "The Endless Tankard will be just opening."

The Nemedian set off down the street, and Conan fell in behind. Every step Drusus took was tentative and seemed to cost him dear, as though he were walking barefoot over broken glass. Conan doubted whether any amount of golden lotus tincture could fully mitigate the torment those wounds were causing him. At most it could make them just a little less unbearable.

Drusus's shambling figure turned down an alleyway. Conan, a few paces to the rear, followed him in. It occurred to him that this was not the most direct route to the Endless Tankard, but perhaps Drusus knew a shortcut to the tavern that he did not.

There were men waiting at the alleyway's end. They were armored and helmeted, and bore halberds and short swords. Conan instantly knew them to be guards from the city watch, an identification confirmed by the bronze eagle molded onto their breastplates of their steel cuirasses.

He halted, only to find Drusus turning towards him. The Nemedian's hand was outstretched, palm up, with a small heap of gray-green powder cupped in it. Drusus blew hard, and the powder blasted into Conan's face.

Even Conan's pantherish reflexes could not save him. The powder clogged his nostrils and mouth, and he choked.

Next thing he knew, the world was teetering sickeningly and his vision had begun to blur. He reached for Drusus, meaning to clamp both hands about the man's neck and throttle him. Drusus, however, seemed to be a hundred yards away and growing more distant by the second.

"Oh, Cimmerian," said he, his voice reaching Conan's ears faintly and echoingly as though from across a deep ravine. "You have a fundamental decency that is all too easy to exploit. 'Come and drink with me, Conan. A dying man's request, Conan. Let bygones be bygones, Conan.' Fool. You betrayed me! Deserted me! Why should I forgive that?"

"Dog!" Conan rumbled. "Louse! Scoundrel!" He lunged again for Drusus, but his own feet became entangled with each other and he staggered, colliding with the alley wall. "I shall kill you. I shall wrench your spine out and beat you to death with it."

"You shall do nothing, Conan, other than pass out. That powder is Derketa Dust. It is a dried distillation of a fruit the Kushites call the Apples of Derketa, the juice of which brings about almost instant death if it touches your body. Fittingly, it is named after a death goddess. Derketa Dust, however, is the fruit in a much diluted and weakened form, and does not kill. What it does do is induce almost instantaneous catalepsy in the body of even the strongest of men. Are you limbs feeling numb? Is your brain turning to fog? Can you feel your heartbeat slowing? You are moments away from insensibility."

Conan was indeed experiencing the very symptoms described. He made one last desperate attempt to seize Drusus, but in vain. He was aware of the men of the city watch moving towards him. He let out a howl of sheer infuriation, even as his legs gave way under him and he tumbled to the alley floor.

The last thing he saw before darkness closed over him like a black blanket was one of the guards looking down at him with an inscrutable expression on his face.

That same guard, leader of his unit, was Sergeant Alzhaak, and he gazed now on the Cimmerian's comatose form with studied professional dispassion.

"This is he?" he said, straightening up and addressing Drusus. "This is the one who caused the furor last night?"

Drusus brushed his hands together, ridding his palm of Derketa Dust residue. "I assure you, this is Conan, who slew that Khitan at the gambling den and injured two others."

"He certainly looks a likely candidate. What of the Æsir who was with him? We have orders to bring him in too."

"About him, I know not, Sergeant. I told you I could find you your Cimmerian, and that I have done. Now, as to my reward? The money I was promised?"

The Nemedian held out an expectant hand, and Sergeant Alzhaak dropped a small purse full of gold into it.

"I thank you."

"Don't thank me," said Alzhaak. "Thank Baron Caliphar. He put up the bounty on the Cimmerian's and Æsir's heads. He insisted to my captain that we drop everything else and scour the city all night long for those two."

"Then it's a good thing I got wind of that and came to find you," Drusus said. "Without me, your job would not be done."

"Half done," Alzhaak corrected.

"Half is better than none."

The sergeant thrust a hand at him, vertical, as though shutting a door. "Away with you now, Nemedian. You have your blood money. Begone from my sight."

"Blood money? I earned it righteously."

"If you say so. I do not doubt, though, given the animosity with which I have heard you have speak about the Cimmerian, that you would have led us to him for free."

"No question," said Drusus. "Payment is merely a pleasant bonus. Now then, a celebration is in order, methinks. To the

Endless Tankard I originally purported to go, and to the Endless Tankard I shall go."

Hefting the purse in his hand, Drusus the Nemedian shuffled away.

"He is a giant, this barbarian," Alzhaak said, eyeing the huge slab of muscled virility lying inert at his feet. He looked at his men. "I am glad there are four of you. Any fewer, and we might struggle to get him to the Eyrie. Each of you, sling your halberd and take a limb. And… lift!"

Straining, teeth clenched, the four guards lumbered along with the sedated Conan hanging prone between them, making for their headquarters, with Sergeant Alzhaak stolidly leading the way.

8

A Valiant Sacrifice

Bjørn Hunwulfson waited all morning for Conan to return. "Soon," his Cimmerian friend and tutor had said. "I shall return soon." But what did *soon* mean? An hour? Two? Three?

Patiently Bjørn bided his time, trusting that Conan would be true to his word.

By midday, however, doubt was beginning to set in. The boy pecked at some lunch and watched the sun outside the window slide past its zenith. He started to worry. Conan would not have abandoned him. It was inconceivable. Why, then, this ever-lengthening absence? Had he been waylaid? Hurt? Taken captive somehow? Bjørn could not fathom what event or agency could possibly overpower that mighty-thewed Cimmerian and bring him low. Conan, to him, was more force of nature than man.

Yet the evidence that he had got into difficulties appeared incontrovertible. Either that, or he had lied and had departed without any intention of coming back—which, as far as Bjørn was concerned, was ludicrous. Conan would rather have died than break faith.

As the day shaded into afternoon, Bjørn became firmly convinced that Conan was in trouble. Had he not mentioned that he suspected villainy from the fellow he was meeting? Could it be that the danger he had feared had come to pass?

Thus Bjørn arrived at an inescapable conclusion. If Conan was in trouble then someone must rescue him, and someone, in this instance, could only mean Bjørn Hunwulfson. Bjørn's parents were elsewhere, and there was no saying when, or even if, they would return. They had raised their son to be self-reliant, to think for himself and to take the initiative if need be. Now, without a doubt, he was confronted with the kind of crisis they had been preparing him for. Would they want him to stay cowering indoors like a weakling, when a friend was in need? Or would they rather he sallied forth boldly and did his best to set things right? Bjørn knew the answer to that.

Such logic passed through his young mind, and as a rock rolling downhill sets other rocks rolling and creates a landslide, it gathered momentum until it was unstoppable and swept all else—qualms, objections, reservations—away.

Bjørn went about collecting whatever armaments he could find in the house. His parents had made off with every weapon the family owned, but there was a small mallet of his father's and a whittling knife with a deer antler handle, both of which might be put to use offensively.

Bjørn thrust the implements into his belt and went to the door. As he turned the key, he hoped against hope that Conan would choose this moment to make his reappearance. The Cimmerian would chide him severely for disobeying his injunction about staying put, but Bjørn would not care. He would be too delighted at seeing his friend again to mind the tongue-lashing.

Conan was not in the house; nor was he in the street outside. Bjørn peered around him, blinking in the afternoon sun. At this hour, Eruk remained busy as ever but there was a marked slowing down in the usual bustle, for when the heat of the day was at its most oppressive, hurrying was ill advised.

Bjørn entered the dream-leisurely amble of the passing crowds, wondering where he should go and in what places he should look for Conan.

He first tried the stables, scene of his combat lessons, but nobody there had seen the Cimmerian today.

He then began inquiring in various taverns, on the grounds that Conan had said he was catching up with an old acquaintance, and what did old acquaintances do when they met but sup strong drink together? No sign of his friend did he unearth in any of the places he tried, however.

He asked around in marketplaces and meeting halls, courthouses and temples, invariably receiving the same negative result.

With humans failing him, Bjørn fell to wishing that his affinity for animals was more sophisticated than it was. He could calm a ferocious dog, make a bird fly in circles at his bidding, get a tarantula to dance and prance in his hand, simply by thinking about it. He imposed his will on the beast, and it submitted.

What he could not do was converse with creatures at anything but the most primordial, elemental level. He was privy to their thoughts and feelings but could make requests of only the simplest sort. He could not, for example, instruct a raven to soar above the city and search for a specific individual, in this case Conan, and get it to ask its corvid brethren whether any of them had seen the Cimmerian lately. That required far more advanced communication than he was capable of.

One day, when he was older, he might be able to command such a power. Perhaps, with practice, he would. For the time being, however, he must resign himself to his current pedestrian method of investigation.

More by luck than judgment, Bjørn ventured into a brothel.

There, women as excessively made-up as they were excessively underdressed clucked over him. They cooed at how handsome he was, following this with a litany of lewd, suggestive remarks.

One of them told him to come back in a few years' time, promising that she would then do him a great favor, "on the house," and relieve him of a burden he would be glad to get rid of. Bjørn grasped her implication and was both alarmed and excited.

This same harlot—whose hair, complexion and accent betokened an origin in Punt, Keshan or one of the other Black Kingdoms—proffered another suggestion, one that struck Bjørn as particularly useful and left him wondering why he hadn't thought of it himself.

"You should try the Eyrie," said she. "If your friend has got into some sort of bother, perhaps the city watch will have taken him into custody. If not, they still might know what has become of him."

"Thank you," Bjørn said. "I'll pay them a call."

The harlot bestowed a brilliant smile upon him. "You are a fine young man, and your friend is lucky to have someone like you looking out for him. Oh, and when you get to the Eyrie, be sure to give Captain Gerrilah my regards. Tell him Shorana misses him and would love to see him again soon." She gave a knowing, throaty chuckle, and a number of her colleagues joined in.

Bjørn turned his footsteps towards the Eyrie, that large and somewhat forbidding building that perched atop one of the low hills Eruk was founded upon. Its dozen or so turrets had many windows and were visible from almost any point in the city, giving the impression that its inhabitants observed all the goings-on below and there was no hiding from their scrutiny.

The truth, as even a comparative innocent like Bjørn knew, was that the city watch was a corrupt institution and, far from being all-seeing, would turn a blind eye to any wrongdoing if bribed sufficiently and, by the same token, would zealously conduct arrests and prosecutions, regardless of a suspect's actual guilt, if given the appropriate financial incentive. Its guards were not so much policemen as mercenaries, beholden less to law and more to lucre. There might be a few honest ones among them, but they were the exception rather than the rule.

Bjørn was halfway to his destination when he spied a group of men walking towards him with a purposeful gait.

There was nothing particularly unusual about this, save for the fact that all of them—they numbered five—were northerners.

More to the point, they were all, if Bjørn did not miss his guess, Æsir: tall, blond, with long, sharp noses and thick, partly plaited beards, their torsos clad in linen tunics, their feet in fur boots. Two of them bore facial tattoos similar to that which Bjørn's father sported, while another wore a bronze torc around his neck with a wolf's head wrought at either end in the classic Æsir style. They strode in a line across the street, with one of them to the fore, the largest and fiercest-looking of their complement.

Bjørn froze to the spot. These men surely could not be who he thought they were! Panic threatened to overwhelm him. He ordered himself to be calm, keep a cool head, take the appropriate measures.

If this really was Ragnar the Relentless and his band of men, the last thing he should do was stand there gawping out in the open where they might espy him.

He darted into a nearby shop, a goldsmiths.

The proprietor took one look at him and ordered him to leave.

"This is no place for children," the goldsmith sneered.

"Prithee, kind sir," said Bjørn in clumsy, rather over-formal Shemitic, a language he had only just begun to pick up, "I must needs hide. Men without endanger me."

"Liar," the goldsmith retorted. "There is only one reason someone your age would come into my shop, and that is to steal." He gestured at the glittering array of wares around him. "Well,

I'll give you one chance. Go. Now. Before I have to get physical."

When Bjørn didn't budge, the man rushed out from behind the counter, brandishing a cudgel. "I've beaten shoplifters to a pulp before, you know," said he. "Don't think I won't do the same to you."

Bjørn cast a frantic look out through the door. Ragnar and his men, if it was them, were passing by right outside. His choice was either to stand and fight here in the shop or take his chances back out in the street and hope the group of Æsir did not spot him. In the former instance, he might have to take a beating, but that would surely be better than falling foul of Ragnar Leifson.

He turned to face the goldsmith, who was almost upon him. There was no time to draw one of the weapons in his belt. Urgently Bjørn summoned up every ounce of combat knowledge his parents and Conan had taught him.

A man with a cudgel needed to get in close. Bjørn, therefore, should move inside his arc of swing before he could bring the implement to bear.

He closed the remaining distance between himself and the goldsmith, and as the cudgel came down he deflected it with a forearm, then slipped that same arm around his attacker's weapon hand, pressing it hard against his hip.

This put the cudgel temporarily out of use, and Bjørn had a brief moment of opportunity to mount a counterattack. He punched the base of the goldsmith's sternum. He felt a satisfying crackle beneath his fist and heard an even more satisfying gasp of pain from his opponent.

But then the goldsmith wrenched the cudgel free from Bjørn's control and, with a loud curse, lashed out with the weapon.

Bjørn failed to deflect as effectively this time as last, and the cudgel caught him on the side of the head.

It was a glancing blow, and yet a gong seemed to reverberate through his cranium and fireballs went spiraling across his vision.

He reeled backwards, stumbling out through the doorway. His legs crumpled beneath him, and he fetched up on his backside in the dirt and dust of the street.

For several seconds that gong continued resounding in his head, above which din he was just able to hear the goldsmith as he yelled, "Stay out and don't come back, brat, or next time it'll go worse for you!"

Dimly, as though through a haze of mist, he saw the man limp back into his shop, tenderly holding his chest where Bjørn's blow had fractured a fragile little projection of ribcage bone.

Bjørn struggled to pick himself up. Wherever those Æsir men were, they must not see him lying there. He must get up and run.

Bjørn did indeed rise, but not of his own volition. Rather, he found himself being hauled up by both wrists until he was suspended in midair, his feet dangling inches off the ground.

He writhed, hoping to wriggle free from the clutches of whoever was holding him, but dazed and disoriented as he still was, his efforts were feeble and ultimately futile.

"Well, well, well," said a voice right behind him, using the language of Bjørn's parents. "What have we here? No Shemite urchin, this. One of our own race, more like."

Bjørn thrashed all the more strenuously in the speaker's grasp, but with no greater success.

"Yes, an Æsir, unless I am much mistaken," said the man. He was holding Bjørn easily with just one hand, as though he weighed next to nothing; and now he spun the boy around through a half-turn so that they were face to face.

The fellow was the one Bjørn had seen moments earlier walking ahead of the other four. He had wild, wide eyes that spoke of a terrible, implacable determination, and of something else, something more, a kind of madness perhaps.

"Can it be?" he said. "Can it possibly be that I am holding none other than the spawn of Hunwulf and Gudrun?"

Bjørn answered him with an oath, at which the Æsir and his cohorts chortled.

"How does one so young know so mature a phrase?" Bjørn's captor said.

"Let me go, Ragnar Leifson!" Bjørn cried. "Let me go, or I swear, I'll kill you!"

The man's glaring eyes narrowed, and in that moment Bjørn realized he had blundered. He had put it beyond all doubt that he was who the other suspected him to be. Who else but the son of Hunwulf Ivarson and Gudrun Ingensdóttir would know of Ragnar Leifson?

At the same time, from the sly look that came over the man at the mention of his name, Bjørn at least now knew for certain that he had fallen into the clutches of Ragnar the Relentless: foe of his family, pursuer of blood-feuds, holder of a decade-long grudge.

There was horror in that knowledge, but also a modicum of relief. After all this time, so many years spent living in dread and awe of this nightmare figure, whom he had never met, never seen, only ever heard about—now at long last Bjørn was in his presence.

With that sudden revelation came clarity. Bjørn's senses returned to him in full. He had mastery of himself again.

And he kicked.

He aimed for a certain soft, vulnerable part of Ragnar's anatomy, just where the legs met at the top. It was a spot Conan had encouraged him to strike when the circumstances were dire enough to warrant it—and if these were not dire circumstances, then what were?

His foot connected smartly with its target. Ragnar let out a whoosh of breath and creased up in agony. His grip on Bjørn eased a fraction, and that was enough.

Bjørn shook himself free and began to run.

A hoarse command from Ragnar set the other four Æsir off in hot pursuit. "Grab him! Bring the little bastard to me!"

Bjørn sprinted as hard as he could, weaving in and out through the milling throng in the street. He could hear the men behind him, hot on his heels. They were barging straight through the crowd, eliciting shouts of distress and protest as they shoved passersby out of their way.

Bjørn ran on, but he knew he was not losing them, to judge by the ruckus behind him, which grew steadily louder and closer. The Æsir were gaining on him with every second.

He hurtled round a corner, whereupon he came across perhaps the most gods-blessed sight he had ever seen.

It was a dog, the stray he had been busy befriending when he met Conan for the first time, the one he had dubbed Wolfblood.

The great, ragged, lupine mongrel, which had been squatting in the gutter, licking itself assiduously, leapt to its feet immediately upon catching Bjørn's scent. It wagged its tail in recognition and delight.

Bjørn diverted towards it, and Wolfblood intuited straight away that its young human comrade was in peril. Looking at Bjørn's four pursuers, in a flash it identified them as predators and knew they meant the boy harm.

Obeying the same instinct which prompts any of its species to protect a fellow pack-member, the dog launched itself at the nearest of the oncoming men. It leapt for his throat, snarling, jaws agape.

The Æsir went down with a strangulated yell, and Wolfblood, straddling his chest, sank fangs deep into his neck.

The Æsir fought back, to no avail. With a powerful sideways wrench of its head, Wolfblood tore its victim's gorge wide open. Blood jetted across the road. The man shuddered horribly as his life spilled in torrents from his eviscerated throat.

His spasming death throes continued even as the dog stepped off him with gore-dripping muzzle, peering around for its next target.

Another of the Æsir had drawn his sword, and giving vent to an ululating battle cry, he hurled himself at Wolfblood, blade extended before him.

Bjørn, who had looked on with glee as Wolfblood sent the first man to Valhalla, now voiced a terrified shout of warning to his canine ally.

The dog, either oblivious or unheeding, sprang at the Æsir, only to be impaled on the point of his sword. Its shrill yelp of pain lasted but a split second. The sword had pierced its heart, and the light vanished from its eyes, to be replaced by the blank emptiness of death.

The Æsir withdrew his sword from Wolfblood's limp, vanquished body, and spat upon the animal in contempt.

"He was my brother," the man growled, "my twin, Knut. He is dead, and now so are you, vermin."

Bjørn, for his part, could only stand there and gape in dismay. He knew he must start running again, but the slaying of Wolfblood had shocked him to the core. The dog had been noble, it had defended him, and now it lived no more. Poor thing.

But there was no time to mourn, he knew. Not now. He stirred himself back into action—but too late.

The momentary delay had cost him any advantage Wolfblood's valiant sacrifice might have gained him. One of the remaining Æsir seized him roughly. Bjørn looked up to see a huge fist swinging for his face.

For a long while after that, things were just pain, and dizzied confusion, and swirling grayness.

Perched on a nearby rooftop was an unseen spectator to the fight between the dog and the Æsir men.

This was the same cloaked, misshapen figure, who days earlier, from a similar vantage point, had observed Bjørn's meeting with the dog and then with the barbarian. Since then it had been biding its time, awaiting the right moment to take action.

Now it looked on as the three surviving Æsir made off with Bjørn, one of them carrying the stunned boy slung over his shoulder like a sack of corn.

The figure followed, keeping pace with them as they threaded through the city. It moved from roof to roof in a series of mighty bounds, each leap longer than any ordinary person could manage.

The Æsir men rejoined their leader, and there was a certain amount of argument and angry remonstration. Eventually tempers cooled, and all four found their way back to their horses, which they had left at Eruk's outskirts. With the still-unconscious Bjørn slung across saddle of their fifth, now-riderless horse, they headed out into the desert.

Atop the city wall, the figure checked to make sure there was nobody else around. Then it shrugged off its cloak, revealing a pair of batlike wings that spanned some fifteen feet from tip to tip.

Extending these, it took to the air and ascended swiftly to an altitude where, from the ground, it appeared no larger than an eagle.

It continued to follow the Æsir at this height, pleased that they had just made its task easier.

In Bjørn they had gained themselves a prize.

What they did not appreciate, for they could not know, was that he was not *their* prize.

9

That Rare Thing, a Law-Abiding Law Enforcer

C onan awoke to find himself locked in a cell and bound by manacles.

It was not the first time he had ended up in such a situation, and neither, he suspected, would it be the last. In the past he had normally done something to warrant this kind of confinement. On this occasion, there was no fairness to it whatsoever.

It was all thanks to Drusus and his lust for some kind of recompense. That irked Conan, but what irked him even more was that he had fallen so readily for the Nemedian's ruse. He should have known better. He had sensed the possibility of a betrayal, yet he had foolishly ignored his instincts. He should never have gone along with the invitation to have a drink. He should have turned Drusus down flat.

If only he had been able to break the man's neck while he'd had the chance, before the Derketa Dust took full effect.

Well, it was not too late. Once he was free, he would make it his priority to find that snake in human guise and put an end to him.

But first, before that, he must get to Bjørn and make sure the boy was safe and sound.

Still groggy from the dose of poison powder, with a headache pulsing behind his eyes and a mouth feeling as dry as dust, Conan took stock of his surroundings.

The cell was small and filthy, with a tiny, barred window and an iron-banded wooden door. A bowl containing a crust of bread and a rind of cheese sat in the corner next to a water pitcher and a latrine bucket—life's essentials pared down to the bare minimum.

He was, he assumed, in a turret of the Eyrie, the unwilling guest of the city watch. The view outside was of rooftops and a glimpse of sky, and by the position of the sun he estimated the time to be late afternoon.

He staggered stiffly to his feet and began inspecting every square inch of wall, in search of a piece of loose masonry that he might work free, thus creating a hole which he could widen through diligent manual excavation until it was big enough for him to squeeze through.

There was none.

As for the window, even if its bars had not been mortared immovably in place, its dimensions would never accommodate his massive bulk.

That left the door, which was solid, stout, and snug in its frame. He did not think he could barge it down, but this would not stop him from trying. And even if he failed, slamming himself repeatedly against it might bear fruit in another way.

Conan took a run-up and launched himself shoulder first at the door.

The impact made it shudder.

He struck it again and again with all his considerable might, the noise resounding like rolling thunder along the corridor outside.

Soon enough he heard angry shouts. Someone ordered him to cease that racket.

Conan redoubled his efforts. He discerned a hinge coming loose. Perhaps he might prevail against the door after all.

His shoulder was throbbing with pain, but he did not slacken.

There came more angry shouts, then a set of footfalls. The peephole slot in the middle of the door slid open and a pair of irate eyes peered in.

"What's the meaning of this?" the owner of the eyes demanded.

"Release me, or I shall release myself," Conan said.

"Not possible. You are here awaiting trial."

"And when will that be?"

"Tomorrow at the earliest. More likely the day after."

"Not soon enough. I mean to leave today. Unlock this door now."

"Not a chance, Cimmerian."

"Then I'll keep battering it until it falls down." Suiting deed to word, Conan rammed the door a couple more times. The eyes in the peephole looked alarmed. "Which would you rather?" Conan said. "A broken door or an intact one? Either way, I am going to be free."

"I… I shall fetch my senior officer," said the man outside.

"Understood," Conan said, then effected another shoulder barge.

The peephole slid shut, and Conan heard the man scurry away.

A minute and several more shoulder barges later, a key turned in the lock. A voice outside said sternly, "Back away from the door, Cimmerian. We are armed."

Conan obliged.

The door opened to reveal three city watch guards, their short swords at the ready. One of them he recognized as the man who had been staring down at him in the alley when he lost consciousness. The scarlet plume on his helmet marked him out as a sergeant.

"Who are you?" Conan said.

"I am Sergeant Alhaak. I am the one who arrested you."

"Well, Sergeant Alhaak, I don't deserve to be your prisoner. You must know that as well as I. I was sold out by an enemy, Drusus the Nemedian, in an act of petty revenge. I'm going to leave this place, and if it has to be over the dead bodies of you and your junior officers, so be it."

"Are you saying you did not kill that Khitan last night?" said Alhaak.

"Is that why I am under arrest?"

"Principally, yes."

"It was self-defense," Conan replied flatly. "Had I not killed him first, he would have killed me. Is that against the law? Taking a life to preserve one's own?"

"Well, no," admitted the other. "But there is also the matter of affray and breach of the peace."

"I see far worse crimes every day in this city, Sergeant. I am occupying a cell which by rights belongs to another."

"Is this your argument, Conan of Cimmeria? You are not a criminal because there are those who merit the description more?" Alhaak gave a scornful laugh. "That is not how the law works, my northern friend. A wrongdoer is a wrongdoer, and must be treated accordingly."

"You strike me as a fair and moral man," Conan observed.

"I like to think so."

"A rare thing in your job."

"I would beg to differ."

"Would you? Eruk's city watch are not famous for their impartiality or their independence. They seldom act without money first changing hands."

"You impugn us."

"Not unjustly," Conan said. "Tell me, do you truly in your heart of hearts think that I should be behind bars and facing trial?"

"It is not for me to determine your guilt or your punishment, Conan. That is down to the magistrate."

"No, true. Your job is to do your paymasters' bidding, whoever they be."

"I resent that comment. I serve the law, first and foremost."

"Even if the law can be bought and sold? Sergeant Alhaak, I barely know you, but if I am any judge of character, I don't think you believe I should be detained, especially on such flimsy grounds. In fact, I think you wouldn't mind me walking out of the Eyrie a free man. And that is better, surely, than me walking out with city watch blood on my hands…"

Sergeant Alhaak fixed him with a coolly appraising stare. "You appeal to my better nature but back it up with a threat? An interesting tactic, Conan. For a barbarian, you are unusually sophisticated."

"Where I come from, 'sophisticated' is an insult."

At that remark, Alhaak seemed genuinely amused, and Conan was strongly of the view that he had won the fellow over.

This was confirmed a moment later when Alhaak spoke to his subordinates thus: "Put your swords away, men. I am inclined to think that we have got the wrong man."

The other two guards hesitated.

"I shall take full responsibility for your actions, as well as mine," Alhaak added.

This was enough to convince them to obey. They sheathed their swords, as did Alhaak his.

"You," Alhaak said to one. "Unlock his manacles."

Conan, unshackled, massaged his wrists. "I thank you, Sergeant Alhaak."

"I don't want your gratitude, Cimmerian. I just want you out of here."

"Show me the way."

Alhaak escorted Conan down several winding flights of stairs to a central vestibule, and thence to the Eyrie's main entrance.

As they went, he confided, "You are correct in as much as bribery and corruption are endemic within the city watch. I myself am not wholly immune to the lure of money, not least since our pay is derisory. But I like to think I have retained a portion of my integrity nonetheless. Your arrest was sanctioned by Captain Gerrilah, our commanding officer, at the behest of Baron Caliphar."

"Aye," said Conan. "I can see why that might be."

"Caliphar also requires that we apprehend an Æsir associate of yours, but we have not located him yet."

Conan nodded. Hunwulf would be out of the city at least until nightfall. When he got back, Conan would warn him that there was an arrest warrant out for him. It seemed as though the family would have to quit Eruk whether or not Hunwulf and Gudrun had managed to slay Ragnar the Relentless. A shame.

"To say that Gerrilah is in Caliphar's pocket," Alhaak went on, "would be an understatement. The only consolation, if one may call it that, is that Gerrilah is in the pocket of every rich person in Eruk, so shares out his purchasable allegiance equally. To be frank, I find it hard to abide."

"So if you can undermine your captain in any way, however small, you take it. For instance, by freeing me."

"I shall doubtless catch hell for it," Alhaak said with a resigned shrug. "I am long overdue for promotion, and Captain Gerrilah will now see to it that I remain a sergeant for the foreseeable future, and, if I continue to cross him, perhaps until I retire. But..."

"But sometimes these small victories are worth the price."

"Such is the cost of having a conscience when I hold a position that would rather I had none."

Out front, Conan shook Alhaak by the hand. "You have done right by me, Sergeant. I'm glad there are some in law enforcement who are law-abiding."

"Just tell your Æsir friend to make himself scarce," Alhaak said. "Understood."

"And please, Conan of Cimmeria, try to stay out of trouble from now on. It's unlikely you'll find me in so lenient a mood the next time."

"I make no promises," Conan said with a grin. "One last request."

"Have I not done you favor enow?"

"Where might I find Drusus?"

Alhaak grasped Conan's implication. "Last I heard, he was going to the Endless Tankard for a celebratory drink. But that was hours ago, and I should be surprised if he were still there."

"It's somewhere to start," said Conan, and turned and loped away.

He ran across the city, with every step praying that young Bjørn was where he had left him. The boy would not have been so imprudent as to leave the house, would he? Conan thought not. Yet a worm of doubt gnawed at his mind. It was as though some sixth sense was telling him that while he had been in the city watch's custody, some terrible calamity had occurred.

Reaching the boarding house, he hurried to the family's rooms and was appalled to find the door unlocked. Worse yet, Bjørn was not within.

"Curse you, lad!" he growled to the empty lodgings. "Do you wish your mother to kill me? For that's what she will do. You have murdered me as surely as if you yourself drove the blade home."

He hastened outside. There was no alternative but to start combing Eruk for Bjørn. Evening was falling, and if he had to spend the entire night hunting for the boy, that was what he would do. Then, when he found him, he would tan his hide.

He had not gone far when who should appear but Hunwulf and Gudrun.

This, for Conan, was perhaps the worst possible turn of events. He would rather have met them after he had got Bjørn back home. Better to have to account for Bjørn's absence once the boy was safe and sound than while he was still missing and his fate as yet unknown. Then the mishap could perhaps be laughed off. Things would certainly not seem as dire in retrospect as they did right now.

The Æsir couple looked disheveled and saddle-stiff. Conan hailed them warily, asking, "Is it done? Is Ragnar finally dealt with?"

Hunwulf sullenly shook his head. "When we arrived at the derelict fort in the Tabaarak Valley, I immediately saw that it was not the same one as in my vision. We rode back to a junction and followed one of the other eastern roads until we came to the ruins of a different roadside fort. This was the right fort, the one I had seen during my trance, and we descried sets of hoofprints going past it, heading citywards. If these belonged to Ragnar and company, then clearly we had missed our chance to ambush them. We lay in concealment at the fort anyway for several hours, keeping vigil, but saw no one go by save for a couple of merchant caravans and a lone religious eremite. Eventually there seemed to be nothing for it but to return to Eruk. In sum, the whole trip was a waste of time."

"One can only assume Ragnar and his men are somewhere in the city by now," Gudrun said. "We shall take Bjørn and go, tonight, before they can find us."

"Aye," Conan said tentatively. "Regarding Bjørn, I must come clean. He—"

"What, Cimmerian?" said Gudrun, cutting him off. "What about Bjørn?"

Swiftly Conan explained how he had been drugged and arrested, and how he had only just recently gained his liberty, and how, for all the precautions he had put in place, Bjørn had somehow disappeared in the interim.

The blood drained from Gudrun's face. "Where is he, Conan?" she hissed. "Where is my son?"

"Would that I knew."

She struck him hard. Conan accepted the blow, and the others that followed. Gudrun pounded him mercilessly, and he bore the pummeling with stoic grace, without even attempting to shield himself. To some extent he deserved it, and if venting her anguish on him made Gudrun feel better, then it was doubly beneficial.

Eventually, when her ire had run its course, she desisted.

"This is all your fault, Cimmerian," she said through gritted teeth, "and you will help us set it right."

"Believe me, I want nothing more than that myself," Conan said, wiping blood from his lips. "I swear to Crom, I shall not rest until Bjørn is recovered."

"Nor shall we," said Hunwulf. "But where do we start looking?"

10

The Tongue of Set

The answer to that question arrived far sooner than any of them might have anticipated. A messenger came jogging up and inquired if they knew where the residence of Hunwulf Ivarson and Gudrun Ingensdóttir lay. He mispronounced the names, for they sat unfamiliarly on his Shemitish tongue.

"I know that they live around here, but not precisely where," he said. "Are you two Æsir they, by any chance?"

"We are," said Hunwulf.

"Then this is for you." The messenger handed over a slip of paper and went on his way.

Gudrun leaned close to her husband as he read the note. Conan looked over their shoulders. The text was in the script used by the peoples of Nordheim, that string of sticklike letter forms which had a crudely efficient look.

"What does it say?" he asked.

"It is from Ragnar," said Gudrun icily.

"He has Bjørn," said Hunwulf. "He says our son is alive and well, and tells us to meet him at a location a couple of miles northeast of the city, a point where two dried-up riverbeds converge. He will wait for us there all night, and we are to come unarmed. If we follow his instructions, there is a chance, he says, that Bjørn will live."

"The dog!" Conan declared. "How low can a man stoop? To use a child as a hostage!"

"Not a hostage," said Gudrun. "Bait in a trap."

"But we have to go," said Hunwulf. "We've no choice, and Ragnar knows it."

"Of course we have to go, and there is every chance that by springing his trap we will die. But..." Gudrun looked grimly thoughtful. "The note is addressed to you and me, Hunwulf."

"It is. So?"

"There's every chance Ragnar knows naught of Conan. He will be expecting the two of us, you and I, to walk into his snare. He will not be expecting a third party."

"A third party," Conan chimed in, "who may catch Ragnar and his men unawares. A third party who won't be unarmed, either. I know of the place he describes. The locals call it the Tongue of Set. There is a crag on one side which would afford me plenty of cover. With stealth, I can get to within a stone's throw of Bjørn's kidnappers, and they won't even know I am there."

"When I think of stealth, Cimmerian," said Hunwulf, "I do not think of someone proportioned as you are."

"By the time I was your son's age I could steal up on a deer from downwind without it bolting, until I was close enough to caress its neck or else plant a knife in it. The skill has not deserted me."

"Conan," said Gudrun, "we are relying on you to deliver us from Ragnar's clutches—all three of us, not least Bjørn. You are our one possible hope for redemption."

"If I redeem you," Conan declared, "I shall redeem myself."

"We need fresh horses," said Hunwulf. "I will go and see if the stables are still open for business. If not, I will make such a commotion outside that the owner will have to let me in."

"If his piebald mare is still there, I want her," Conan said. "And while you're busy about that, there's something else I must attend to."

"Something more important than rescuing our son?" said Gudrun.

"I shall be no more than quarter of an hour." Conan hastened off before the Æsir woman could raise any further objections.

Minutes later, he was at the Endless Tankard.

It was highly unlikely, he knew, that Drusus would still be at the tavern, but he had to check. The Nemedian had no reason to think that Conan was not still in custody, but he must also realize that as long as the Cimmerian was alive, his own safety was not assured. He would surely, if he was sensible, quit Eruk as soon as he feasibly could, so this might be the only opportunity Conan would get to catch him.

By some miracle, Conan's venture paid off. In a corner of the tavern sat Drusus, deep in his cups, with a plump, bosomy trollop fawning over him, doubtless because he was being free with his newfound riches.

Conan crossed the crowded room in a few swift strides and snatched the girl away from the Nemedian. She began venting her annoyance with some very choice words, until a fierce glare from Conan silenced her. As for Drusus, he looked up, and the sottish glazedness ebbed from his eyes as his startled expression turned to one of dread.

"I'd call you a rat, Drusus," Conan snarled, "but I know rats to be intelligent and loyal creatures. You are neither."

Cringing, the Nemedian stammered, "C-Conan! Do—do not wax wroth. I merely saw a way to make a little profit. I was certain the city watch would not hold you for long and you would suffer no serious repercussions for being arrested. Here, you may have a share of the bounty. I—I saved some for you."

He proffered a few coins in a trembling hand.

Conan slapped the hand aside, scattering the money across the sawdust-strewn floor.

Drusus's doxy dove for the coins, scooping them up into her skirts.

"I want none of your spoils, Nemedian," Conan said. "I want only one thing from you."

"And th-that is…?"

"Your life."

So saying, Conan seized Drusus by one arm and one leg and hoisted him high into the air. Drusus screamed at the pain this caused his lacerated back.

He screamed harder as Conan raised a knee and brought him down onto it sideways with all the might in his body. Under the impact, Drusus's ribcage shattered and his spine snapped in twain. Blood blurted from his mouth and nose.

Conan discarded the Nemedian's bent, broken form on the floor and gazed down impassively at him as he shuddered through the final few seconds of his life.

Then, turning on his heel, he wended his way back through the ranks of startled and awed drinkers and out into the night air.

The woman Drusus had been consorting with cast a look over her now-deceased cash cow, sniffed, and went in search of another drinker with deep pockets and generous hands.

Someone followed him out of the tavern.

Conan walked on a few paces, pretending he was unaware. This was to confirm that the man did not merely happen to be going the same way as him but was actually dogging his footsteps. From the purposeful sound of his stride Conan determined that he was, and he swung round abruptly, fists knotted.

"State your business with me, fellow," he snarled. "If you are a friend of Drusus's seeking redress, be very sure of your next move. I'm happy to dish out the same treatment to you as I did him."

"Nay, Conan," the other replied, holding his hands up, palms out. "No friend of Drusus's."

It took Conan a moment to recognize Sergeant Alhaak of the city watch. "You again. You are out of uniform."

"Very observant," said Alhaak.

"Since releasing me, you've been keeping a covert eye on the Nemedian, knowing I might come for him."

"Not 'knowing.' Strongly suspecting."

"Very astute of you."

"Hardly. You more or less stated that was your intent when you asked me where I thought he might be."

"But you did not prevent me from killing him."

"Would I have been wise to try? No."

"No," Conan agreed. "Will you arrest me now for his murder?"

"I ought to, but…" The sergeant shook his head. "Some would argue Drusus had it coming. I cannot, however, countenance you remaining within my purview any longer, Cimmerian. I did ask you to stay out of trouble."

"And I said I would make no promises," Conan rejoined.

"So now I am asking you, for everyone's sake, not least mine, kindly leave this city. Eruk is done with you."

"That is fortunate," said Conan, "because I am done with Eruk. I thank you for your civility, Sergeant. You should feel flattered, for that is not a thing I say often."

Sergeant Alhaak smiled. "Why does that not surprise me?"

As Conan took his leave of the city watch man for the second time that day, he marveled at the rarity of a police official who knew the difference between the law and justice, and tempered the one with the other.

Conan's own notion of justice was clear-cut indeed, and he thought now of Ragnar the Relentless and his cronies, and how he would soon be visiting that justice upon them.

At the Y-shaped intersection of dry gullies known as the Tongue of Set, Ragnar Leifson was congratulating himself on his extraordinary stroke of luck.

To have chanced upon Hunwulf's and Gudrun's son within an hour of arriving in Eruk—truly the gods had smiled upon him! It was as good as encountering the pair themselves. Nay, it was better. Now he had a new weapon in his arsenal, perhaps the most effective imaginable, one which ensured their full compliance. Hunwulf and Gudrun would do anything for their boy.

Ragnar knew this not least because they had spent a decade fleeing from him, and if not for the child they would undoubtedly have stopped and confronted him years ago. The only thing that could have kept them perpetually on the run like that was the all-consuming parental imperative to keep one's offspring safe from harm.

He looked across to where Bjørn Hunwulfson now sat, slumped against a boulder, bound hand and foot, his mouth gagged.

Bjørn met his gaze and held it. By the light of the small campfire Ragnar had lit, he saw how the lad's eyes blazed pure fury, conveying eloquently that which his stopped mouth could not. Were he free, those eyes said, he would be doing his level best to kill Ragnar.

He even had the tools for it: a whittling knife and a small mallet lodged in his belt. It had amused Ragnar to leave these items where they were instead of confiscating them. It demonstrated to Bjørn how little Ragnar feared him and how hopeless his situation truly was.

Ragnar's cousin Halfdan was pacing round in circles. "Are they ever going to come?" he said, letting out a snort of impatience. "Surely they should be here by now."

"They will, fear not," Ragnar reassured him. "They are not going to leave their son to our tender mercies."

"Well, they're taking their gods-damned time about it," Halfdan grumbled.

"We have pursued them for nigh on ten years, cousin. After so long, we can easily wait a few hours more. Think on it. Our quest is almost over. After tonight, we will be free men again."

"It feels as though I have spent my entire life chasing that accursed couple," said Halfdan. "I can scarcely remember a time when we were not on the move, journeying from one country to the next, traversing the world back and forth, hunting for the least trace of them..." He sighed. "How strange it will seem not to have that purpose anymore."

Sten, the most staunchly loyal of Ragnar's men, gave a nod of agreement. He seldom spoke, did Sten, and Ragnar cherished that about him. Not a word of complaint had the fellow uttered over the past ten years, whereas the others had each, at one time or other, voiced doubts about their mission and questioned Ragnar's wisdom, governance, and even sanity. Ragnar had been able to keep them in line with cajoling, goading, exhortation, and sometimes threats and bullying. Sten, alone of them all, had just kept on going, stoic and imperturbable.

"I say we should kill the child." This was from Njal, who had his sword in his lap and was sharpening its blade with a whetstone. "Slaughter the wretched brat now and have done with it. If not for him, my brother would still be alive. Bjørn led us to that dog which tore out Knut's throat and which I in turn slew. I will happily slit *his* throat, and thereby the scales will be rebalanced." Njal half-rose, sword in hand, as if preparing to make good on his statement.

"Sit," Ragnar commanded him. "The boy does not die now. But you will get your chance, Njal, I promise you that. What is the point in killing him if Hunwulf and Gudrun are not here to see it? Would it not be preferable to watch the anguish on their faces as the boy is executed before their very eyes, and they helpless to prevent it?"

Njal realized the sense in this. "As long as it is I who does the deed. I am owed that at least."

"Who am I to deny the wishes of so keen a volunteer?" said Ragnar. He looked over at Bjørn again and divined a touch of terror now in the boy's eyes. It was swiftly masked, Bjørn fixing Ragnar once more with that defiant, hate-filled stare.

Ragnar found himself, in spite of everything, admiring the youngster. He was exhibiting a remarkable toughness and resilience. It was almost a shame to have to kill him.

Yet it was necessary, if Hunwulf and Gudrun were to suffer before they themselves died. Ragnar would hurt them physically, of course, by blood-eagling them, but their pain would be all the greater if they underwent the excruciating torture with the corpse of their son lying in front of them.

His thoughts went back to the day Hunwulf slew Heimdul, his much-loved older brother, and made off with Gudrun.

Hunwulf had once been Ragnar's bosom friend, so the betrayal was doubly acute. Ragnar recalled the many times Hunwulf told him how deeply in love he and Gudrun were; and when the tribal elders assigned her as wife to Heimdul, he was all but inconsolable in his grief and anger. He confided to Ragnar that he and Gudrun intended to elope, but Ragnar counseled against it.

"You are taking Heimdul's side because he is your brother," Hunwulf said accusingly.

"No, I am trying to help you," Ragnar replied. "You cannot go against the wishes of the elders. If they so much as knew what you were planning with Gudrun, you would be banished forever from the tribe. And I should not wish to lose you, Hunwulf. I should not like to be deprived of my very best friend. For that selfish reason, I implore you not to embark on this rash course of action. Forget Gudrun. There is many another comely maiden in the tribe who would make you a fine mate. Astrid the Silver-haired, for one. I know for certain that she is fond of you."

"She is nothing to me. I want only Gudrun, and she wants only me. Heimdul the Strong could have his pick of women, and Gudrun and he are not meant to be together the way she and I are. She will never be happy with him."

"And I tell you, you are mad. I cannot allow you to be so foolish."

"Will you apprise the elders, then, of what I mean to do?" said Hunwulf.

"If it comes to it, although I would rather not."

In hindsight, Ragnar could see that this was the moment when Hunwulf made up his mind: he and Gudrun would not just elope but he would slay Heimdul too. His jealousy was just too strong, and Ragnar's threat to reveal his intentions to the elders merely reinforced his sense that the fates were conspiring against him.

That very night, Hunwulf murdered Heimdul and fled with Gudrun.

For a decade since, Ragnar had dedicated himself to finding his brother's killer and avenging himself upon him. What had started out as mourning had turned into a seemingly endless quest for retribution, in which he had embroiled his four closest comrades.

Now that it was nearing its culmination, Ragnar felt some regret. He was sorry that Knut was dead, and sorry, too, that Halfdan, Sten and Njal had given up so much of their lives to his cause, however willingly. When this was all over, would they even be able to return to their tribe? They had been away from for so long, perhaps they would not be welcomed back. Perhaps they had become strangers to their own kin, eternal exiles.

Ragnar could accept some of the blame for that, but most of it, he thought, lay with Hunwulf and Gudrun. It was another misdeed for which the pair would have to pay.

"Hsst!"

This sibilant warning came from the usually taciturn Sten. His expression was quizzical.

"What is it?" Ragnar asked.

Sten held finger to lips and cocked his head. He was listening hard for something.

"Is it them?" Ragnar wanted to know. "Can you hear them coming?" Out of anyone Ragnar had met, Sten's ears were the sharpest. Perhaps because he spoke so little, he heard so much more.

Sten shook his head, and now his demeanor turned anxious. He got to his feet, unsheathing his sword. Their horses, meanwhile, which were tethered nearby, started whinnying disquietedly.

Sten cast an eye upward to the starry heavens.

Next thing Ragnar knew, an immense dark shape swooped in, and Sten gasped. The fleeting shadow was there and gone in the space of a heartbeat, passing in front of Sten so swiftly that Ragnar was not even sure he had seen it at all.

And now Sten—large, quiet, long-suffering Sten—stood there with his sword drooping in his hand and a look of incomprehension on his face. By the flickering firelight Ragnar saw that three ragged red lines had opened up across his chest. They were deep slashes, streaming ribbons of blood pouring out from each. Sten's ribs were exposed, and he opened his mouth to emit an inarticulate howl of distress.

The shadow swooped again, and Ragnar caught a glimpse of leathery wings and gleaming talons.

Then Sten's head was gone, sheared clean off at the neck. His decapitated body sagged to the ground, and a moment later his head itself fell from the sky to land with a thud beside it.

"What in hell's name...?" said an astonished Halfdan, and then he was next to fall prey to the strange, swooping winged figure. It dived down and lifted him up into the air by his arms.

Halfdan screamed in shock and panic as he was carried higher and higher, disappearing into the darkness above in a matter of seconds. His voice faded then returned as a shriek of terror increasing in volume, only to be cut short abruptly by a loud, sickening thump. This was the sound of Halfdan hurtling downward from a great height and hitting the ground.

His body made an inches-deep impression in the dry silt of the riverbed and spattered blood in all directions around it. His mangled remains, with bone shards protruding at various angles from a shambles of flesh, scarcely resembled a human being anymore.

That left just Ragnar and Njal, along with the trussed-up Bjørn.

The two men instinctively moved together until they were back to back, swords out in front of them. Both scanned the sky. The horses were stamping back and forth, wrenching at their restraints and neighing their distress.

"What is happening?" Njal said. "Who is attacking us? It cannot be Hunwulf and Gudrun."

"Nay," said Ragnar, "this is something else, some unearthly monstrosity. Did you see its wings? They looked like the wings of a giant bat."

"I think I saw a scaly hide. What manner of creature is it?"

Bjørn, meanwhile, was straining at his bonds in sheer terror. Of the three of them remaining, he was the one least able to defend himself, and thus the most vulnerable to this airborne predator's assaults. Try as he might, however, he could not free himself.

"Ragnar!" Njal cried, pointing. "I see it!"

Ragnar looked over his shoulder to follow the direction of Njal's forefinger.

There, silhouetted against the stars, was a manlike figure, hovering aloft on beats of huge, jointed wings that sprouted from its back. The head was somehow misshapen, far narrower at the base than at the top, and the hands and feet terminated in long, wickedly curved talons.

That was as much as Ragnar was able to glean before the creature descended once more, coming at them almost too fast for the eye to follow.

Njal collided backwards into Ragnar, and the impact knocked him flat on his face. He lay there, winded, beneath his fellow Æsir. He could hear Njal groaning and making weird, wet sucking noises.

He pushed himself up onto his hands and knees, rolling Njal off his back. The other man lay supine beside him, and he no longer had a face. The skin had been torn completely off, exposing cartilage, glistening muscle, and here and there a glimpse of white skull. Njal's lidless eyes rolled in their sockets, and his lips smacked moistly together as he tried to frame his agony in words.

Even as Ragnar looked on, the winged entity looped round and glided back towards them. It raked its lower set of talons along Njal's torso as it flew past, ripping him open from collarbone to navel as easily as one might cut a piece of sackcloth with a sharp knife.

Ragnar sprang to his feet. The blood was pounding in his ears. Fury had supplanted horror in his heart. In under a minute this winged abomination had slain all three of his comrades, seemingly without effort.

He understood that he was very likely to be joining them in death tonight, but the thing, whatever it was, would not take his life cheaply, and not at all if he had any say in the matter.

"Come and get me, you hell-spawned demon!" he yelled. "You had the element of surprise before, but now I am ready for you. I'll show you how an Æsir fights!"

He braced himself for the creature's next sally.

As for Bjørn, he had ceased to struggle. He had no hope of getting himself loose. All he could do was look on in powerless, horrified resignation. He did not know who was going to win, Ragnar or the winged beast, and either way, it did not make much difference for Bjørn.

Whichever of them survived, he himself was going to die.

Kidnapping From Kidnappers

Conan crept on all fours to the edge of the crag that overlooked the Tongue of Set.

"Crom!" he swore under his breath, as he peered down.

Moonlight revealed a scene of butchery. A hundred feet below him lay four bodies in various states of dismemberment, ranged around the embers of a dwindling campfire. Tethered horses stood close by, tails swishing in agitation.

He set off swiftly down the rocky precipice, the time for stealth clearly now past. The side of the crag he had climbed up was a shallow-angled slope. This other side was far steeper, almost sheer, but afforded enough handholds and footholds for an easy descent, not least for an agile Cimmerian who had been scrambling up and down mountainsides since he was old enough to walk.

Lowering himself into the riverbed, he examined each of the bodies in turn. They were all Æsir, as expected, and they all appeared to have been torn apart by some wild animal.

What he did not see was Bjørn, and he could not decide whether this was a good sign or a bad one. He called out the boy's name, in case he was hiding somewhere nearby, but no response did he receive.

He then shouted at the top of his voice to Hunwulf and Gudrun, who he knew were approaching on horseback from the direction of Eruk. They were not in sight yet but could not be too distant. He had parted company with them a mile or so back, leaving his own horse, the piebald mare, tied to a scrubby little acacia tree and continuing on foot, taking a circuitous route to the other side of the crag.

"Ho! Make haste!" His voice carried far in the nighttime stillness of the wilderness. "Ragnar and company are no longer a danger."

A faint answering cry was followed shortly by a rattle of cantering hooves. Hunwulf and Gudrun reined in, dismounted, and joined Conan down in the riverbed.

"In the name of all the gods..." Hunwulf said, casting an incredulous eye over the slaughter.

"Bjørn," said his wife. "I cannot see Bjørn. Where is he?"

A low moan caught their attention. One of the Æsir, it transpired, was not as dead as the rest.

"Ragnar," Hunwulf breathed.

The man had been brutally savaged. There remained few parts of him intact. Yet somehow, improbably, he continued to cling to life.

"H-Hunwulf," he rasped. "Is that you? Finally, after all this time..."

"Where is Bjørn?" Hunwulf demanded.

"Taken. Gone."

"Gone where?"

A ravaged arm rose. A bloodied finger gestured skyward. The arm fell. "Monster," said Ragnar. "Bore him away. Into the air. Into the night." He coughed, ejecting a lungful of blood.

"What nonsense is this?" said Gudrun. "Where is my son, Ragnar?" She kicked the prone figure in his flank, prompting more blood to bubble from his lips. "And no more tall tales about monsters."

"True," Ragnar croaked. "All true. Winged monster. Killed us all. Took Bjørn. I swear it."

"Took him which way?"

"South."

"But why Bjørn? Why kidnap him but slay the rest of you?"

"Don't know. Hunwulf…"

"Yes?" said Hunwulf.

"I am dying."

"That much is abundantly clear."

"I… I have spent years… hating you. Hunting you. Hounding you. But now that I see you again… I remember only my friend from before. My good friend Hunwulf. Would that… things had been different."

Hunwulf gave a mournful nod. "Would that they had. But it's too late now."

"Too late. Far too late." Ragnar's voice had become little more than a ragged whisper. "One favor, I beg of you."

"Do you wish me to forgive you? I am not sure I can find it in my heart to do so."

"Nor can I… forgive you. But would you send us off… the four of us… according to the custom of our people? Would you… do that for me… at least? So that our souls… are received properly in the afterlife? Promise me you will."

Hunwulf sighed and said, "Very well. I promise."

Ragnar seemed satisfied with this answer, and now he could keep death at bay no longer. A stillness settled over him, his eyes closed, and his suffering came to an end.

Hunwulf stood over him with head bowed for a full minute, then straightened up.

"We must burn them," said he.

"We must go after our son," countered his wife.

"I made a promise. It's the right thing to do. We burn them, and then we go after Bjørn."

Gudrun conceded, and she, her husband and Conan set about collecting brushwood and tree branches. Hunwulf and Gudrun erected a low, makeshift bier over the campfire, rekindled the embers, added the gathered wood, and soon had a pyre going. Onto the bier they piled the Æsir men's bodies one after another, and Hunwulf murmured a prayer in his native tongue as the corpses were consumed by the flames.

In the meantime Conan went to fetch the piebald mare. By the time he returned, Hunwulf and Gudrun had freed their compatriots' horses to go wheresoever they wished and were mounted on their own.

The three of them turned southward and, with the funeral pyre still crackling and blazing at their backs, kicked their steeds into motion and galloped off.

They rode south all night long. There was precious little conversation among them. All three kept a constant lookout for a winged creature in the sky bearing Bjørn in its talons, but saw no sign of any. They did this though fully aware that it might well be futile.

Near dawn, Conan broke their silence. "Perhaps it has gone to ground. A creature like that must have a roost, a lair of some sort. There could be a cave hereabouts where it is wont to take its prey, or else a structure like that tower you described, Hunwulf, when you told me about the winged beast that abducted Gudrun."

"Prey," said Gudrun. "I would rather you did not use that word when referring to our son."

"It was not my meaning. I was talking in generalities. I do not believe Bjørn even is prey."

"What makes you say that?"

"Why did the monster kill four men but take Bjørn alive? What about him is different from the others?" These were rhetorical questions.

"His youth," said Hunwulf.

"That is one answer, aye," said Conan, "and if it is the creature's intention to eat Bjørn, then I can see how it might prefer the tender flesh of a youth to the gristlier meat of an adult. After all, who does not prefer lamb to mutton?"

Gudrun looked daggers at him. "Are all Cimmerians so crass and tactless, Conan, or is it just you?"

"But in that case," Conan went on, unperturbed, "why not eat him on the spot? Why not, moreover, eat Ragnar and his followers? There were no signs of those four being consumed—no teeth marks, no chunks of missing, chewed-off flesh. Few predators wait to gorge themselves. They feast unthinkingly and move on. Nay, Bjørn has been chosen. First, the monster slew those holding him captive. Then it made off with him."

"But if chosen, why?" said Hunwulf.

"To that I have no answer. All I can tell you is that I believe your boy remains alive. This creature is no mindless, ravening animal. Look at how it killed the Æsir men. Those were precise, methodical strikes, to judge by the wounds. Beheading. Gutting. It even tore one man's face off. It attacked with intelligence and clear cunning, not to mention relish. Whatever it is, it possesses wits like you or I. It must want Bjørn for some other purpose than food. That makes this a kidnapping. It has kidnapped him from his kidnappers."

"And you are certain of that?" said Gudrun. "You are not saying it just to give us comfort?"

"I am not a man who coddles," Conan retorted.

"Could the monster be connected somehow to the winged thing Gudrun and I confronted all those years ago?" said Hunwulf. "Close kin to it, even?"

"I do not know. Perhaps." And perhaps, Conan bethought himself, it could be connected to the apelike, demoniac ogre which slew Bêlit and which he in turn slew. That was the likelier of the two possibilities, seeing as how here in Shem they were much closer to the Black Coast than they were to the lands just south of Vanaheim. What if that red-eyed travesty of nature had not been, as he had believed, the last of its kind? What if there were more?

Yet Shem was still a very long way from the Zarkheba inlet, and the notion that a creature had flown all those hundreds of miles in order to wreak revenge by kidnapping the son of Conan's friends beggared credibility.

No, any link between Bêlit's murderer and Bjørn's abductor, or for that matter Gudrun's abductor all those years ago, had to be happenstance. The world was awash with bizarre, inhuman beings, as Conan knew all too well, and one winged abomination was not necessarily related to another.

The only thing the coincidence suggested to him was that the ways of fate were riddled with concordances and patterns which seemed to imply much but actually were empty of meaning. If there were some great significance to the recurrence of winged monsters in their lives beyond luck—and ill luck at that—Conan would be very surprised.

As the sun broke the horizon, the trio arrived at a waterhole situated on the edge of a parched desert plain. They let the horses drink, and themselves drank too.

"We need a plan," Conan opined, shading his eyes as he surveyed the rippling sandy emptiness ahead. "We can't search all of Shem in the vain hope of coming across the monster's trail. The creature flies, hence leaves no spoor."

"Maybe we'll find someone who witnessed the massacre," Gudrun said.

"That is far from guaranteed."

"And besides," said Hunwulf, "what is there around here?

I see only nothingness. No human habitation, that's for sure."

"In other words," said Conan, "we could wander from now until doomsday and never find the beast." His face turned wry and insightful, as though a certain idea had just occurred to him— although, in truth, it had been circulating in his mind for some while. "Hunwulf, your power of foresight is required," he said.

He fixed Hunwulf with a very meaningful stare.

"My abilities do not work that way," Hunwulf said. "It is one thing to foresee the results of a dice roll. It is quite another to be shown the farther future and discern the outline of some forthcoming major event."

"How is it different?"

"I told you. My prophetic visions arrive unbidden. I can achieve a state of mind wherein I can see what is due to happen in the next few moments, as at the gaming table, but the visions are different. Those, I cannot induce. They do not come unless my incarnations wish it so."

"Why not?"

"How should I know? That is just how it has always been."

"But might you not be able to produce them to order?" said Conan. "Beg these so-called incarnations of yours to reveal something from the days to come?"

"So-called," echoed Gudrun softly. "Still he doubts."

"No," said Hunwulf, in answer to Conan's question.

"Why not?" said Conan.

"They don't answer to me. I answer to them."

"That seems very disobliging of these other selves of yours. Don't you think they would help if you asked, not least since you are they and they you?"

"I... I cannot say. I just know they won't."

"You know this," said Conan, "only because you haven't tried."

The Æsir man shook his head, but the action turned into a reluctant nod of acknowledgment. "Granted. But consider this.

Even assuming I were able to prevail upon my incarnations to lay bare my immediate future to me, it is possible that that future does not contain finding Bjørn. My other selves cannot remember anything I do not experience personally. If we are not destined to find him, then all I will learn from them is that very fact."

"But look at it another way," Conan argued. "Consult them, and you can make sure that we do find Bjørn. They are able to give you the guidance you seek, and through that you are able to accomplish your goal."

"By Ymir's frostbitten pizzle!" declared Gudrun, with a hint of admiration. "Hunwulf creates a loop, like a serpent eating its own tail. That is knotty thinking, Conan, worthy of a philosopher, but I like it."

"Bah! Philosopher! Insult me not, woman."

"My apologies. What an easy thing it is, to hurt the feelings of a barbarian."

Gudrun was teasing him once more, and Conan deemed this a good sign. She was mastering her fears about Bjørn, putting them in a place where they would impel rather than hinder her.

"What I find embarrassing," she went on, "is that Hunwulf and I have never thought of the idea ourselves."

"As I've already explained, Gudrun," said her husband, "and as you well know, I only receive information; I cannot solicit it."

"So do as Conan suggests and try."

"I would not even know how to begin."

"Begin as you do when you are at the gaming table and you allow time to become elastic around you," said Gudrun, "and then expand from there. Invite your incarnations to parley with you. Open yourself up to them. Become a conduit rather than just a vessel."

Hunwulf looked unconvinced, but it was obvious that Gudrun was not going to let the matter rest. What Conan had proposed was their best and perhaps only chance for locating and rescuing

Bjørn, and even if it was doomed to fail, Gudrun would never forgive her husband if he did not at least make the effort.

Hunwulf's shoulders slumped. "Very well," said he. "I shall give it a go."

Hunwulf took himself off to a spot in the shade of a juniper some hundred and fifty yards from his wife, Conan and the horses. Here, there would be fewer distractions.

He sat cross-legged on the ground and willed himself into the frame of mind he adopted when gambling. He let his eyes become unfocused and allowed his thoughts to drift and lose coherence.

He was well practiced at this, so much so that it was almost second nature. Within moments he could feel time's grip upon him loosening. He saw himself taking his seat beneath the juniper. He saw himself standing up afterwards. He saw himself moving towards the tree. He saw himself walking away from it. He held these events from the immediate past and future in his mind like water cupped in his hands. They were happening both disparately and at once.

Always, whenever he entered this state of temporal flexibility, Hunwulf would hear the dim, distant whispering of his other incarnations. It was as though a membrane dividing him from them thinned and their voices seeped through.

He had learned to disregard their susurrant babel, treating it as an irrelevance; but now, for a change, he gave it his full attention. He listened to them speaking in dozens of languages. It was the sound of men living their lives, conversations they were holding, expressions of joy and agony and rage and despair, all of it bleeding through time from past and future, funneled into the present. At some point during the long march of history, whether in bygone ages or ages yet to come, these were words he himself had uttered or would utter.

He addressed his other selves, using his own inner voice. He asked them collectively to lend an ear. He had a request to make. He recounted what had happened to Bjørn. He beseeched his incarnations to let him know if they had any inkling of his son's whereabouts. They were his and Gudrun's only hope. He impressed upon them the urgency of the matter. Before now, his incarnations had aided him without his asking. Just this once, he wished to initiate a message from them and not have to wait optimistically for one.

Did they listen? Were they hearing him? Hunwulf thought he detected a brief lull in their massed murmuring, but perhaps he imagined it. He braced himself for a vision to arrive in direct response.

But there was nothing. He reiterated his appeal a couple of times further, with no more success.

Resignedly he committed himself back to the here and now, and time again became remorseless, unidirectional, fixed. He stood up. He walked away from the juniper tree.

He collapsed to the ground as though poleaxed.

Gudrun saw Hunwulf stumble and fall. She sprinted over to his side, Conan trailing in her wake.

"Husband!" she said, patting his cheek. "Speak to me!"

Hunwulf replied in a senseless mumble.

"Has he had a vision?" Conan wondered.

"The symptoms seem the usual ones," Gudrun said.

"How long before he is able to tell us its contents? Last time it was some while."

"It can take anything from a few minutes to an hour. We'll simply have to see."

"Let us get him back into the shade," Conan advised. "The sun is strengthening."

Between them they carried Hunwulf over to the tree and laid him down. They waited, and the wind sifted across the sand dunes on the plain, and the horses nickered to one another.

Eventually Hunwulf stirred. Gudrun fed him some sips of water, and when he was ready, he spoke.

"Kush," said he. "We must travel to Kush, and a city called Ghuht."

"Ghuht?" said Conan. "I have never heard of it."

"I neither, and I know not whereabouts it lies in that country. Nonetheless, at Ghuht shall we find Bjørn." A troubled look entered Hunwulf's eyes. "But we must consider this also."

He picked up a fallen twig and sketched a symbol in the dirt, thus:

"What is it?" said Conan.

"It is a sigil representing an eye," said Hunwulf. His lip quivered like that of a man overcome by a nameless dread. "I know not whose, nor why my incarnations felt moved to inform me about it. I know only that it is important and it is terrible. It is an eye which sees much and to which emotion of any kind is wholly alien. We must be wary of it. We must avoid catching its attention."

He scrubbed out the symbol with his heel, as if he could not bear the sight of it. He did not stop until it was thoroughly obliterated.

His voice dropped to a hushed whisper.

"Wherever that sigil is," he said, "there too is death."

12

A Fixed Heading After Months Adrift

O f their southerly journey through Shem, there is little to tell. Skirting the desert, they joined one of the well-trodden roads that led towards Stygia.

Things were pleasingly uneventful on that road, save for an incident when they were beset by bandits while filing along a narrow, lonesome pass. The would-be plunderers outnumbered the three travelers by a multiple of at least five and thought they would be easy pickings. They did not foresee much resistance. This overconfidence was, in part, their undoing.

Without hesitating, Conan goaded his mare to a gallop and charged straight into the thick of the bandits, his broadsword swinging in glittering silver arcs right and left. Hunwulf unshipped a double-headed axe and joined the fray, while Gudrun snatched up a bow, nocked an arrow and let it fly. She followed it up with a succession of further arrows, each of which found its mark, even as Conan and Hunwulf cut a bloody swathe through the bandit ranks.

In next to no time what had been a gloating, heavily armed criminal gang was reduced to a frantic, mewling rabble. Only two of their complement got away with their lives. The rest were cut down mercilessly. They simply had not bargained on meeting people who were quite such formidable warriors, nor who had such a level of pent-up rage and frustration in need of an outlet.

After four days' ride through Shem's lower reaches, the wayfaring trio arrived at the River Styx, which served as the border between that country and Stygia. A ferryman took them across in his barge one at a time, each with horse.

On the far bank, while waiting for the Æsir couple to join him, Conan reflected on the fact that he had finally left Shem. It was time. He had spent long enough there honoring the memory of Bêlit.

This did not mean that he was being disloyal to his lost love by moving on, merely that he had grieved for her sufficiently. Bêlit had been someone who embraced life with a ferocious zest, and if there was any lesson to be learned from her death, it was that he, her erstwhile paramour, should continue to do likewise. It helped that he had a purpose again, a mission to pursue, a fixed heading after months adrift.

They got on their way again, with Conan frequently and snarlingly expressing his dislike of the land they now found themselves in. Stygia was a place of strange religions and dark magics, presided over by theocrats in thrall to malign gods, most notably Set. The ruling class curried favor with their deities by means of regular human sacrifice, which also served to reinforce their own authority over their subjects through the time-honored tradition of keeping them cowed and obeisant with fear. The blood-soaked holy rituals were conducted by a debauched priestly caste who seemed to take a rare, indeed lascivious, pleasure in wielding the ceremonial knife and eviscerating their living offerings.

The three travelers now veered southwest, following routes in the direction of Kush. They gave Luxur, Stygia's royal capital, a wide berth, and likewise Khemi, the ecclesiastical capital, eschewing these cities as places to rest and resupply in favor of villages and small provincial towns. This was at Conan's urging and in accordance with his personal prejudices, for as far as he was concerned the fewer sorcerers, nobles and monarchs one had to rub shoulders with, the better.

Within a week and a half they were nearing Sukhmet, down by the border with Darfar, a nation perhaps even more sinister than Stygia, where cannibalism was commonly practiced and dragons were known to roam. They went no closer to it than twenty miles: that was plenty close enough.

By now, after so many days in the saddle and nights in a variety of hard-bedded inns or sleeping under the stars, the three companions were becoming increasingly travel-weary. They were tough, all of them, and inured to hardship, Conan most of all; but the road takes its toll.

They pressed on regardless, growing dustier and more bedraggled with every mile. Thanks to Hunwulf's vision they knew Bjørn was to be found in Kush, in the city known as Ghuht, which meant they knew they would find him. This spurred them on and made the privations they endured bearable.

It was in a town not far from Sukhmet, the slaver city, that they chanced upon a version of the eye sigil.

The symbol was rendered crudely on the outer wall of a house in red paint and was near identical to the one Hunwulf had etched in the dirt after his vision. When Conan spied it, he straight away pointed it out to the Æsir couple.

There was a sharp intake of breath from Hunwulf. "Ymir take me!" he declared, reining in his horse. His eyes bulged and his chest started heaving.

"Husband, calm yourself," said Gudrun. "This show of fear is unseemly, ill befitting an Æsir."

"You don't understand," came the hoarse, quavering reply. "My incarnations spoke with one accord, and they were insistent. That thing is unearthly and represents everything that is hostile to life."

"Let's find out what it is doing here," Conan said. "You." He seized hold of a local man passing by along the street. Gripping him by the front of his tunic, he indicated the sigil. "What does that mean? Why is it on this house?"

"Unhand me, barbarian," said the Stygian, affronted.

"Not until you answer my question." To this statement Conan added a glowering look with his baleful ice-blue eyes, which convinced the Stygian to comply.

"I know not its import," he said. "I believe it is there to ward off evil. Why not ask indoors yourself? That is Abrax the carpenter's house. He can tell you, I'm sure."

Conan let the man go, and he scurried off with a disgruntled curse. The Cimmerian thundered on Abrax's front door with the side of his fist.

A woman opened the door. "Yes?" She was not old, no more than twenty-five, but she was gaunt and her hair hung lankly, lending her the air of someone twice that age. Her eyes were swollen and red-rimmed, the eyes of someone who had been crying for a long time and often.

"The image daubed on this dwelling," Conan said. "Account for it."

"It…" The woman faltered. "I cannot put it into words. My husband can explain better than I. He put it there."

"I would talk with him."

The woman hesitated, then acquiesced. "He is within. Enter. Your Nordheimer friends too."

She ushered them into the house, which was a plainly but

comfortably furnished abode. A table and set of chairs were especially well made, presumably Abrax's handiwork. Two small boys, identical twins, played listlessly with carved wooden toys in one corner of the main room, while out in the rear yard a man sat slumped and disconsolate. Next to him was a heap of lumber and a workbench upon which sat the tools of the carpentry trade: handsaw, plane, adze, hammer, chisel, and so forth. They all bore a layer of dust, denoting disuse.

"Abrax? These people wish to know about the eye."

At the sound of his wife's voice, the man looked up bleakly. His hair was styled in the Stygian fashion, bald apart from a long topknot. He had neglected to shave his scalp as he ought in some while, for the skin was covered in a fur of stubble.

Conan introduced himself and the Æsir couple and reiterated the question he had posed to Abrax's wife.

"Thereby hangs a tragic tale," said the carpenter dolefully, "and I am loath to tell it."

"You will find us an attentive audience," said Conan.

"How come?"

"That eye sigil is a matter of great interest to us."

Abrax studied the three of them. "Aye," he said. "I see it in your faces. This is no casual inquiry. You know something of the symbol's provenance." He steeled himself. "Where do I begin? It was a month ago. Our daughter, our precious Layla, eldest of our three, was out with her friends. There were a half dozen of them, all around the same age as her, eight years old. They were a stone's throw from here, over by the town well. A cat had lately given birth to a litter of kittens there, and you know how children are about kittens. I was at home, working, and I heard screams, loud and shrill. I somehow knew from that sound that Layla was in trouble. I went running. Aminah wished to come with me." He gestured at his wife. "But I told her to stay with the twins."

"I consented," Aminah said. "They are still too little to be left unattended, and besides, I did not want them witnessing whatever might have provoked those screams."

"I arrived at the well," said Abrax, "along with various other townspeople who had been drawn by the commotion, to find Layla's friends milling about in terrified confusion. Of Layla herself I could see no sign. I demanded of the children what had happened. Eventually one sobbing girl told me about a winged monster that had descended upon their group without warning and plucked Layla up from the ground in its talons. The monster flew off with her, rapidly vanishing from view."

Conan exchanged meaningful looks with Hunwulf and Gudrun.

"I was stunned," Abrax continued. "I could not believe my ears. I interrogated another of the children, and another, and received the same story. All agreed: there had been a winged monster, shaped like a man but with skin and facial features that were distinctly lizard-like, and it had swooped out of nowhere and borne Layla away. They were too patently terrified to be lying. One child provided a further detail. The winged thing had been wearing an amulet about its neck, and upon the amulet there was a peculiar design, which the child sketched for me."

"The eye sigil," said Conan.

"Just so. I scoured the countryside for days, without finding any clue to Layla's whereabouts. It was a lost cause, and eventually I gave up in despair. And that is now our situation. Our daughter—our sweet, strange little Layla—has been taken from us, and there is no rhyme or reason to it. We know not where she has gone, nor what has become of her, nor why she alone of all her peers was taken. We must just accept that we are never going to see her again. Our lives have become a constant trudge of sorrow and torment. I refuse to let the twins go outside, much to their aggravation, lest the same fate befalls them as befell their sister. I cannot work.

I hardly sleep. The heart has been ripped from our family, and I fear we shall never recover."

Gudrun stepped forward and embraced the man. "It has happened to us also," said she. "Trust me, I share the pain you feel. I can offer you no other consolation than that."

Abrax burst into tears at her touching gesture, as did Aminah. Their shoulders heaved as their misery spilled out.

Conan had formed a view of Gudrun as a fierce, stern woman, so her display of tender compassion surprised him. It also made him like her more. He said to Abrax, "You believe the eye you have painted will prevent the winged monster from returning?"

"Can it hurt to try?" the carpenter answered. "It shows we have been marked already, and perhaps the monster will take pity and pass us by next time. I would do anything to protect our boys."

"You called your daughter your 'strange little Layla,'" said Hunwulf quizzically. "An unusual choice of words."

Aminah said, "Layla is... she was a dreamy child. Oftentimes she seemed not of this earth."

"And then there was her love of fire," said Abrax. "More than a love. She was drawn to it, and on occasion she was able to control it."

"Control?" said Conan.

"Aye. With her hands. With her mind. By concentrating, she could manipulate fire between her fingertips and make it do her bidding."

"She was a witch?"

"You can hardly call an eight-year-old girl that. Layla just had a peculiar trick she could perform, that's all. Flame danced to her will. She could bend it, shape it, make it grow large or shrink, and took delight in doing so. Once, in error, she nearly burnt the house down. The cooking fire grew too strong under her playful ministration and threatened to engulf everything. Thankfully, I managed to extinguish the blaze with a bucket of water, in the nick of time." Abrax half-smiled at a memory that clearly elicited both happiness and sadness. "After that, she confined herself to toying with candle flames."

"Tell me, do any of the friends who were with Layla have gifts like hers?"

"You mean controlling fire?"

"Or similar."

"Not that I know of."

"No," said Aminah authoritatively.

"And all this happened a month ago, you say?"

"Thereabouts," said Abrax. "I lose track of the days."

"Twenty-seven days," said Aminah.

"We have intruded upon you enough," said Conan. He turned to Hunwulf and Gudrun. "Come."

Having taken their leave of the devastated household, Conan consulted with his two companions. "I think the same beast that took Bjørn took the Stygian girl beforehand. What say you?"

"It certainly looks that way," Hunwulf said.

"Moreover, I think I know why. What do the two children have in common? Both possess a preternatural ability. This Layla manipulates fire, and your boy communicates with animals."

"You know about that?" said Gudrun.

"He told me himself."

She sighed, with a touch of exasperation. "Bjørn is quite proud of his talent but we have encouraged him not to show off about it. It might bring unwelcome attention."

"He only confessed to it after I had seen him, with my own eyes, make a lapdog of a stray feral mongrel," Conan said.

"We think it may be hereditary. Hunwulf's father, too, was

born with an affinity for animals. It is part of the reason he became tribal shaman. It is a role requiring a close kinship with the natural world in all its forms."

"It skipped a generation with me," Hunwulf said. "Instead, perhaps as compensation, I was bestowed access to my incarnations."

"I believe this winged reptilian devil is choosing people who have magical abilities, and youngsters at that," Conan determined.

Briefly, he wondered once more whether there were some connection here with Hunwulf's winged monster of a decade ago and his own such beast at the Zarkheba river. As before, he dismissed the notion. Fate did not weave such intricate webs, although it was known sometimes to speak in rhyme.

"That," he went on, "is why the thing took only Layla and none of her friends. Both of them, she and Bjørn, were kidnapped to order, methinks. But for what purpose?"

"And also," said Gudrun, "are they the only ones?"

Gudrun Ingensdóttir's question was answered a few days later as the three travelers arrived one morning in yet another small town, this one in Stygia's marshy southern lowlands, very close to the border with Kush. They were drawn towards a commotion in the town square, the roaring of a crowd.

"I know that sound," said Conan. "It is the sound of a mob."

It was indeed. A couple of hundred angry people thronged the square, clamoring for blood, baying and braying like animals.

The object of their wrath was a woman dressed in filthy rags who was being hauled by two men towards a wooden stake set upright into the earth. The woman's arms and legs dangled floppily like a stringless marionette's, clearly broken in several places. Blood caked her body, dried black. She was semiconscious, doubtless in shock from the agony of her shattered limbs, but still sufficiently aware of her predicament that her eyes rolled in mad terror. Her lips writhed wordlessly, perhaps pleading for clemency. None would be forthcoming, to judge by the way the mob kicked and spat at her as she was hauled through their heaving, jostling midst.

Her part-bared breast revealed a symbol that had been cut into the flesh just below the collarbone. Crudely and raggedly incised though it was, it was clearly Hunwulf's—and Abrax's—eye sigil. As soon as Conan spied this, he went rigid.

Gudrun had seen it too, and nudged her husband.

Conan leaned towards a woman near him who was screaming shrill words of hatred at the focus of the mob's ire.

"Who is she?" he demanded. "What has she done to earn such enmity?"

"Why, only killed her own daughter, outlander," the woman replied. "And for that, she has suffered, and will suffer further before she dies. She is to be stoned to death, and we will take our time over it."

"Killed her daughter?"

"Oh, she swears she did not. Even under torture ordained by the magistrate, she has maintained that the girl was stolen. But we know better. Heqet—that is her name—has always been touched in the head. She's a good healer, able to cure a whole host of ailments just by the laying on of hands, and her daughter looked set to follow in her footsteps when she was older; but there's a streak of lunacy in Heqet. Lunacy and magic often go hand in hand. And the two of them living in a shack in the swamp outside town, all alone, after Heqet's husband perished in a hunting accident—isolation like that can do things to a mind, bad things."

"Did she insist that her daughter was snatched by a winged creature as much reptile as man?"

The woman looked at Conan with wild curiosity. "It so happens she did. But what a preposterous tale! Just the kind of thing a madwoman would say. And to talk about a mysterious eye symbol the monster sported upon its clothing! No wonder the magistrate's inquisitor carved it into her body, just as she described it. Serves her right. Heqet killed the poor girl and buried her somewhere where no one can find her. But how did you know about her insane excuse anyway? It was only a week ago that she came into town wailing that her daughter was gone, spirited away. Has word of her crime spread so far, so fast?"

"I have heard similar claims," Conan said curtly.

By now Heqet was being tied to the stake. She screeched like a soul in hell as her arms were lifted up above her head so that the bindings around her wrists could be attached to an iron ring near the stake's top.

The crowd's revelrous frenzy was mounting, and many of them were gathering up rocks, pebbles and stones from the ground in readiness for the execution.

Hanging by her wrists, and her broken legs unable to support her, Heqet sagged dismally. The hour of her death was at hand, and she knew it would be a prolonged ordeal. Nobody among the townspeople was going to do her the courtesy of finishing her off swiftly with a heavy stone to her head.

Conan held out a motioning hand to Gudrun. "Your bow," said he.

The Æsir woman immediately grasped his intent. "You will not make us popular."

"I care not," Conan replied.

Gudrun nodded and passed him the bow and an arrow to go with it.

Conan clambered onto a low wall to give him a clear line of sight above the heads of the mob. He was not an expert archer—he was certainly no Bossonian—but he was proficient enough. It was an easy shot, besides: thirty yards, no great range.

Stones began to hail down on Heqet, small ones designed to hurt but not cause serious harm. The crowd cheered jubilantly as the healer woman writhed and moaned in her wretchedness.

Conan knew he could have done little to deter these townspeople from their course of action, given the mass hysteria that had overcome them; and anyway, even if he could have saved her, Heqet had been so badly injured as a result of her torture that she would never survive long.

The simplest thing he could do for her was put her out of her misery.

The arrow flew. Its tip pierced Heqet's heart. She died instantly.

It took the mob several moments to realize they had been deprived of their vicious, vindictive entertainment. They turned this way and that, scanning for the arrow-shooting spoilsport.

"Time we beat a retreat," Conan advised Hunwulf and Gudrun, and the three hurried to their horses, which they had left just outside the square.

They remounted and fled at the gallop. The incensed mob chased after them on foot, pelting them with leftover stones, but the trio rode swiftly out of range.

"A murrain on your town!" Conan yelled over his shoulder at their pursuers. "May your crops fail and your aquifers run dry! You persecute an innocent and think it justice! You are no better than hyenas!"

The frustrated howling of the fast-receding mob seemed proof that the comparison was accurate.

"That makes three," Conan said after they had put the town far behind them and felt it safe to slow their horses to a walk. "Three children taken, each born with some sort of magical power: Bjørn and his animals, Layla and her fire, and now Heqet's daughter, who shared her mother's abilities as a healer. The pattern is clear."

"They are being sought out," Gudrun said. "Reaped like a harvest. But we still do not know for what end."

"It can only be a sinister one," Hunwulf chimed in. "The eye sigil confirms it."

"Then onward we must go," said Conan, urging his horse to a canter with a tug on the reins. "The sooner we reach Kush and find this Ghuht place, the better."

Within a day they were through the marshlands of southwest Stygia and crossing over into Kush.

Swamp gave way to savannah, yellow grassy plain dotted with high-crowned, multiple-trunked trees. The sun bore down fiercely on the three travelers' heads, little alleviated by a sluggish, oven-hot breeze that whispered across the terrain.

The horses' pace slowed, as it had to. There was no hard riding in unremittingly high temperatures like these. They plodded along, and at every river or mud hole they came to, their riders let them drink their fill, while making sure to replenish their own waterskins.

Now and again, as they trekked along, the trio caught distant glimpses of spear-carrying Kushite hunters who stood statue-still and watched them go by with frank curiosity. These people were tall and rake-thin and, when they moved, moved with a graceful, loping gait, both purposeful and unhurried.

The three also passed a herd of elephants who were similarly watchful and cautious. Conan had seen these giant beasts once or twice before in the course of his voyages up and down the Black Coast aboard the *Tigress*, and every time he was reminded of the creature he had met in the wizard Yara's tower in Zamora's City of Thieves, the strange transcosmic being called Yag-Kosha. Not only did that godlike entity have many of an elephant's physical attributes, he also had an elephant's dignity and majesty.

When one of the herd raised its trunk now, as though in salute, Conan was tempted to return the gesture, feeling that somehow the soul of dead Yag-Kosha lay behind the creature's wise, wrinkled eyes and was hailing him as a friend.

The first night in Kush, the trio slept out in the open, and Conan insisted they take it in turns to keep lookout. Lions prowled the area. You could hear their eerie yowls from miles away in the dark.

During his watch, he even glimpsed one of them by the light of their campfire. The great cat slipped all but silently through the tall grass, a shadow among dappled shadows, and Conan gripped the hilt of his broadsword, anticipating attack.

Luckily, the lion showed no further interest and padded onward. Its musky, pungent scent lingered in Conan's nostrils for some time afterward.

The next day they came to a village, and it was there that they learned about the Rotlands.

13

A Leprosy of Terrain

The village was a huddle of thatched huts, a couple of dozen all told, home to a handful of extended families. The residents were happy to offer the three northerners board and lodging, and that evening they all shared a meal outdoors consisting of antelope meat, cassava, yam, and cornmeal.

Conan had picked up Kushitic during his swashbuckling years with Bêlit, and while not fluent in the language, he could speak it conversationally. Many of the Kushites had a smattering of Stygian, which Hunwulf and Gudrun also had, and thus everybody present could more or less make themselves understood to one another.

The elderly village headman, Jaalu, was curious to know what brought the three strangers to his neighborhood.

Conan saw no harm in responding with the truth. There were expressions of sympathy and dismay from the villagers as he delivered his account of recent events, and when he mentioned Ghuht there was a collective appalled gasp. Several of the Kushites moaned piteously, and a few gesticulated and muttered under their breath in a certain formal manner, invoking their gods to preserve them from evil.

"Ghuht," Jaalu intoned solemnly. "Only a fool goes thither, and anyone unwise and unwary enough to do so never returns. I counsel you, my new friends, to abandon your quest. Your boy is lost, as are those other children."

"I do not accept that," said Gudrun.

Jaalu gave a sad shrug. "Whether or not you accept it, it is fact. We know of these winged monsters. All too well do we know of them."

"Either I've misheard or my understanding of your tongue is faulty," said Conan. "You said 'monsters' plural. There are more than one?"

"There are many, northerner. They dwell in Ghuht, and thence do they sally forth in search of younglings to abduct. They have been doing this consistently for many months now. Communities throughout Kush have been raided by them, children seized out in the open or even dragged from their homes, often beneath their parents' very noses. They are swift, bold and determined, these airborne lizardly abominations, and any who dare oppose them or interfere with their mission are savagely slaughtered. It would seem that their supply of victims in Kush has been exhausted, if they have ventured into Stygia and even as far afield as Shem."

"And in every case, the children they take are ones with some form of magical gift?"

"In every case," Jaalu confirmed. "We know of a child in a village not too far from here, a girl no older than fifteen, who was abducted shortly after the rainy season ended, two months past. Zevia is her name, and she was renowned for seeing spirits and elementals and being able to converse with them. Her mother and father attempted to protect her when the winged lizard-man came, and both were rent limb from limb for their pains. Once more, I urge you to turn and go back." He fixed the Æsir couple with a stern, pitying look. "This boy of yours, this Bjørn, cannot be rescued. None of the children can."

"With all due respect, Jaalu," said Hunwulf, "you have no notion quite how resolute we are."

The headman shook his wizened, hoary-locked old head. "I am a father myself, and a grandfather, and I understand that we will do anything, brave anything, dare anything, on behalf of our young. But what use is it, dying for a hopeless cause? Better, by far, to carry on living."

"What use is living," Gudrun shot back, "if we have not done all we can to retrieve our son?"

"Well, your lives are yours to throw away as you wish."

"Why can we not enter Ghuht and rescue Bjørn?" said Conan. "What is so dangerous about the city?"

"Other than that it is home to hundreds of winged lizard-people?" said Jaalu. "Why, only this. Ghuht lies at the heart of a region that has come to be known as the Rotlands, and nobody who has entered the Rotlands has ever returned. Nobody human, that is. You think you are the only ones who have journeyed after the stolen children in order to get them back? Others have. But never have any of these intrepid folk met with success. Rather, the upshot of their efforts has just been further disappearances, more losses, more lamentation. The Rotlands are death. I can put it no more plainly than that. They swallow up all who enter and never spit them out again. Derketa herself, goddess of death, is not half so avaricious as the Rotlands."

"What sort of a place is it, then? Why so lethal?"

"As to that, I cannot accurately say. This much I do know, from accounts passed on via word of mouth. The Rotlands lie in a remote valley some twenty days' journey hence, and the landscape within their boundary is a ghastly perversion of nature. Animals and vegetation are no longer as we understand them. Thanks to some unknown force, they resemble nothing that is found on this earth or should be. Worse, the limits of the Rotlands are slowly expanding, spreading to encompass yet more territory. Inch by inch, day by day, good land is turning bad, as though blighted by some disease. A leprosy of terrain, you might call it. Perhaps in time the Rotlands will cover Kush entirely. Perhaps eventually they will encompass the whole known world."

Jaalu gave a despairing sigh.

"We can only pray that does not happen," he said.

Conan, Hunwulf and Gudrun rode on the next morning, their spirits little buoyed by the headman's words.

At midday they entered another village, and the sun was now so boilingly intense that they took refuge for an hour or so beneath a vast baobab, which sat centrally among the encircling huts. Its close-clustering branches cast a great dark pool of blissful shade.

There was nobody else outside, and an uncanny feeling hung over the place. People peeped out at the new arrivals from their doorways, but none emerged to accost them, and it was almost as though everybody was eager for them to depart. Whereas at the last village they had been shown great hospitableness, the atmosphere here seemed one of mistrust verging on hostility.

"This must be the village Jaalu spoke of," Conan reasoned, "where the little girl was taken from. No wonder they're treating us so cagily. Anyone out of the ordinary is now suspicious."

"Let us move on, then," said Gudrun. "There's little point upsetting them just by our presence."

As they were preparing to leave, a boy ventured out from one of the huts. He could not have been more than fifteen years old, just on the threshold of manhood. He had a long, handsome face and his body was lean, well-muscled, and lithe. Around his neck hung countless strings of beads in a vast array of colors, and there were patterns of ritual scarification in dots and lines across his cheeks and chest.

He approached the three northerners sidelong, his hands held up with the palms out in a supplicatory gesture.

"Greetings," said he. "X'aan is my name. You are the foreigners who seek the city of Ghuht, am I correct?"

"How do you know of us?" Conan asked.

"You visited Jaalu's village yesterday and stayed overnight," said X'aan, as if this was the answer to the Cimmerian's question.

"But we've only just come from there. How can word about us have reached this village before we did?"

The boy smiled briefly. "News travels fast in Kush. Hunter speaks to hunter, through the darkness, through the dawn, using a code of clicks and whistles that carry far in the stillness. But it is no matter. What matters is that I would like to go with you."

"Into the Rotlands?"

"Into the Rotlands, all the way to Ghuht."

"What ever for?" said Hunwulf.

X'aan's expression darkened and his eyes hardened. "Simple. My sister is there."

"Your sister," said Conan. "And her name would be Zevia, am I right?"

"You are right. My little sister Zevia. A winged lizard-man made off with her, and murdered our parents into the bargain. I wish to get her back, and if I can obtain some measure of reprisal for our parents' deaths too, so much the better." X'aan illustrated his determination with a clenched fist. "I will gladly kill a dozen of those inhuman creatures, a hundred!"

"It's out of the question," Gudrun stated. "You cannot come with us. You are too young. We cannot be responsible for you."

Conan was of a different view. "You are young, aye, but I was your age when I had my first taste of battle at the siege of

Venarium. I don't see why you shouldn't accompany us, X'aan. You know the way to the Rotlands, yes?"

X'aan nodded. "They lie in the eastern hills, past Lake Dhakela. Let me be your guide. I can show you the route. You will get there quicker with my help."

"No," said Hunwulf. "We cannot reasonably allow it."

"You are just a child," Gudrun added.

"I can fight," X'aan declared, "and I am afraid of nothing."

Conan averred, "I think we should give him a chance."

"And I think we do not need any burdens," said Hunwulf. "We have enough to contend with already, without having to keep an eye out for this lad as well."

"Were you a parent yourself, Conan, you would agree with us," said Gudrun.

"I'm thinking only of the practicalities," Conan said. "X'aan is local. He knows the lay of the land. We should take advantage of that."

"And," X'aan chimed in, "I am an orphan, and Zevia is my only close kin. Without her, I am alone in the world. You three seem my best chance of finding her. You will be helping me even as I help you."

The Æsir couple were adamant in their refusal, however, and there was little Conan could say to win them round to his way of thinking. In the end, he offered X'aan an apologetic shrug.

"I am outvoted," he said. "When we get to Ghuht, we'll be sure to look for your sister and save her if we can."

X'aan's shoulders slumped. "I thank you for that, at least," he murmured, crestfallen.

As the three travelers were riding off, Conan looked back. The Kushite boy was watching them forlornly.

The Cimmerian made a subtle beckoning gesture, unseen by Hunwulf and Gudrun.

X'aan caught his meaning, and immediately set to following them. He walked fast along the dusty track they took out of the village, keeping pace with their horses at a distance of some fifty yards.

Minutes later, Conan made a show of turning in the saddle and seeming surprised that X'aan was behind them.

"By Crom!" he said. "The boy isn't leaving us be."

The Æsir couple voiced their discontent.

"Go back," Gudrun called out to X'aan, and kicked her horse into a trot. Hunwulf and Conan did likewise. The latter, however, made sure to wink surreptitiously at X'aan over his shoulder, and the boy returned the wink.

A mile farther on, X'aan was still trailing them, jogging gamely and tirelessly along.

"I don't believe it," Conan said, feigning bemusement. "Still with us. How can we ever shake him off?"

"He's persistent, I'll give him that," said Hunwulf.

"Are you surprised? He has as much reason to go to Ghuht as we, perhaps more. I doubt there is aught we can do to deter him. He will follow us until he drops down dead from exhaustion. I wouldn't care to have that on my conscience. Would you?"

"We settled this already," said Gudrun. "I am not changing my mind."

Another mile passed, and another, and X'aan showed no sign of flagging. The lad certainly had stamina, Conan thought. Such dogged determination would, he reckoned, wear down the two Æsirs' resistance in the end.

Their horses were lathered in sweat and becoming balky. The blazing afternoon sun was sapping the animals' strength and willpower, even though they were only trotting. Perforce, their riders slowed them to a walk, and X'aan tempered his own speed accordingly.

An hour later, they still had not lost their Kushite tail. By now, even stubborn Gudrun was beginning to relent. "I pity him," she said. "He is willing to leave behind everything he knows, for the sake of his sister."

"For my part, I find myself admiring him," Hunwulf said. "He must realize the risks he may run if he enters the Rotlands."

"Hmm," said Conan musingly. "A young man prepared to quit his tribe and face untold hazards, all in the name of what he feels is right. It reminds me of something. I can't quite put my finger on it..."

"Very droll, Cimmerian," said Hunwulf.

"Did you perchance put X'aan up to this?" Gudrun inquired.

"I?" said Conan. "Never!"

"I think you did. All these displays of surprise and bewilderment. You are no great actor, and I see them now for the clumsy charades they are. You secretly encouraged X'aan to follow us, didn't you? You sly dog." She laughed, amused by his effrontery in spite of herself.

"Even if I did," Conan said, "has X'aan not proved his worth amply? One so steadfast and single-minded will make a useful addition to our party."

Gudrun exhaled a longsuffering sigh. "Oh, very well. He can come with us. But you, Conan, are solely accountable for his welfare. Have you got that? And if he turns out to be a liability, I shall have no hesitation about abandoning him."

"Those are fair terms. I shall give him the good tidings." Conan waved to X'aan. "Lad!" he cried. "You can join us after all. Come along. Hurry. You may sit behind me."

X'aan sped up to cover the ground between him and them, grinning all the way. Conan hauled him up by the arm and deposited him on the mare's hindquarters, immediately to the rear of his seat.

Thus did three travelers become four.

14

The Odor of Things That Had Seen Better Days

J ungle enclosed them on all sides, dense and humid. Rippling birdsong and the strident, cacophonous calls of primates resounded above their heads, while insects chirred and whined in the undergrowth. Sunlight filtered by the tree canopy cast everything in shades of green. Lichens, lianas, bark, the mud of the track they rode along, and anything else not naturally green, were all green. Even the air itself took on a shimmering emerald glow.

It had been nearly three weeks since the trio of northerners met X'aan, and they were now in the easternmost region of Kush— low-rolling slopes caparisoned in lush, sweltering forest.

The Kushite boy had shown himself to be a deft and well-informed guide. He had led them safely through a province presided over by a brutish tribe said to be drinkers of human blood, who defended their territory at spearpoint and took no prisoners. He had brought them to the shores of Lake Dhakela, where edible fish swam in abundance and were easily caught, so long as one was willing to risk being attacked by the crocodiles that loitered in the shallows. He had steered them into the jungle and kept them steadily on course for the Rotlands.

When Conan asked him how someone so young had such a comprehensive knowledge of a whole country, X'aan explained that Kushites habitually told one another stories which described their national geography. Landmarks, natural features, place names, types of terrain, peoples, dialects—all these were folded into campfire tales about scheming hyenas and lazy leopards and foolish monkeys. The relation of one locality to another in terms of direction and distance formed an essential part of each narrative, and thus, from infancy onward, every Kushite developed a mental map of all of Kush and, having memorized this, could in theory never get lost.

Gradually the four of them neared the Rotlands and Ghuht. The city was ancient, so X'aan said, and had fallen into decline and decay several centuries ago. Long believed uninhabited, it had always been best avoided, a place of rumor and superstition, the haunt of demons.

One of the folkloric tales—the only one to mention Ghuht directly at all—told of a lion cub who strayed from his pride as they rested beside a set of rapids at a river bend. The cub, no longer a weanling but not yet an adult, was an impetuous sort who refused to listen to good advice. Walking due north for a couple of hours, he strayed toward the ruins of Ghuht.

On the outskirts he met Amra-kuu, the lion god. Amra-kuu warned him away from the city, saying it was a dangerous place, but the cub ignored the admonition and went on ahead. He began excitedly exploring Ghuht's broken, vine-wreathed buildings and shattered, weed-strewn streets, until all at once he was surrounded by demons, who capered wildly around the cub and taunted him about his fur, whiskers and tail.

The cub fled, but as he left the city he began to feel distinctly unwell. When he returned to his pride, they reacted to him with a surprising animosity, flattening their ears, baring their fangs and hissing at him. Every time he approached, they lashed out with their claws, driving him back.

The cub wandered miserably away, unable to understand why his family had rejected him. Then he happened to catch sight of his reflection in the river water. What he saw was himself but horribly diseased and disfigured: covered in growths, patches of fur missing, blood trickling from nose and mouth.

As the day wore on, the cub felt sicker and sicker, and by dusk he knew he was dying. The last sight his ailing eyes saw was the sun sinking between the sides of the valley where Ghuht lay, like a morsel of food disappearing into a set of jagged-toothed jaws.

Thus did the reckless cub pay for his deity-defying hubris.

"From this," said X'aan after relating the tale to Conan, "we know that Ghuht is a couple of hours' walk north from rapids at a river bend, and that the valley it sits in runs east-to-west—and also, that it is to be steered clear of. That is how the stories work."

On the quartet went, and daily the jungle grew thicker and more overgrown and the ground underfoot more uneven. The track petered out, and they made the difficult decision to ditch their mounts. The going would be just too treacherous for them. They removed the horses' tack and saddlebags and sent them on their way with a slap to the hindquarters. Conan was sorry to see the piebald mare go. She had been, as he had predicted, an excellent steed, stoically indefatigable under not just his weight but X'aan's too.

Loaded with as much food and equipment as they could carry, the foursome forged onward on foot. Conan took to using his sword to clear a path through the vegetation. It was a time-consuming and laborious task, and the sweat poured off his body in glistening runnels, yet he went at it tirelessly. Every step they took was hard-earned. It was almost as though the jungle was fighting them, or perhaps, from a kindlier perspective, deliberately trying to discourage them from going farther, for it knew their ultimate destination.

There seemed to be an incremental dimming to the air, although the sun's rays still beat down as fiercely as ever. The jungle's green was darkening and becoming murkier, just as the color and clarity of seawater do the deeper one dives.

Conan noted a muting of animal noises, as well. The birds, the mammals and the insects were all quieter, as if there were fewer and fewer of them about. And when the wind blew from a certain direction, it carried a peculiar odor. It was not quite that of decomposing flesh, nor quite that of stagnant water, nor quite that of mildew, although it had elements of all of those. It spoke of things that were dwindling and atrophying, things spoiling, things that had seen better days.

"This," Conan opined, "must be the smell of the Rotlands. I have known no smell like it."

X'aan concurred. "We are close now. The wind direction is assisting us, telling us which way to go. We follow the scent."

"X'aan," Gudrun said, "you have brought us as far as you need to. There is no reason for you to continue. We can make it the rest of the way on our own."

"You don't get rid of me that easily," replied the Kushite. "I am coming with you to Ghuht, and that is that."

"And what if I were to knock you out cold and we left you here and went on without you?"

"As soon as I came to, I would simply get up and carry on," X'aan said, with all the brash imperiousness of youth. "Would you actually do such a thing?"

"It crossed my mind," the Æsir woman admitted, "but I thought it through and came to the same conclusion you have. It would only slow you, not put you off, and I would rather have you with us in the Rotlands, where we may shield you from its perils, than roaming through them on your own."

"I know you mean well, Gudrun. But you still don't seem to understand. I will stop at nothing to find Zevia. If, as a consequence, death claims me, so be it. I will happily go into Derketa's arms, knowing I tried my hardest to get my sister back. After she was taken, I spent two months sunk in despondency, pining for her and mourning our father and mother. Two months bemoaning the fact that I was not present when the lizard-man came, for then I too would have been there to defend Zevia, as our parents did, and perhaps that might have made a difference. Two months trying to summon up the courage to go after her and wishing there was someone who could help. No one in my village would; they were all too frightened. Then you three happened along, and I knew the gods had brought you to me, and I knew I must not pass up this opportunity. In short, I am not giving up now. Nothing could make me."

"Well put, lad," said Conan, slapping X'aan on the back. "To die fighting for a worthy cause is the best way to die. Rather that than wither away, old and decrepit and full of regrets about what one didn't do and should have."

"Not that any of us are intending to die here," Hunwulf pointed out. "Our aim is rescuing the lizard-people's captives."

"Granted," said Conan, "but it is Æsir tradition, is it not, that the highest, noblest form of death is death in battle. It assures you of a place in Valhalla, your people's heaven, where all is combat and swordplay and roistering."

"Maybe so," said Hunwulf, "but I am in no hurry to get there just yet."

"Not that you, of all people, need worry about the afterlife," Conan went on, a mocking inflection to his voice. "Your soul is destined to occupy other bodies from now until the end of time, or so you say."

Hunwulf grimaced. "Perhaps not as desirable a fate as it sounds. Given a choice, I might prefer the rambunctious certainties of

Valhalla, or even just everlasting oblivion, over endless reiteration. From what glimpses I have had of my other incarnations' lives, all there ever has been or ever will be for me, it appears, is strife, strife, and more strife."

"Do Cimmerians have a heaven?" X'aan asked Conan.

"Nay, lad!" said Conan. "For us, there is nothing to look forward to when we die, merely an underworld of cold, gray mist for all eternity."

"It sounds miserable."

"It is. Which is why, while alive, my race strive and fight, and drink and love, and seek to vanquish, because we know what awaits us the other side of death—a purposeless void."

"But you must have gods, must you not? Beings you venerate and fear?"

"We have Crom, who cares naught for mortals," Conan said. "He demands nothing from us, least of all worship, and invariably he ignores our prayers. Thus are we free to live as we choose, answerable only to our consciences, with no divine power holding us as slaves."

"As gods go, he seems hardly a god at all."

"And hence he is the best kind of god," Conan declared.

The strange, moribund smell grew stronger as Conan continued to plow through the ever-resisting jungle, hewing a tunnel for the others to follow.

With the next dawn, the four companions were finding the odor chokingly repugnant, and they wrapped cloths around their noses and mouths in the hope of mitigating it.

An hour later, Conan hacked through some dense thorny bushes to a small clearing, wherein they discovered the corpse of a baboon. The animal looked not to have been dead long, but its belly had already begun to bloat.

Conan thought it peculiar that no flies were alighting upon the cadaver, but he supposed that the odor of the Rotlands, akin to that of death and decay, was confusing their senses. Either this was the case or else flies, as with practically all other animal life, shunned the area.

All at once the baboon's body convulsed, and its belly split open with a sound like hessian being rent. The wound disgorged a great slimy mass of intestine.

So it seemed, at any rate, but the entrails were as black as pitch. They were also moving of their own volition, heaving and writhing.

"Crom and his devils," Conan breathed. "What foulness is this?"

It transpired that what appeared to be inner organs was in fact a single, huge, greasily black tapeworm.

The thing squirmed nightmarishly in the daylight and began uncoiling itself. A flattened, lobate head, sporting a rudimentary mouth fringed with suckers, rose up cobra-like from the ground.

With a spasm of utter revulsion, the Cimmerian whipped out his sword and embarked on a frenzy of chopping and hacking. Within moments he had reduced the giant tapeworm to a soup of ragged segments, each of which thrashed and writhed in its individual death throes.

He continued shredding the parts of the parasite until all lay still.

"The baboon must have wandered into the Rotlands, overcome by curiosity," Gudrun observed. "There, it must have eaten something containing a tapeworm egg, which hatched and grew at an unnatural rate to an unnatural size."

"Is this what awaits us ahead?" said Hunwulf.

"This, I would say, is just a taste of it," X'aan replied. "From what I have heard, everything in the Rotlands exists to kill you, or eat you, or maim you, or all three. Once within, we must be on our mettle."

As a rule, Conan feared little and was confident there was no threat he could not defeat through sword arm and sheer brawn; but even he now felt a prickling of anxiety in his gut. What with that unnamable stench polluting the air, and the sight of the dead baboon and its erstwhile parasitic passenger, he was starting to wonder whether this expedition was quite so prudent after all.

The odds on a successful outcome seemed to be lowering by the minute. His hackles were up. Every instinct in his barbarian frame was warning him of impending menace and urging him to retreat.

It took an enormous effort, both physical and mental, to resume cleaving through the jungle.

And now, after a further half-hour of slashing and severing, Conan paused, ears pricked. No sound had caught his attention; rather, the absence of sound. There was silence all around, save for leaves softly rustling in the breeze and the rasp of his and his companions' breaths beneath their makeshift masks. A stillness filled the forest, too profound, too absolute, to be normal or natural.

The hush was profane, the Cimmerian thought. It was *wrong*.

Minutes later, the four of them got their first glimpse of the Rotlands.

They had come to a wall of dead plant life, where what had been green and burgeoning was now brown and decaying. Everything crumbled to the touch, foliage gossamer-fragile, wood as brittle as spun sugar. Conan's sword made short work of penetrating this delicate, flimsy barrier.

Beyond lay a band of bare soil, some dozen yards wide, running leftward and rightward as far as the eye could see. Here, nothing grew at all. Sheer proximity to the Rotlands had eradicated the living flora.

On the other side there were trees, but they were trees unlike any Conan had ever seen. They were gnarled and twisted as though they had been warped by a dozen contrary prevailing winds, their trunks and boughs jet-black and their leaves of similarly dark hues, from deep crimson to tawny orange to midnight blue, with here and there a streak of tallow-like yellow and storm-cloud gray.

Growing around their bases were what appeared to be flowers, some of which had pulpy fat blossoms, and others petals that looked razor sharp, and again their colors tended towards the funereal and the sickly.

There were fungal things too, proliferating across the ground or clinging onto other plants: toadstools with glossy dark green caps, mosses that extruded thin wavy filaments in the air, mushroom-like blobs covered in webbed integuments.

As for animal life, none was visible, but there was aural evidence nonetheless. Faint, distant hoots echoed across the treetops, interspersed with weird stuttering whoops and odd, coughing, crackling barks. Conan could identify the cries of most beasts, and none of these ones were familiar.

The vista of unrecognizable landscape stretched for miles around. Were it not for the sun overhead—unmistakably the same burning orb that shone down on every corner of the world—one might imagine one had stumbled onto a different planet. Nothing here was of this earth. Nothing here *belonged* to this earth. Tens of thousands of undulating, hilly acres were now the domain of the Rotlands, a whole other environment.

"I never could have imagined..." said Gudrun. "So alien."

"This must be what hell looks like," said her husband.

As for young X'aan, all he could do was gawp in dumbstruck amazement.

Without a word, Conan stepped forward, broadsword at the ready, out into the gap between the jungle's edge and the Rotlands. The ground crunched dryly beneath his sandaled feet.

At the opposite side of this no-man's-land, hard by the perimeter of the Rotlands, shoots had pushed up through the soil, new plants budding and uncoiling, as aberrant and unearthly as the full-grown ones adjacent.

He saw how this worked. The Rotlands destroyed by their very proximity, like a fire scorching everything around it with its radiant heat. Then they replaced with their own life forms that which they had eliminated. Thus did they encroach little by little upon their surroundings, creeping outward, remaking the world in their own hideous image.

He took a deep breath. This was his last chance to give up and turn back—the last chance for all of them.

Into the Rotlands did Conan go, and Hunwulf, Gudrun and X'aan went with him.

15

Relaxed and Sedentary

"Touch nothing," Conan said to the others as he led the way. "Handle nothing. Approach nothing."

The advice was easy to give but hard to follow. The vegetation of the Rotlands was densely packed. To move through it without making contact, one had to alternately weave, duck, sidle or step high. Branches seemed to reach for them. Flowers seemed to lean towards their legs as they passed.

And always that miasmic stench clogged their nostrils, despite the masks—a smell one just could not become accustomed to. Nothing in particular seemed to be generating it; it was simply the massed odor of the place, the tainted air.

Eventually they discarded their face coverings, which restricted breathing and were hardly blocking out the smell anyway.

The foursome had not penetrated far into the Rotlands when they came across a pair of human skeletons. These lay side by side, their skulls grinning lopsidedly at the sky. Scraps of clothing clung to them, and weapons glinted in their bony white clutches. Grasses and other weeds had grown up through their ribcages, entwining around as though laying claim to them.

"Our predecessors, no doubt," Conan remarked. "One of the parties that came this way in pursuit of kidnapped children."

"Are those tooth marks?" said X'aan querulously.

"Aye, of various kinds. The meat has been gnawed clean off the bones by creatures both large and small. The bones themselves still look fresh. These two died within the past month."

The sight of the skeletons—whose armaments had clearly availed them naught against whatever had caused their demises—sent a chill through the Cimmerian. The fate of the baboon earlier had offered some foretaste of what the Rotlands held in store. This stark memento mori before them, however, was a clear, unignorable warning, all but shrieking at him and his companions to turn back.

"We press on," he said, as much a directive to himself as to the others.

Moments later, something suddenly scurried through the undergrowth.

Conan held up a hand, bringing the three behind him to a halt.

The unseen thing stopped, then scurried again. Conan glimpsed a small, striped mammal—like a hybrid of squirrel and tabby cat—darting across an open space ahead. It cast a frightened look backward at the party of humans, evidently alarmed by their intrusion.

Next moment, a huge mushroom in front of it split wide open, revealing a hollow interior. The unheeding animal ran pell-mell into it, and the mushroom, large as a man's head, snapped shut like the jaws of a trap, enclosing the squirrel-cat thing within.

The creature gave a series of shrill, panicked yelps, muffled by the mushroom. One could see it struggling inside its fungal prison, and gradually its efforts subsided, as if it had become resigned to its fate, or else was simply suffocating. Conan could only assume the mushroom was carnivorous and would be busy digesting its meal for some while.

"Well," he said, "we now know plants here are predators, but at least that one is too small to bother us."

Scarcely had he uttered these words than X'aan let out a cry. A vine dangling from a tree had lashed itself around the young Kushite's arm and was hauling him upwards.

Conan did not hesitate. He lunged forward and slashed the vine in twain. X'aan tumbled to the ground.

Conan looked up and saw something immense squatting in the tree's upper branches. It was somewhat like a jellyfish but also like a bristling ball of mistletoe, and he perceived that what had appeared to be a vine was in fact a tentacle, of which there were dozens attached to this miscreant atrocity.

Others of the vine-like extrusions descended now, threading through the tree and groping for the humans below. The Cimmerian whirled his sword, truncating each one that came close. This released sprays of a sap-like substance and shortened the tentacles but failed to deter them.

Hunwulf and Gudrun joined in, and there was a protracted period of hacking and chopping and whittling by all three, until at last the monstrosity in the tree seemed to decide the effort was no longer worthwhile. It withdrew all its tentacles upwards, mutilated and intact alike, furling them up beneath it, almost resentfully.

Conan glimpsed a puckered hole in the thing's underside and inferred this to be its maw, into which it would have dragged X'aan and the rest of them had it had the chance.

They were all spattered with its tentacles' yellowish juices and panting hard. Conan wiped himself clean as best he could. The stuff had a vile, vinegary reek.

"Did I not tell you?" said X'aan. "Everything in this place wants to kill you, eat you or maim you."

They had gone no farther than another hundred paces when an enormous animal came crashing through the trees towards them.

It was as big as a bull, with thick, powerful legs, a wrinkled leathery hide and a mouth which when it gaped, as now, exposed row upon row of serrated teeth like a shark's.

Conan reacted almost without thinking. He sidestepped out of the beast's path and dug his sword into its flank, ripping skin and shedding blood. The thing bellowed deafeningly and turned mid-stride to face him.

"Come at me," Conan growled to it. "You think yourself fearsome, but you have not met a Cimmerian."

The bullish monster charged, faster than he expected. He moved again, but a mite too slow. The animal's shoulder butted into him and sent him flying.

He was on his feet again in a trice, cheetah-swift, even as the creature hurtled at him with terrifying speed, jaws wide. Its mouth looked large enough to swallow him whole.

Instead of evading, Conan rushed to meet the monster, intending to combine his momentum with its so that his sword would sink in all the farther when they clashed. The interior of its mouth looked soft, and this was his target.

But at the last instant the creature seemed to realize it had a point of vulnerability and snapped its jaws shut, leaving just its teeth bared. Conan's sword glanced judderingly off that fence of interlocking fangs, and only by dint of a sudden, sharp twist of his body did he avoid being barged into again.

He heard a heavy, wet thud, and saw an arrow sprout in the monster's eye. Gudrun was already stringing a fresh arrow as the monster, with an enraged shake of its head, launched itself at her, the human who had just half-blinded it and caused it fresh pain.

Conan did the only thing he could think of and sprang onto the beast's back. He clamped his thighs around its thick neck as one does when riding a horse bareback in order to stay mounted, and bracing himself against its rocking motion, he raised his broadsword high, point downward. He thrust with both hands, ramming the sword into the top of the monster's head.

Its skull was thick but Conan put every ounce of his iron-thewed might into the thrust, piercing deep through bone into something soft within. The creature shuddered to a halt and collapsed.

As it toppled to one side, Conan rolled off in the other direction so that his leg would not get trapped beneath its bulk.

There was a great, explosive sigh from that tooth-filled mouth, a final expulsion of air, and the monster died.

Conan picked himself up and shook the hair out of his eyes. "I wasn't sure if that thing even had a brain, and if so, how big it was. But my blade found it." He wrenched his sword from the monster's head, and cleaned and sheathed it. "Are we all well?" The others nodded. "How far do we reckon we have gone?"

"It can't be more than five hundred yards," said Hunwulf.

"And twice we have been savagely attacked," Conan observed, "and we have no idea how much farther there is to travel. We will die if we continue on this path. Hunwulf, you must use your clairvoyance to guide us."

"It can be done, I suppose."

"You sound dubious."

"The trouble is, when I am gambling, I am relaxed and sedentary. I have nothing else to concentrate on except the task at hand, which makes it easy."

"And 'relaxed and sedentary' is the very opposite of the current situation," said Gudrun. "Hunwulf will have difficulty getting into the appropriate frame of mind and remaining there."

"And," her husband added, "I can sustain it for perhaps three hours, four at most, before it becomes too exhausting to continue."

"I have an idea, then," said Conan. "I shall carry you. That's the sedentary part taken care of, and as for relaxed... Well, you shall just have to have faith that the three of us, not least myself, can shelter you from harm as we go."

"You are asking a lot," said Hunwulf.

"It's this or die. Which would you rather?"

"Put like that, there really isn't any alternative, is there?"

Conan picked Hunwulf up in a piggyback. The Æsir man was no lightweight but the Cimmerian hoisted him like a sack of feathers.

"Can Hunwulf really see the future?" X'aan asked Gudrun.

"To a limited extent, he can," Gudrun replied. "Conan's plan is a good one, if it works. Hunwulf should be able to forewarn us of dangers as long as he does not lose focus. Once the four hours are up, however, we will be back where we started, reliant on just ourselves again."

"Gudrun," said Conan, "you are at the front. X'aan, you take the rear. Onward!"

They marched ahead in that order, Conan in the middle with Hunwulf. Conan felt Hunwulf's limbs slacken as the Æsir willed himself into that time-malleable state of his.

Moments later, Hunwulf said, "Stop."

A few seconds passed, then something reared up from the ground inches in front of Gudrun. It was like a leech, with a mouthful of concentric teeth, and it was as long and thick as a grown man's leg.

The Æsir woman's sword whirred through the air, bisecting the creature. The two parts of it fell to the earth, and all at once thousands of tiny, scuttling insects appeared, seemingly from nowhere, and crawled over the still twitching remains.

They were beetles of a kind, with bright golden carapaces, beautiful in their way, and they feasted on the leech creature's flesh until, in mere minutes, there was practically nothing left. Then, glutted, the insects scuttled away again, vanishing down into the tiny holes in the soil from which they had emerged.

So it went for the next few miles. Hunwulf would call out a warning, the four-strong procession would come to a halt, and some nightmarish incident would ensue.

A host of flowers simultaneously unleashed bursts of pollen which billowed up into a single acrid cloud in front of the travelers, perhaps a defense mechanism triggered by the tread of their feet.

A brightly colored creature—part parrot, part bat, part monkey—came screeching down at them from above like a falcon diving, its beak as sharp and thin as a rapier.

Something amphibian, half submerged in a mire, shot out a vast tongue like a length of pink, fleshy cable across their path.

Dozens of termites, each the size of a rat, flooded out from the mouth of a cave, clacking their pincers menacingly.

An earthworm of whale-like proportions burrowed through the ground just below the surface, leaving a gully several yards wide and similarly deep in its wake.

In every instance, the companions knew in advance that something was about to happen and were ready for it.

They held back as the flowers spat their pollen and saw the tiny powdery granules singe every living thing they landed on.

Gudrun shot the parrot-bat-monkey animal in midair and watched in satisfaction as it flopped down at her feet, a flailing clump of feathers, fangs and prehensile tail, transfixed by her arrow.

Conan sliced clean through the amphibian's tongue so that it failed to snag any of them and drag them into its domain.

X'aan had, at Hunwulf's urging, carefully scraped up some of the deadly flower pollen into a pouch, and he tipped this over the giant termites, laughing uproariously as its contents made them sizzle and shrivel.

The whale-worm passed the travelers harmlessly by, whereas if they had been just a few paces farther on it would have undermined them and they would have fallen into the depression created by its tumultuous subterranean passing.

All good things must come to an end, however. Hunwulf held out for as long as he could, but eventually he gasped, "That's it. I can manage no more. Set me down, Cimmerian."

"It's getting dark anyway," Conan said, briskly divesting himself of his Æsir load. "This place is bad enough in daylight. At night, predators are more wont to prowl, and there's no telling what could come our way in the dark. We make camp here. No fire. Crom knows what its glow might attract. After we eat, we sleep in square formation, sitting back-to-back and facing outward. We keep watch in shifts. Two of us must be awake at all times."

Conan himself did not sleep at all, even when he was supposed to. He stayed awake the whole night through. The more pairs of eyes there were on lookout, the better.

The Rotlands were far from quiet in the dark. Creatures were constantly on the move. Footfalls soft and loud could be heard all around. Stealthy beasts padded and crept, less stealthy ones thudded. There were snufflings and shufflings and muted nocturnal cries. The undergrowth rustled and shivered.

Above, a near-full moon rode high in a cloudless sky. The face which men say can be seen on its surface seemed, to Conan that night, to have a sneering cast as it looked down upon him.

"Why do you do these things, Cimmerian?" he fancied it was saying. "Why put yourself in hazardous situations again and again? Why chase adventure and peril and glory so remorselessly?"

The only answer he could think of was that to do otherwise would be anathema.

Conan was driven by many motivations but one of the foremost was a dread of dullness. He was never more alive than when at risk of death.

It was something which civilized folk, with their etiquette and their niceties and their need for comfort, would never understand. They wrapped themselves in material concerns and called it safety. Conan knew it to be quicksand in which one was slowly sucked down and drowned.

At one point during that long night, while he was pretending to slumber, Conan's sharp ears picked up Gudrun murmuring to Hunwulf.

"Husband, something has been troubling me. I have been reluctant to ask, fearing the possible answer. You say that we are going to find Bjørn in Ghuht, but I must know this: are we going to find him alive? You have not specified."

"Neither did my vision," Hunwulf responded. "Does it matter?"

"I take your point. Either way we will learn his fate, and then we can act accordingly. If he is alive, we rescue him. If not, we teach those who took him the error of their ways. Them, their homes, their loved ones—we burn the whole Ymir-damned lot to the ground."

Bjørn was alive. That much the boy was certain of, though little else.

He was in a small chamber—a cell—with a tiny window set too high for him to see out of, even standing on tiptoe. Every so often the door opened and a dish of food was shoved in. The viands, meat and fruit mostly, tasted odd, like none he knew, but he was always too hungry to mind.

How long he had been held here, he could not say for sure. It must have been at least a month, if not more.

Of his airborne journey with his reptilian abductor, his recollections were vivid, although fragmentary too, like shards of a mirror.

They must have spent a total of four days flying southwest from Shem, with Bjørn dangling precariously from the creature's talons the whole way.

At first he was terrified of being dropped, whether on purpose or by accident, but the winged man kept a firm hold on him and after a while he was able to, if not relax, then at least acclimate to the unusual mode of transportation.

At night they landed at places inaccessible to anyone without wings.

The first time, on a narrow ledge projecting from near the summit of a towering pinnacle of rock, Bjørn asked the winged lizard-man to undo his bonds, for his limbs were cramping and he had lost all feeling in his hands and feet. His abductor obliged, refastening the ropes more loosely.

Then, to Bjørn's surprise, he spoke.

"I see that knife in your belt," said he in a voice that was mostly croak. His reptilian lips seemed to find it hard to form words properly. "That little mallet too. Some might say you are armed. But those are hardly weapons at all."

"Enough to hurt you with, if I like."

"Certainly. But I am sure you have thought it through. Let us assume you were able to kill me with one or other of those implements, which I doubt. Do it while we are here, and then how will you get down? You will be stuck. You will starve to death and the vultures will pick your bones clean. By the same token, do it while we are in flight, and you will plunge to your doom. So I shall leave you your petty tools. Now eat."

From a small satchel strapped to his back the winged lizard-man produced some strips of jerky. Bjørn gnawed on one with an odd sense of gratitude. He understood now that he was not to be killed, at least not yet. Why else would his abductor be feeding him? The notion cheered him somewhat.

"What's your name?" he inquired.

"Why do you ask?"

"I am Bjørn Hunwulfson. Somehow I feel I should thank you. Those men who were holding me—you saved me from being murdered by them."

The lizard-man let out a guttural laugh. "Saved you! Well, you might call it that. Or you might not. You'll see." After a pause he said, "Krraa-Bhaak."

"I beg your pardon?"

"My name. Krraa-Bhaak. It will be difficult for you to pronounce."

Bjørn tried, and it was. There was a weird inflection to it that demanded a contortion of the throat he struggled to make.

"Now get some sleep," Krraa-Bhaak said. "We have a long way yet to go." And precipitously perched though they were, Bjørn did manage to sleep.

Throughout the journey, the landscape below them changed almost by the hour. On average they flew twice as fast as the fastest horse could gallop, and when the wind was at their backs, they attained a nigh-unimaginable speed. The lizard-man seemed not to tire, the beat of his wings steady and consistent.

During their nighttime sojourns there were further conversations between the two of them, but they were sporadic, brief and, for Bjørn, none too enlightening. He learned nothing about where he was being taken or why he was being taken there. He asked but Krraa-Bhaak kept mum.

On the third night, as they ate dates together atop a sheer-sided mesa, Bjørn said, "Why me?"

"What do you mean?" said Krraa-Bhaak.

"Why did you choose me to take on this journey to wherever we're going? What's so special about me? Can you at least tell me that?"

The lizard-man blinked, and it was a queer slow double-blink. An outer set of scaly eyelids went down and up like an ordinary human's, while at the same time an inner set consisting of two white membranes closed and parted sideways, sliding across the black vertical slits of his irises.

Then he said, "I saw how you quietened an angry dog. I could see you have some strange, magical influence over animals. You do possess just such a power, do you not?"

"I do," said Bjørn.

"I kept watch over you for several days afterwards, awaiting my moment, but you were almost always in crowded places and with your parents or that hulking, black-maned giant of a man."

"Conan."

"Aye. That was what I heard you call him. It was preferable to remain unseen, so I needed you away from the city, isolated, before I could act."

"Therefore it was good for you when Ragnar and his men kidnapped me."

Krraa-Bhaak nodded.

"You went through the four of them like—like a scythe through wheat," Bjørn said.

"Humans are weak compared with my kind."

"Maybe. But I'm still thinking about killing you."

"You are? But I thought we had settled the matter."

"I don't mind dying if it means you're dead too."

"Interesting," said Krraa-Bhaak. "Well, if you are going to try, Bjørn Hunwulfson, do it now."

"No. But perhaps there'll come a time."

The lizard-man made a guttural sound that Bjørn realized was laughter. "I admire your pluck, child. I think you will make a useful addition."

"To what?"

"Never mind."

"No, to what?" Bjørn insisted.

But Krraa-Bhaak merely shook his head. "It won't be long," was all he said.

On the fifth day they crossed over jungle and then an expanse of dark, tangled vegetation of a kind Bjørn had never beheld before. The air here carried a noxious odor, not unlike that of a decomposing carcass. So rank was it, he almost retched.

They descended into a valley, and Bjørn caught glimpses of a broken, ancient city. As they flew above this, the mephitic smell exuded by the strange jungle diminished somewhat, to his relief.

Krraa-Bhaak brought them to their final destination, a partially collapsed building wherein others of his race awaited.

By that stage, after so many days of hard and wearisome journeying with very little food to sustain him, Bjørn had grown exhausted and even a little delirious. He nevertheless managed to reach for the whittling knife in his belt the moment the lizard-people undid his bindings. He attempted to stab the one nearest him, but a powerful hand grabbed his wrist, staying it.

"I had an inkling you might try something like that," said Krraa-Bhaak. He twisted the wrist sharply, and the knife tumbled from Bjørn's fingers. "You are a spirited creature, child. I hope that fire of yours never deserts you."

Krraa-Bhaak picked up the knife and took Bjørn's mallet from him too.

Other lizard-people then dragged Bjørn down several flights of stairs to a lower story and thrust him into the meager chamber where he now resided. The door was locked, and here in this cell he had remained since, for days on end, waiting for he had no idea what.

Often he would hear doors nearby opening and closing, and occasionally there came voices, muffled but identifiably those of other children. They were sometimes plaintive, sometimes defiant, and now and then there was abject, helpless sobbing.

Bjørn was not alone, at least, but he did not know whether to be reassured by this or not. As one captive among many, did that make his survival more likely or less? And what had Krraa-Bhaak meant when he had described him, up on that mesa, as a "useful addition?" Bjørn had pondered long and hard on the phrase but could not fathom its meaning. It sounded both intriguing and ominous, albeit more the latter than the former.

A single thought sustained him in his state of imprisoned misery and kept him from lapsing into total despair.

His parents would be coming for him. They would never leave him to languish here. His mother and father were on their way, and perhaps Conan of Cimmeria too, and they would let nothing hinder them.

Bjørn only hoped they would arrive before whatever was due to happen to him happened.

16

A Ghostly Echo of Magnificence

Dawn sucked a mist up from the ground, so thick that Conan could scarcely see his hand in front of his face. It made travel through the Rotlands trickier still. The party of four picked their way over the treacherous terrain, moving as slowly and carefully as blind men. The dangers of the place, bad enough when they could be seen, felt ten times worse for being hidden. Every gray shadow looming in the mist was a potential threat. Every sound—every swish, every creak, every rustle—seemed freighted with deadly significance.

At last the sun started to burn off the vaporous shroud, and then Conan spied something overhead. Three shapes moved through the sky, accompanied by the sound of wingbeats. He hissed a warning to the others. "Keep still."

The figures in the air passed above them, and their silhouettes were those of three men borne aloft on batlike wings. They flew in triangular formation, unhurriedly.

When they were gone, Conan remarked, "Denizens of Ghuht, I'll be bound."

"That looked like a patrol," Hunwulf said. "Their slow speed, the way they were keeping equally distant from one another and looking around all the time…"

Conan grunted agreement. "Dispatched to keep an eye out for people like us. We aren't the first to enter the Rotlands to recover stolen children. But their presence is good news nonetheless."

"How?" said X'aan.

"It is early morning. The patrol will have departed from the city only recently to begin their day's work. That implies we are nearing Ghuht itself."

The patrol passed back their way a half-hour later. The mist was all but dissipated by then, and the travelers might have been spotted had Conan not heard the heavy whump of multiple wingbeats in time.

With an urgent sweep of his arm he indicated that they should take refuge in a thicket close by. Hunkering down, the four watched the winged lizard-men fly past in that almost leisurely manner of theirs.

Conan scowled as he saw Gudrun draw an arrow from her quiver.

"Would you have them know we are here?" he whispered.

"Just in case they spy us and attack," she whispered back.

Conan nodded. He had mistaken the Æsir woman's prudence for overzealousness.

He looked up again at the lizard-men, who were no more than twenty feet above. This was his first clear view of the enemy. Their reptilian hides glistened in the low sun and were various shades of green and brown. Their faces were passably human, although their noses were snubby things with narrow nostrils and their mouths lipless gashes, and where people had eyebrows, they had thick lumpen ridges of scale. They wore crude clothing, and embroidered on the shirtfront of one Conan saw the eye sigil, while another of them had an amulet around his neck upon which, though small, he could just about discern the same symbol.

The lizard-men paused, hovering in midair. They were scanning below with evident suspicion, and instinctively the four allies crouched lower within the thicket.

A part of Conan yearned for the lizard-men to spot them and for battle to be joined. At last he would have a chance to test his mettle against these creatures. One of their brethren had made light work of slaughtering those four Æsir. How lethal, then, would three such lizard-men be? The prospect ought to have given anyone pause. Yet still the Cimmerian's battlefield-born soul longed to engage in hostilities with them.

In part this was because they and their kind had kidnapped Bjørn and a host of other innocent youngsters, for who knew what vile reason.

In part it was the memory of the winged abomination that had killed his beloved Bêlit—even though these three resembled that one only superficially—its distant cousins, so to speak, from some earthlier, more human-looking bloodline.

In part it was the visceral repugnance Conan felt for all miscreated monstrosities like these.

A war cry was bubbling up in the back of his throat, and it took every ounce of his self-restraint to withhold it. He wanted the lizard-men to descend to him and taste his blade. He would show them how a true man fought.

But whatever had made the patrol curious, they seemed to decide it was of no import. Off they flew, the tension eased from Conan's body, and he tried to ignore the pang of disappointment he felt.

The companions tramped onward through the Rotlands, warier than ever; and close to noon Conan's ears detected the far-off hiss of rushing water. A little way on they came to a broad river.

The current was mighty, the water gliding turbulent and deep over a rocky bed. There was no possibility of crossing it safely here, and anyway they did not know if they needed to cross it at all. Their only option was to follow the bank and see where that led them.

Conan made the decision to head upstream, for no other reason than the river was wont to be narrower nearer its source and thus more easily fordable.

Farther up its course, the river turned whiter and more torrential, and they arrived at a bend where the water leaped and bounded thunderously across a barrage of exposed boulders, sending up shafts of spume and great crashing bursts of spray. In the lee of the bend, on the other side, there lay a thin strip of beach.

X'aan could not suppress a yelp of excitement. "Conan! This is it. Do you not see?"

"See what?" the Cimmerian queried.

"These are they. The rapids in the story. The story of the lion cub who met Amra-kuu in Ghuht. They must be. They are on a bend in the river, and there, on that beach, will be where the pride were resting when the cub wandered off. Now we know where we are. Ghuht is due north of this spot, and only a couple of hours' walk."

Conan found it hard to gainsay what the boy was telling them. Had X'aan not seen them safely halfway across Kush? Had his knowledge of his country's geography not proved extensive and accurate, thanks to his people's folkloric tales? There was no cause to think Ghuht did not lie exactly where he claimed it did.

If nothing else, what harm could it do to head north and see where they ended up? It was as good a plan as any, and better than simply roaming the Rotlands in hopes of stumbling across the city.

"Very well," said he. "But north lies yonder." He pointed across the river.

"Moving from boulder to boulder, we might just be able to make it," X'aan said.

Conan's response was a noncommittal grunt. Any other river, in any other place, and he would have said their chances were good. But this river, which flowed through the hellish heart of the Rotlands, was surely fraught with perils. Anything might be lurking in that water. The water itself, for all they knew, might be poison.

"We make a rope," he decided. "Gather vines and plait them together—and be sure that they are just vines and nothing else," he added, remembering the shapeless thing lurking in the trees the previous day. "I will go first with the rope and attach it to something sturdy on the other side. You three will have the other end of the rope and can pull me back to shore if I fall in."

In short order, the Cimmerian was venturing across the torrent with the vine rope fastened around his waist. Hunwulf, Gudrun and X'aan held the rope securely, paying it out as he went.

The boulders were slippery; in jumping from one to the next, Conan had to make extra sure of his footing both when he sprang and when he alighted. Even then, though possessed of catlike agility, he almost slithered off more than once into the river. The water spray soaked him to the skin and plastered his hair to his scalp. The roar of the rapids was a constant booming thunder.

The last section he had to cross was boulder free. The water looked to be only chest deep. It was flowing terrifically fast nonetheless. Conan drew his sword, held it high and lowered himself in.

Immediately he felt the current trying to whisk his legs from under him. He planted his feet squarely and took a first laborious step, then another. All the while his gaze roved, watching for some additional disturbance in the water that might presage danger.

He had still several yards to go before gaining the other side, but the river was shallowing, only up to his navel now. It looked as though he would make it safely across.

Then a portion of the river to his left boiled, and all of a sudden a large bestial head reared up above the surface.

It was box-shaped, like a coffin, with a beaky, toothless maw and a blunt sawtooth crest along the crown. Behind it Conan glimpsed a wrinkled, leathery neck and a humped ridge of shell, and he realized he was facing some sort of enormous turtle, roughly fifteen feet long and about nine broad. Its small, deep-set eyes were fixed on him, and there was sheer hungry malevolence in them.

Dimly he could hear his three companions shouting from the far bank. He felt a tug on the rope. They were hauling him back, which they felt was the correct course of action. But in fact, all they were doing was pulling him off-balance, even as the turtle homed in on him with sweeps on its mottled fins, snapping its gummy jaws greedily together.

Though it lacked teeth, there was no question its hard-edged mouth was capable of crunching through a man's limb, and if Conan did not kill the beast, that limb would be his. The trouble was that, in trying to help by reeling him in, his friends were hampering him. He was losing his footing on the riverbed, and without stability, his swordplay would be severely compromised.

Quickly he did what he had to and hacked through the rope. Then he braced himself as the turtle plunged towards him. Its shell was inches thick, obviously impenetrable to his blade, but the creature's neck looked vulnerable, and Conan thrust at it while the turtle swam around him in a circle, lashing out at him with its beak.

His strikes hit home, and thin streams of blood trickled out of various cuts in the creature's wizened hide, to be swept away by the river.

Yet the turtle only grew fiercer and more determined in its assaults. Its fins thrashed the water.

In return, Conan's sword sheared and slashed, shedding glittering arcs of water droplets with every swing.

The turtle made a sudden sally and almost caught his arm in its maw. Anyone with fractionally slower reflexes would have been lost, but Conan managed to snatch his arm out of the way and the turtle's jaws clamped shut on thin air.

Another cut, and another, and yet another, and now the beast's throat was a mass of dangling, ragged fleshy strips. But still its onslaught continued, and the effort of combating both it and the river current was taking its toll on the Cimmerian's energies.

Then, all at once, the turtle seemed to change its mind. It was badly damaged and bleeding heavily, and perhaps it thought its prey was no longer worth the trouble and now was the time to cut its losses. With something like a snort of disdain it turned away from Conan and finned downriver, sinking below the surface, leaving crimson billows in its wake.

Conan, panting hard, watched it go with exhilaration roiling in his breast.

Once he had caught his breath, he waded over to retrieve the rope, which had become entwined around a boulder, its severed end flailing in the current. He toiled the rest of the way to shore with it, and there, on the beach, he sank to his knees and recouped for a while before getting up again and attaching the rope to a tree trunk.

With their end fastened similarly on their side of the river, his companions now had a lifeline to cling onto as they crossed. They came over one by one, without incident. All the while Conan kept watch in case the giant turtle returned for another foray, or some other riverine monster decided to follow its example.

"I despise everything about these Rotlands," Conan offered as X'aan became the last of the three to join him on the opposite side of the river.

"I doubt there's one among us who would disagree," said Hunwulf.

Taking their bearing from the sun's position, they headed northward, away from the beach and the river.

It might have taken the lion cub in X'aan's tale just a couple of hours to reach Ghuht from the river bend, but that was only a story, a tapestry stitched together from fact, hearsay and guesswork, with threads added and removed over the years until it ended up only distantly resembling the truth. For whatever reason, there was no mention of the Rotlands in it, likely because in the days when the story first budded and started to bloom, the "leprosy of terrain," as Jaalu had termed it, had been far smaller or even nonexistent. Hence the cub's journey was a comparatively easy one.

Whereas now the same journey passed through territory where any incautious step might kill, so that one had to walk at a snail's pace, making sure of every foot placement and arm movement.

Thus the four travelers toiled along for half a day, traversing a succession of ridges, with nary a sign of a city.

Then, cresting yet another hill brow, they saw it.

Before them lay a valley, running east–west just as the story said; and in that valley's basin there nestled the ruins of what must once have been a mighty metropolis.

Towers that would have been of remarkable height, grasping for the firmament, now stood half-collapsed, with their own shattered debris heaped around their feet. The remnants of impressive colonnades leaned haphazardly in their rows like drunken soldiers on parade. Roofs had gaps, and their fallen tiles filled cracks in the ground. Lintels slanted and porticos slumped. Vegetation sprouted everywhere, its unnatural Rotlands coloring forming a garish palette with the stonework around it, which was uniformly of a pale greenish hue.

Ghuht had surely been extraordinary in its heyday, the seat of some great civilization, but all that was left was a ghostly echo of magnificence, just as an aged, decrepit man lying on his sickbed, all skin blemishes and wasted muscles and papery skin, is a ghostly echo of his pristine, beautiful youth.

Conan surveyed the city, looking for lizard-people. He saw none. Ghuht appeared deserted; but just because it looked that way did not mean it was.

"We go carefully," he said to his three companions. "We do not make a sound. If you have anything to say, use gestures."

They crept down the hillside and infiltrated the city's outskirts. Weeds thrust up through every paving-stone crack. Insects crawled and swarmed, as if they owned the place. A hot jungle wind drifted along the streets, stirring spirals in the dust. The sun, starting to set, cast lengthening shadows between the buildings, as daylight turned to gloom. At least the stench of the Rotlands was diminished here, no longer as pervasive and nauseating as it had been in the thick of the jungle.

The first eye sigil they came across was carved into a wall. It was one of what would prove to be many.

The farther they penetrated into Ghuht, the more frequent the symbol's presence became. Sometimes it was finger-painted on a building, sometimes etched with a chisel or other sharp implement. On one occasion it was modeled out of twigs and vines and hung in an open doorway, twirling in the breeze. On another, it was a pattern formed from morsels of broken masonry laid out on the ground.

After a while the sigil became such a commonplace feature that even Hunwulf was no longer so disturbed by it. The clear impression was that it obsessed the citizens of Ghuht. Whatever it represented to them, they deemed it of signal importance.

But where were they? This was the question plaguing Conan. Jaalu had said that Ghuht was home to hundreds of the winged lizard-people, and all around, there were abundant indications that the city was not unoccupied. Conan spied a pile of freshly discarded fruit rinds, alongside spat-out seeds, still moist. Taloned footprints in the dust spoke of reptilian pedestrians who had passed by not long ago. He peered through an unglazed window into a house, and inside there were items of simple furniture and some earthenware pots and crockery that looked well used.

He could only infer that Ghuht was not abandoned, and its citizens must be congregated at a single site somewhere within its bounds.

He was correct. As he and his companions proceeded deeper still into the city, a drone of distant voices was carried towards them on the wind. They were joined in unison, hundreds of throats intoning words and phrases. There was a rhythm to it: a rumble of massed noise, then a brief lull during which a lone voice shouted, then another rumble, and so on.

"It sounds like worship," said Gudrun. Silence no longer seemed paramount. "One person calling, the rest responding."

"Or a rally," Conan said.

"Should we take a look?"

"Of course. If the lizard-people are assembled together, we must learn why. It may give us a clue as to where Bjørn is."

"And Zevia," X'aan added, "and the other children."

"Moreover," Conan continued, with a nod to the boy, "if the lizard-people are concentrated in one place and look set to stay there for a while, searching for the children will be that much simpler a task."

They followed the hum of voices, which was emanating from the very center of Ghuht. They came to the edge of what appeared to be a crater, a bowl-shaped indentation in the earth about half a mile in diameter. Crouching, they peered over.

The crater's sides, which sloped at a shallow angle, were littered with tumbled chunks of broken building. Fluted columns teetered against other fluted columns. Houses looked to have collided with one another.

To Conan's mind, it was obvious that some terrible natural disaster had occurred many years ago: an earthquake had struck, or a gigantic sinkhole had suddenly appeared, and this part of Ghuht had subsided into the depression thus created.

At the very bottom there was an expanse of flat ground. Here, the damage had been made good. Flagstones had been laid, with rising tiers of seating in a semicircle around it. It was a kind of amphitheater, and it was thronged with lizard-people—a good three hundred of them, perhaps as many as four hundred, a mix of male and female adults, all dressed in simple clothing.

Some stood, some sat, some hovered a few feet high in the air, and their focus was directed towards one of their kind who was stationed on a dais in the middle of the amphitheater.

This one was clad in long, flowing robes, upon which the eye sigil was prominently displayed in gold braid. He was unmistakably a high-ranking religious figure, some kind of priest. Not just the robes suggested it; the posture, the self-important carriage, the fervor with which he waved and gesticulated. He might not be wholly human, but the traits were universal, it seemed.

He was addressing his fellow lizard-people just as any holy zealot would his disciples. He shouted, they answered. He exhorted, they exulted.

The four traveling companions understood that they had happened upon a ceremony of some sort, and with ever-widening eyes, from their vantage point on the crater's rim, they watched it unfold.

17

The Genesis of Metamorphosis

"Tell me, my people, my faithful," cried the priestly lizard-man, his voice amplified boomingly by the acoustics of the crater. "Tell me again: *who is your leader?*"

"*Khotan-Kha!*" the others yelled, as one.

"Tell me who is here to deliver us, the Folk of the Featherless Wing, from decline."

"*Khotan-Kha!*"

"Tell me who loves you, who wants what is best for you, who knows what is best for you."

"*You, o Khotan-Kha! You! You!*"

The priest, Khotan-Kha, acknowledged their approbation with his arms held aloft.

"I," he said, "as your elected Hierophant, chosen by you to be your spiritual guide and mentor, have been laboring long and hard to bring about a change in our race's fortunes. You know this. You respect me for it. You love me for it."

At that, the crowd burst into paroxysms of joy. Their howls and cheers were deafening. They slapped the backs of their wings together above their heads to generate a deep, reverberantly thudding applause.

Khotan-Kha waited for the ruckus to abate, meanwhile strutting to and fro across the dais, hands linked behind his back, lapping up the acclaim.

This religious figure, Conan thought, this Hierophant, was no mere cleric. The Cimmerian had seen dictators behave in much the same way, rabble-rousing demagogues who knew what to say and how to say it in order to win over the populace and keep them on-side. To them, the adoration of the public was an addiction; they craved it like lovers of the yellow lotus craved the narcotic dreams that the fumes of that flower induced.

"And tonight, my people, my beloved people," Khotan-Kha said, "my work will at last come to fruition. The sun is going down. The moon is soon to rise. And it will be a special moon, my friends. Have I not promised this countless times? Has it not been foretold through the auspices of the sacred Granite Orrery? It comes at long last. Tonight is to be the Night of the Obsidian Moon, when the Folk of the Featherless Wing's fortunes will finally change for the better."

He had them in the palm of his taloned hand. The so-called Folk of the Featherless Wing were in raptures.

When the crowd were quiet again, Khotan-Kha dropped his voice somewhat. He could still be heard clearly, but he wanted closer attention.

"Many generations ago," said he, his demeanor now somber, "Ghuht was rocked by catastrophe."

"The Rupture," the crowd murmured darkly. "The Rupture."

"Yes. The Rupture. Overnight, a thriving city was all but destroyed. The earth trembled and was rent asunder. Buildings fell. Thousands died. It seemed like the end. It should have been the end."

His congregation keened sorrowfully as he evoked the tragic event.

"But," Khotan-Kha went on, his tone brightening, "we recovered. We forged on. Calamity had struck, but our race survived. We were not the same thereafter. We had changed. A power greater than us was unleashed, and it transformed us. It blessed us, and for that we thank it. You know what I am referring to. It has no name. It can have no name, for it is unknowable, unutterable, ineffable. It—"

"Show us!" someone in the crowd yelled, interrupting. The cry was taken up by the rest and became a chant: "Show us! Show us! Show us! Show us!"

This audience trespass onto Khotan-Kha's speech was, it seemed, not unexpected. Conan had a feeling it was a customary practice at such ceremonies; either that or the lizard-man who started the chant had been assigned the task beforehand by the Hierophant.

Khotan-Kha certainly showed no objection to the crowd temporarily setting the agenda. It was all part of the way he was controlling them, playing them as a musical virtuoso does his instrument. Give your followers the illusion that they were in charge, however briefly, and it would make them feel valued and enfranchised.

"Would you like that?" he said.

"Yes! Yes! Yes!"

Wings beat. Feet stamped. The racket was so loud, Conan felt like covering his ears.

"Then who am I to refuse?"

Khotan-Kha motioned, and several lizard-people who had been waiting out of sight emerged into the open. They, too, were robed, but their attire was less grand and elaborate than the Hierophant's. Acolytes, Conan thought. Junior priests.

Dividing into two groups, the acolytes picked up a pair of heavy iron chains that ran up out from a pair of slots in the flagstones to the rear of the dais. Then, flapping their wings, they rose in a choreographed fashion, hauling the chains with them.

By this means some hidden pulley mechanism was operated which drew two large sections of the amphitheater floor slowly apart.

From the rumblingly widening aperture a coruscating light spilled out. Its color was like none Conan had ever beheld. It had hints of lilac and pink, and carried a pearlescent luster, but overall he was hard pressed to compare it to anything at all. It was an unearthly light, an otherworldly light, and its beams shimmered and rippled in the air as they lanced upwards and outwards.

When the gap in the amphitheater floor was fully open, he could see that the origin of the light was a jagged, uneven fissure in the earth some ten feet across at its widest and about thirty feet long, tapering to a point at either end. Within the fissure the light seemed to swirl dazzlingly, like eddying tidal water.

The faces of all the lizard-people present were illuminated by that uncanny radiance. Conan could see their avid eyes reflecting it glitteringly as they gazed upon it with awe and reverence.

"This is it," said Khotan-Kha. "The light that brings wonders. The light that changes. The light that binds us."

"That brings wonders. That changes. That binds us," the crowd echoed.

"It has dwelled in the bosom of Ghuht for lo these many decades. It is the city's lifeblood, its soul, its pulse."

"Lifeblood, soul, pulse."

"It is the genesis of metamorphosis."

"The genesis of metamorphosis."

"We worship it, for it has made us what we are."

"Made us what we are."

The lizard-people had begun moving in synchrony, their bodies swaying from side to side, their wings wafting up and down at the same tempo. Some had their hands clasped in front of their breasts. A kind of pious ecstasy had overcome them.

"And it is the light," said Khotan-Kha, "that will illuminate our pathway to the future."

He gestured again to his acolytes, and they lowered the chains rattlingly back into their slots, thus closing the aperture. There was a collective groan of disappointment from the crowd, much like that of children when deprived of a treat, as the otherworldly light dimmed and then was blanked from view.

"I know, I know," their Hierophant said in what some might think was a tone of sincere regret. "You hate to see it go. But believe me when I say you have not seen the last of the light this day. Believe me, too, when I tell you that I have something else to show you. You know already what I refer to. As I have said, our fortunes are about to change. Our future is to begin anew. For months now I have sent emissaries out into the wider world, brave souls willing to travel far and wide in order to fetch that which we are in dire need of. Their task is complete, and I have here the fruits of their labors. It is time you all saw for yourselves what they have gathered."

He gave a quiet instruction to his acolytes, who disappeared somewhere off to the side. For several minutes his congregation waited in a murmurous hush of anticipation. Khotan-Kha himself stood with his head bowed, like someone dwelling on profound and weighty matters.

When at last the acolytes returned, it was with a gaggle of human children trailing behind them.

Conan stiffened, as did all three of his companions.

The lizard-people, meanwhile, nudged one another and voiced soft whispers of excitement.

The children were a range of ages, with the youngest perhaps no more than five and the oldest around fifteen. As they were led out into the open, they blinked up at the assembled lizard-people in quailing trepidation.

"Here they are," said Khotan-Kha, and his voice was soothing, almost benevolent. "Look on them, my friends. Welcome them. Behold the new generation. Behold our future!"

"Our future, our future," the congregation crooned.

Yet more children emerged. One of them was a Stygian girl who might well have been Layla, the daughter of Abrax and Aminah. Another was a snow-haired Æsir boy of nine. He held himself with somewhat greater confidence than the others, although he still looked anxious and intimidated.

Conan shot a look sideways. Gudrun and Hunwulf were beaming at each other in pure joy. He knew they ached to call out to their son and tell him they were there, but they restrained themselves. They had the sense to know it would be unwise to attract the lizard-people's notice.

Conan himself sent up a small prayer to any gods that might be listening, to thank them that Bjørn was alive and, as far as he could discern, well.

He turned to X'aan, who was still watching the children keenly as they trooped out. So far there had been a few Kushite girls, but none had yet elicited a reaction from him. Conan hoped for X'aan's sake that his younger sister was here. He would be utterly crushed if she did not appear.

The last few youngsters came out, making a total of around thirty in all. Among these stragglers there was a Kushite girl of around fifteen, the right age to be Zevia, and Conan saw X'aan leap to his feet.

He foresaw what was about to happen next, and he moved to prevent it, but too late.

X'aan was callow, lacking the Æsir couple's maturity and presence of mind. Elation got the better of him, and he cupped hands on either side of his mouth and yelled his sister's name.

"Zevia! Zevia, it's me! X'aan!"

His voice carried down into the crater, all the way to the amphitheater. The Kushite girl's head snapped up.

"X'aan?" she shouted back, puzzled, then overjoyed. "X'aan!"

At the same time, several hundred lizard-people swiveled round, including Khotan-Kha. Their gazes homed in on the source of the first shout, the spot where Conan and his companions lay, only partially concealed, on the crater's rim. Mutters of consternation rippled through their ranks.

Their Hierophant seemed genuinely aghast and lost for words, but he recovered his composure soon enough.

"Outsiders!" he bellowed in an indignant roar. "Interlopers! Get them!"

In answer to Khotan-Kha's command, lizard-people unhesitatingly took to the air and swarmed towards the four humans.

Conan fixed X'aan with a furious scowl.

"By Crom!" he exclaimed, rising to a crouch and unsheathing his sword. "Well, you've done it now, boy. This is no longer a rescue mission. This is a fight to the death."

18

The Song of Whirring Steel

The moment chaos broke out in the amphitheater, Khotan-Kha barked an order at his acolytes and they began hurriedly shepherding the children away.

Bjørn and all the others were hustled off into the tunnel through which they had been brought in earlier.

The Kushite girl had to be dragged. It took two lizard-people to hold her, and even then she wrestled and kicked and kept screaming a name repeatedly: "X'aan! X'aan! X'aan!"

"Will you be quiet!" one of the acolytes ordered, but the girl continued to resist, so he slapped her. She fell to the ground with a shriek, clutching her face. The lizard-man stooped, preparing to fetch her another vicious backhand blow.

Bjørn put himself between her and the acolyte. "No," he said.

"Move, boy. Or would you like to be hit too?"

"Leave her alone," Bjørn said. Sounds of confusion and clamor were echoing along the tunnel from the amphitheater and beyond. "I don't know what's happening back there," he went on, "but she's scared. We're all scared." His voice cracked a little, betraying the truth of his words.

"I'll give you 'scared,' boy," the lizard-man growled, raising his hand higher.

Bjørn clenched his jaw and stood his ground, ready to take the blow.

"Bah!" snapped the acolyte after a moment, relenting. "You are not worth it." He lowered his hand and took a step away. "Everyone, carry on. Back to your cells."

Bjørn helped the girl to her feet. "Are you all right?"

"No," she said, still clearly stunned and shaken by the slap. "Actually, yes," she corrected herself. "I *am* all right. Because that was my brother."

"Your brother?"

"He called out to me from the edge of the crater. I heard his voice. He used my name—Zevia. My older brother X'aan has come for me. I want to go back and find him."

"I don't think that's a good idea, Zevia," Bjørn said. "Even if our guards allow it, which they won't, it sounds like people out there are fighting. It wouldn't be safe. We must simply do as we're told, for now."

"Come along!" one of the acolytes cajoled. "Pick up the pace!"

Bjørn put an arm around Zevia's waist to support her and they started walking. She was older than him by a few years, and taller, but she seemed grateful for his assistance.

"I'm Bjørn, by the way," he said. "I've no idea what's going to happen to us, and I fear it won't be good, but I'm glad to meet you anyway, Zevia."

The Kushite girl braved a smile.

"And I have some news for you," Bjørn added, lowering his voice so that only she could hear. "If your brother has been able to find you, then there's a good chance that some people I know will be able to find *me*. And if—no, when—they do, they will rain hell upon these lizard-people."

He had no idea how close to the truth he was.

Conan, Hunwulf and Gudrun adopted battle-ready positions, weapons drawn. X'aan followed suit, pulling out an ivory-handled hunting knife. He looked shamefaced, as well he might. His moment of recklessness had ruined their scheme; it might even prove their undoing.

"My friends," said he to the others, "I am sorry. I did not think. I saw Zevia and could not help myself."

"Save your apologies," the Cimmerian growled. "They're of no use to us. The best thing you can do now is fight like hell and, if it comes to it, sell your life dearly."

"I understand."

Onward the airborne lizard-people came, in a vast flock that all but blotted out the low, reddening evening sun. Arms outstretched, wings beating, they descended on the four humans.

Conan propelled himself forwards to meet them, his broadsword whirling above his head. With a single stroke he removed one lizard-man's foot. With another, he rent through the membranous skin of a wing, rendering it useless.

Left and right he sliced and slashed, as reptilian hands grabbed for him and razor-sharp claws sought to gouge his flesh.

Nearby, Hunwulf wielded his axe like a berserker in full frenzy, hewing and hacking in all directions, while Gudrun sent arrows accurately aloft, piercing a belly here, an eye here, a ribcage here. One after another, Folk of the Featherless Wing plummeted from the sky, brought down by her shafts; but in seemingly no time her quiver was empty, whereupon her hand found her sword hilt and she joined in the mêlée at close quarters alongside her husband,

Conan and X'aan, swinging her blade with her face set in a mask of focused fury.

The Kushite boy, for his part, lashed out with his knife, doing his utmost to hold the enemy at bay. He showed greater zeal than skill, but nonetheless many of his desperate thrusts hit home.

The lizard-people had them fully surrounded, above as well as on all sides, but the four companions fought on.

Talons raked Conan's body, tearing his clothing and spilling his blood in freshets. That blood mingled with the lizard-people blood which coated the Cimmerian liberally, shed by his sword thrusts. He felt the pain of his injuries remotely, as though it did not belong to him. The battle-lust was upon him. He scarce knew where he was anymore, nor why he was fighting, nor who his comrades were. All he knew was the song of whirring steel, underpinned by the percussion of sword strike, the rattle of blood-spatter and the grunts and wails of the injured and the dying.

He was never more truly himself than in these moments, when he cared not whether he lived or died, only that his foes were defeated and slain. His lips were formed in a shape that was both snarl and ferocious grin. His wild barbarian soul, liberated from the notions of honor and chivalry which often trammeled it, screamed its glee.

Amid the scrum of combat he lost sight of the Æsir couple, and likewise of X'aan. The bodies of dead, half-dead and crippled lizard-people lay all around him. He felt himself becoming overwhelmed by the sheer number of opponents attacking. He reckoned this might be his last ever fight, and he accepted that with grace. As long as he went down taking as many adversaries with him as he could, he would consider that a fair and gratifying death.

Then there was a break in the proceedings. Just as a tempest has lulls, often conflict does too. The Folk of the Featherless Wing realized they were taking severe casualties, and many were rethinking the wisdom of assaulting the humans, particularly this one with the long black hair and remorseless sword arm. They withdrew to regroup and reassess.

While they were being newly circumspect, Conan decided to press home the advantage and bring the fight to them again. He broke into a run, which was arrested abruptly when a shrill yelp of terror caught his attention.

He looked over to see X'aan being lifted off the ground by a lizard-man, suspended helplessly by both wrists, facing backwards. His knife was nowhere to be seen. Presumably his foe had disarmed him.

Conan diverted towards them but failed to reach them before they had gained too great a height. The lizard-man was out of sword range.

He was not yet out of dagger range, however, and Conan snatched his poniard from his girdle and hurled it.

The poniard plunged into the small of the lizard-man's back, and he screeched and arched his spine but somehow kept flying, attaining yet greater altitude.

"Damn that scaly devil!" Conan cursed, watching as the wounded lizard-man soared away on an erratic course, with a flailing X'aan still in his clutches.

He had dealt a mortal blow, but the lizard-man seemed determined to carry on regardless. He could only assume his intention was to let go of X'aan when they were sufficiently high up.

X'aan, though, was not content to accept his fate meekly. With a sudden, spectacular effort he levered himself up and wrapped his legs around the lizard-man's waist, bringing the two of them face to face.

Clinging on like this, he leaned back and rammed his forehead onto the other's nose. He must have understood that if he knocked the lizard-man unconscious, they would fall and likely perish. It appeared that he was heeding Conan's injunction to sell his life dearly.

X'aan drove his brow into the lizard-man's face a second time, and a third, and now the two of them did indeed fall, spiraling down towards the base of the crater, locked together in a death-grip, accelerating as they went.

Conan did not see them land, nor much wanted to, for the sight of brave young X'aan being dashed against the ground would be hard to bear.

He was suddenly preoccupied, besides, by a fresh onslaught from Folk of the Featherless Wing.

This time, Khotan-Kha himself was leading the charge. The elaborately robed Hierophant flew towards the Cimmerian at chest height, swift as an eagle, barreling into him before he could bring his sword to bear. Conan crashed onto his back, and all at once dozens of lizard-people were upon him, pinning him to the ground.

"That's it, that's it," said Khotan-Kha to the others. "Hold the miscreant down. We have another two of his kind under restraint. I want all three of them alive."

"Alive?" Conan spat, struggling in vain against the press of bodies on top of him. "You would do better to kill me, Khotan-Kha. Alive, I am a danger to you."

"But alive," came the reply, "is how I need you to be, so that I may interrogate you. The dead answer no questions."

"It is a mistake to spare me."

"But I wish to cross-examine you, human," said Khotan-Kha, "and my wish is my deed." He stepped close to Conan. "Now, will you come willingly?"

"Never!"

"Then unwillingly it must be."

So saying, Khotan-Kha raised a fist and smote the Cimmerian on the skull with brutal, bone-crunching force.

There was a lightning-flash of white, and then for a while Conan knew naught but oblivion.

When Conan recovered consciousness, he was not surprised to find himself bound hand and foot. Were he taking a captive who had shown himself to be as adept and aggressive a combatant, he would have done the same.

He was on his side, on a marble floor, and the first thing he did was test the ropes securing him. They were fastened well. In addition, there was rope wound about his neck, and this was attached to his other bindings in such a way that it tightened when he worked at them. To struggle was to strangle, and so he kept still.

Hunwulf lay nearby, hogtied just like he was, and Gudrun too. The Æsir couple bore copious grazes and lacerations, a sure sign—as if there could be any doubt—that both had given a good account of themselves throughout the battle with the lizard-people.

Conan's eyes met theirs, and in them he saw burning anger and humiliation, the same emotions he felt.

He twisted his head, and his gaze fell upon a throne, where sat none other than Khotan-Kha. Two of his acolytes were stationed on either side of him. The throne was the centerpiece of a room that must at one time have been grandly, austerely imposing; now, its walls were riven with cracks, like forks of black lightning, and the marble floor tiles were tilted askew.

The lizard-people's Hierophant was observing his three prisoners inquisitively, head cocked to the side.

"Awake already, eh?" he said to Conan. "You came to quicker than I thought you might. You must be blessed with a thick skull."

"We'll see how thick *your* skull is," Conan replied, "when I crush it in my bare hands."

Khotan-Kha chuckled. "I am not going to die today, outsider. You three are. But not before you explain how you were able to get all the way into my city."

"Untie me and I'll show you."

Khotan-Kha rose and stepped down from the throne. The back of the chair had the eye sigil inlaid in gold. "Normally, humans never get farther into our territory than a few hundred yards before the jungle kills them. You managed to reach Ghuht. That is remarkable."

"For that you can thank, in part, the boy who was with us," Conan said, "the one your people slew."

"The same boy who so carelessly gave away your position?" said the Hierophant. "After that, I would have thought the three of you might take a rather dim view of him."

Hunwulf piped up. "You are not wrong," he said glumly. "If not for X'aan, we wouldn't be where we are, trussed up like pigs waiting for the butcher's cleaver."

"Aye," Conan acknowledged. "He let us down, badly, and he paid the penalty for it. But don't forget, Hunwulf, without him we might never have made it as far as we did. And," he added, "when all's said and done, he was just a boy, not much older than your son."

"Our son, whom we shall now never see again," said an embittered Gudrun.

"You came to retrieve your child," said Khotan-Kha, nodding, "as so many others have tried to in the past few months, and failed. Which brings us back to my question: your late young friend notwithstanding, how were you able to reach Ghuht? What is so special about you people, over and above the rest of your kind?"

"We tried harder than they," said Gudrun simply.

The Hierophant hummed. "Humans intrigue me," said he, strolling round his three captives. "Compared to us Folk of the Featherless Wing, you are feeble creatures. We are hardier than you, stronger, with tougher skin—not to mention our talons— and capable of flight, of course, where you are not. We are your betters, and yet, if our history has taught us anything, it is that you view us as monsters. As freaks of nature. As something to despise.

Is it any wonder we have kept ourselves to ourselves here in Ghuht for so long?"

"If I had my way," Conan said, "I would slaughter the lot of you."

"There it is. That contempt. 'Slaughter.' As though we are vermin."

"If you are so much better than us, why do you kidnap innocent children?" said Gudrun. "Hardly the mark of a superior race."

"Now there, I admit, you have me," said Khotan-Kha. "I cannot refute the charge, and I can only tell you that I regret doing it but it had to be done."

"Why? What do you need them for?"

"Is it to sacrifice them?" said Hunwulf. "Perhaps as an offering to that thing your people worship, that hideous light from underground."

Khotan-Kha's eyes blazed. "That light is not hideous!" he said in an enraged hiss. "That light is glorious. It is a miracle, a hymn to the beauty of change and salvation."

"Spoken like a true fanatic. I don't know what that light is, but I do know it is unnatural. Cracks in the earth do not glow like that. It is something which doesn't belong in this world."

The two acolytes gasped, appalled. Khotan-Kha drew back one leg and kicked Hunwulf hard in the gut. The Æsir man doubled up, gasping for air and writhing.

"Blasphemy!" the Hierophant cried. "*You* are the ones who do not belong. You three are intruders in our land. Worse, you have interrupted our holy celebration. You have no right to come here and upbraid us for the way we conduct our lives."

"We do when it entails stealing children from their families," said Gudrun. "Those same children you were parading on stage just now like animals in a menagerie."

"Merely giving my people a foretaste of what awaits."

"Here is my offer to you, Khotan-Kha," said Conan, managing with some effort to pivot himself up into a seated position. "You let us go, you allow us to take all of the children with us…"

"And in return?" said Khotan-Kha.

"In return, I will not destroy this entire city and everyone in it."

The Hierophant was superciliously amused. "Ho ho! Grand talk from a helpless man who is shortly to be executed."

"It is no bluff," the Cimmerian stated. "Ghuht is half razed already. I shall merely finish the job."

Khotan-Kha bashed Conan viciously on the side of the head, toppling him. Conan, spitting blood, hoisted himself upright again. His head was ringing. The lizard-man was strong. He could not recall when he had been hit harder.

"And I shall save you for last," the Cimmerian persisted, "so that you may witness the destruction of your race before joining them in death."

Khotan-Kha mused for a moment. "Do you know," said he, "I truly believe that you truly believe you will do that. You are an impressive individual, as humans go. What is your name?"

"I am Conan of Cimmeria, but you may know me as nemesis to the Folk of the Featherless Wing."

"You persist in trying to antagonize me, Conan of Cimmeria, but all you are accomplishing is making me admire you. For that reason, I am going to tell you and your two comrades why we need those children. Under any other circumstances I would send you three to your deaths in a state of ignorance. But you have earned the right to be edified. Consider it a courtesy. My gift to you. This is the story of the Folk of the Featherless Wing—how we came to be and how we have arrived at the parlous state we find ourselves in. Listen well and be enlightened."

19

A Shattered Gem

"Half a millennium ago," said Khotan-Kha, "Ghuht was a marvel. It was a glorious, shining city, remote, self-sufficient, inhabited by humans such as yourselves, and thriving. A place of splendors. Fountains played in its plazas. Lush public gardens abounded. It was girt all round with cultivated land, where crops grew in abundance and cattle safely grazed. Its citizens wanted for nothing and lived in harmony with their surroundings. Then came the Rupture."

"An earth tremor," said Conan.

The Hierophant nodded. "Just so. The land quaked. Ghuht's great towers shuddered and crumpled. Not one building was spared. It was wholly unexpected and unprecedented, and it happened so suddenly, so swiftly, that there was no time to take refuge. Thousands upon thousands of people perished in a matter of moments—crushed or buried alive. An entire section of the city subsided into a cavity which abruptly yawned in the earth. You have seen that for yourselves. It is where our Temple of the Light now lies."

Khotan-Kha paused.

"Perhaps the greater tragedy was not the deaths themselves but the destruction of perfection. Where Ghuht had once been flawless, now it was a place of devastation, a shattered gem. All that remained of its population were a hundred or so souls, a lucky handful who had somehow managed to survive this apocalypse. As they roamed the ruins—scarce able to believe how, in an instant, paradise had turned to hell—they were drawn towards a pulsating glow which originated from a freshly opened fissure at the epicenter of the earthquake, within that cavity I spoke of. None had seen its like before. Their curiosity and wonderment were great as the light bathed them in its brilliance. Little did they realize that exposure to it was altering them—them and everything else it touched."

"As I said," Hunwulf commented. "Unnatural."

"Silence!" Khotan-Kha snapped, even as again the two acolytes gasped. "Keep up that heretical talk, and I shall forget that I am paying you a courtesy and have you executed right now."

"You might be doing us a favor. Better that than having to listen to you pontificate."

"Let him speak, Hunwulf," said Conan. "I, for one, am interested in what Khotan-Kha has to say."

He did not add that the longer the Hierophant's narration went on, the more time there would be to figure a way out of this situation. Covertly he was testing his bonds, seeing if he could somehow tease the ropes loose by working his wrists around inside them—and do this without throttling himself. It was hard, however. The knots were cleverly contrived.

"The survivors could not hope to rebuild the city," Khotan-Kha said. "The task was too great, too onerous, for so few. But neither did they wish to leave. They knew little about the world beyond their immediate vicinity, and besides, Ghuht was their home. They stayed put and made do, eking a living amid the rubble. In due course they procreated, but this first post-disaster generation was born different. They had scales, and talons, and tiny buds on their backs from which, in due course, wings would sprout."

"They were like you," said Conan.

"They were like me. Initially, these infants were regarded with horror and disgust. Some were even, I am sorry to say, murdered at birth. But as more and yet more of them appeared, it became clear that this was how the denizens of Ghuht were going to be hereafter, and thus they gained acceptance. Eventually the day came when the last human inhabitants died out, and then there was only the Folk of the Featherless Wing. They—we—were now the norm."

"The light from the fissure had done something to your people's bloodline."

"Transformed us," Khotan-Kha said, "and not only us but plant life in the city too, and the lower orders of creature, from the largest mammal to the tiniest insect. Its influence spread out from the fissure over the course of decades, through the jungle, slowly reshaping all living things."

"And continues to do so, to this day. The Rotlands keep growing."

"Naturally, the Folk of the Featherless Wing understood that the light was powerful, and the kind of transfiguring force it exhibited could only be considered divine. They fell to worshiping it. Grorr-Prak was the first Hierophant, a chosen intermediary between the Folk of the Featherless Wing and the object of their veneration. Then came Krall-Hrark, and then Klaa-Urhk, blessed be their names."

"Blessed be their names," the two acolytes intoned.

"It was Brekh-Orak, fourth in the Hierophantic succession, who instituted the use of this symbol." Khotan-Kha touched the gold-braid eye sigil on his robe. "He was sitting in contemplation of the light one day, when all at once the shape came to him in a vision. He knew it represented everything about the light. The light sees deep. The light sees far. The light sees all. That is what it stands for."

"Sees deep, sees far, sees all," the acolytes said.

"The same Brekh-Orak had the Temple of the Light constructed in order to house the light and shield it from the sight of the unworthy and the infidel."

"Aye," said Conan. "Ever has it been the practice of priests to control access to their mysteries. Thereby do they prosper, whilst also growing corrupt."

"You are cynical, Conan of Cimmeria."

"I have seen enough of the world to mistrust those who set themselves above others in the name of religion."

"Within which category you include me?"

"If the shoe fits..." said Conan.

He braced himself for another vicious blow from Khotan-Kha, but the Hierophant merely uttered a hollow, patronizing chuckle.

"Oh, human! Your worldview is so limited. You perceive everything through the lens of your own prejudices. Can you not understand that something which renders such improvements, as the light has done with us, must be husbanded and protected? The light made me infinitely better than you." Khotan-Kha thumped his chest. "The light created a race who can withstand the rigors of the environment that now surrounds us. Humans die within moments of entering the Rotlands, whereas Folk of the Featherless Wing are strong and resilient enough to survive there without difficulty."

"*We* survived it," Gudrun said.

Khotan-Kha wheeled towards her. "Yes, and still I have not established how that was possible. You, woman, told me it was because you tried harder than others had, but there must be more to it."

Conan could feel the ropes around his wrists starting to slacken.

It was only by a minuscule amount, and the constriction around his neck was becoming painful, but still he was encouraged.

He said, "Khotan-Kha, you haven't yet told us why you need human children so badly."

"Ah yes," said the Hierophant. "As to that, the answer is simple. It is tragic, too. After the Rupture, as the centuries passed, the Folk of the Featherless Wing flourished. Our numbers never equaled those of the human population that had dwelled here in Ghuht before then, but we could always rely on there being a few thousand of us. In the past hundred years or so, however, those same numbers have gone into a steep decline. The majority of our females are barren and our males infertile, and what few babies are born emerge from the womb with severe physical defects, such that they do not live long. In short," he concluded with a sorrowing sigh, "we are dying out."

"So much for your vaunted superiority," Conan scoffed. "Why didn't you introduce bloodlines from outside, to revitalize your own?"

Khotan-Kha merely shook his head. "Would that it had been possible, but who else is there like us?"

"I once met a specimen of a race similar to yours," Hunwulf said, "though not an exact match."

"As did I," said Conan.

"Did you now?" said Khotan-Kha. "I had always imagined the Folk of the Featherless Wing to be unique."

"But I'll hazard that crossbreeding between your kind and theirs would not have worked," Conan said, "and if it had, it would only have created sterile mules."

"I suspect you would be correct. Nor can we mate with humans. It was attempted. Early on, when the population decline first started to make itself apparent, parties were sent out to capture suitable prospects from the human villages closest by. But their revulsion of us was a stumbling block. It hampered the chances of natural procreation. And even when pregnancies were achieved through coercive means, the results were stillborn abominations."

"'Coercive means,'" said Gudrun with a sneer of distaste. "No need to prettify it. You may call it what it is: rape."

Khotan-Kha blithely ignored her caustic comment. "We sent the captives back to their homes, but I daresay they were quite traumatized by their experiences. I daresay, too, that Ghuht garnered a dark reputation because of it."

"Clearly, Khotan-Kha," Conan said, "your race started out too small in number to last without mingling with other races from elsewhere. You were destined from the outset to become inbred and then to degenerate—and by staying so insular, you ensured that."

"Please don't tell us," Gudrun said, "that those human children are here for the same purpose. I did not think I could feel any greater loathing for you and your kind."

"Not the same purpose," Khotan-Kha replied guardedly, "but a similar one. There are certain occasions when… But it would be altogether easier if I just showed you."

He struck a gong, and a door opened and a half dozen more acolytes filed into the throne room.

"Adjust their bonds," he commanded, "in such a way that they are able to walk, but only just. I am taking them to the Granite Orrery."

"As you wish, sire," said one of the acolytes.

"Start with the big one, this Conan. He may try to resist, but if he is sensible he will not—not while his two comrades are lying helpless and at our mercy. And even if he were able to break free and go for his weapon…"

Khotan-Kha pointed to a corner of the room, where Conan's broadsword and the Æsir couple's armaments lay in a pile, all having been removed from their persons in the wake of the battle.

"Well, I doubt he could reach it in time before his friends perished. In other words, their lives are entirely dependent on his cooperation."

As the acolytes manhandled Conan to his feet and retied his ropes, he assessed his chances of turning the tables and thought them slim. Khotan-Kha was right, damn him. Whatever he did, no matter how fast he did it, Hunwulf and Gudrun would die.

Reluctantly, he submitted to the acolytes' ministrations.

"That, of course, applies to you two as well," Khotan-Kha said to the Æsir couple. "Think carefully, and behave."

Hunwulf and Gudrun came to the same verdict as Conan had, and presently all three humans were standing, alive but still bound. Each now had a short length of rope linking their ankles together, meaning they could only shuffle. The ropes around their necks remained in place, yoked to the ones binding their wrists in front of them.

"Before we proceed," said Khotan-Kha, "I feel I should remind you that, unarmed, any one of us Folk of the Featherless Wing is more than a match for any one of you, and several of us would have no trouble tearing you to pieces. I would recommend you come along quietly. It will go easier for you."

20

The Granite Orrery

Surrounded by acolytes on all sides, the three humans were ushered out of the throne room, with Khotan-Kha leading the way. They passed along a series of corridors and scaled several flights of stairs.

Conan noted a teetering wall that was shored up with timbers, and a doorway that was likewise propped up to prevent it collapsing. The Folk of the Featherless Wing had had centuries in which to renovate Ghuht and restore it to its former glory, but instead their attitude seemed like that of a once-wealthy widow fallen on hard times who must patch and darn her old finery.

As far as he could tell, the sole new piece of construction they had carried out was the Temple of the Light. This said a lot about their priorities. When it came to matters of faith they were fanatical. The omnipresence of the eye sigil was testament to that, as well as the fact that they were ruled by a theocracy. They had elevated religion above all other concerns, so that anything else—a decent standard of living, engagement with other races, creativity, commerce—was immaterial.

The inevitable consequence of this was introversion and complacency, and therein had lain the seeds of their downfall. Every civilization ended in decadence and failure, and religion did nothing but hasten the deterioration.

The procession arrived eventually at a huge chamber lit by tall braziers and dominated by a fantastic structure. It comprised a set of concentric stone rings standing upright, the biggest some twenty yards in diameter, the smallest a couple of feet across.

Each ring was engraved with markings—mainly large dots but also thick lines, some curved, some straight—apart from the central one, which was a solid disc sculpted to resemble the moon.

"The Granite Orrery," Khotan-Kha announced. "This, like the Temple of the Light, was the handiwork of Hierophant Brekh-Orak. He was perhaps the shrewdest of all Hierophants, understanding more than any of us before or since. He always credited the light with granting him insight into the workings of the universe. The light enhanced him mentally, he said, as it enhanced the rest of us physically."

"What in Crom's name is that thing?" Conan inquired, eyeing the stone structure.

"A map," said Khotan-Kha. "It charts the motion of the stars in the sky, showing how they go in cycles. Their cycles, you see, correspond with fluctuations in the strength of the light. There are times when it shines more brightly and times less so, and the stars' positions relative to one another mark the fact. This—the manner in which it and the heavens are intrinsically associated—is proof of the light's connection to the very essence of the universe. On certain very rare occasions it shines brightest of all, blindingly so, and its power grows exponentially vaster."

"When?"

"When the moon is obscured by shadow."

"You mean a lunar eclipse."

"Not just any lunar eclipse, Conan of Cimmeria. That is a commonplace enough phenomenon. I am referring to a lunar eclipse accompanied by a certain specific stellar alignment. It occurs only twice or thrice every century, and we call it the Night of the Obsidian Moon."

Conan recalled Khotan-Kha using the very same phrase during the ceremony. "Which is happening this very night."

"Indeed so," said the Hierophant. "The Granite Orrery is designed in such a way that it foretells when the next Night of the Obsidian Moon is due. Here, let me show you."

There was pride in Khotan-Kha's step as he went over to an arrangement of brass levers embedded in the floor beside the Orrery. He seemed keen for the three humans to think well of him, perhaps even to admire him. His faith was fundamental to everything he did and justified his actions, and he wanted them to understand this and therefore, perhaps, no longer regard him as a monster.

He manipulated the largest lever, and the Granite Orrery ground into life. Its nested wheels within wheels turned ponderously, gratingly, rotating both clockwise and counterclockwise, driven by unseen weights and chains.

"Each dot represents a star," Khotan-Kha said, raising his voice to be heard above the din of churning machinery. "The lines are of Brekh-Orak's design. I can set the dots so that they reproduce the positions of the stars as they are right now. Every Hierophant is taught the technique as part of their initiation into the role."

He worked the levers deftly.

"And when the dots are positioned correctly and I do this..."

He pulled another lever, and the moon at the center of the Orrery spun round on its vertical axis in a half-turn, showing its reverse, which was plain save for a single line dividing it down the middle.

"Then the arrangement of all the lines will confirm whether a Night of the Obsidian Moon is imminent. If they do not match up precisely, the answer is no. But when, as now, they do..."

The Granite Orrery came to a shuddering halt, and the lines on the rings, in tandem with that on the central disc, now formed a pattern stretching from top to bottom.

It was the eye sigil.

Conan permitted himself a wry smile. "Why am I not surprised?" he said. "Everything in this place revolves around that symbol."

"Ho! A witticism."

"I meant none."

"But the Granite Orrery literally revolves around the symbol," said Khotan-Kha.

Conan shrugged uncaringly.

"Humans," the Hierophant muttered in a disparaging tone of a haughty sophisticate. "The finer points of everything are wasted on them." He resumed his thread. "On the Night of the Obsidian Moon, the light's metamorphic power is at its peak. Thus it may, in minutes, wreak transformations that would otherwise be subtle and take far longer to have effect."

Gudrun was the one who put it all together first. "The children," she said, aghast. "You are going to change them."

"Very good," said Khotan-Kha. "The human younglings are to be exposed to the light, and it will convert them into Folk of the Featherless Wing. The transformation will take place in just moments."

"No," breathed Hunwulf.

"Then," the Hierophant continued, "they will become the new blood that propagates our race. Some of them are old enough already to procreate. Others will soon be of age. We have gathered as many as we can, and we have chosen only children with a propensity for magic."

"Why magic?" Conan asked. "Why not ordinary children? Why children at all, for that matter? Why not adults?"

"Because," explained Khotan-Kha, "in times past the conversion process was tried on ordinary humans, without success. On the last two Nights of the Obsidian Moon, my forerunners as Hierophant collected such subjects and bathed them in the light. The only effect was to mutate them in various undesirable ways. Their bodies grew deformed and diseased, riddled with maladies— cankers and buboes and the like. The first time, it was adults, and they perished swiftly. The next time, under the auspices of my immediate predecessor Hierophant Yurr-Drrak, it was decided to try children, since children are in general better able to cope with physical changes. The results, alas, were just as disappointing. The children, too, sickened, and those few who survived were left severely damaged and incapacitated. We took them to the edge of the Rotlands and set them free. How they were received when they returned to the outside world, I know not."

Conan's mind went to X'aan's story about the lion cub who wandered into Ghuht. He could see now how it had come about. Accounts of what the Folk of the Featherless Wing had done would have become widespread, and a narrative would have emerged, a veiled warning. The story was a partly sanitized version of an awful reality, as fables often were.

"My hope," Khotan-Kha said, "is that the inherent magical abilities this new batch of children have will protect them, just as contracting certain diseases gives one immunity. Their exposure to the light will not have the same detrimental outcome. It will merely make them like us."

"Your hope?" said Gudrun. "You don't even know if this scheme of yours will work, and yet you are ready to risk harming—even killing—thirty-odd children, purely on the off chance that it might?"

The Hierophant was phlegmatic. "Our race is at an impasse. When all other avenues are exhausted, desperate measures are called for. I have no doubt that your own people, under the same circumstances, would act likewise."

"And suppose your desperate measures fail, Khotan-Kha. Suppose all you succeed in doing tonight is destroying children. You will have let down the Folk of the Featherless Wing badly. Won't they turn on you?"

"There is nothing angrier," Conan said, warming to Gudrun's theme, "than a populace when their leader promises them the world and fails to deliver."

"That is not..." Khotan-Kha faltered, his smooth assuredness lapsing momentarily. "I have faith," he said, recovering his composure. "My people have faith. They will understand that I tried my best for them. They will forgive me."

"You had better hope they do. More likely they will tear you apart."

"Not if I don't first." So saying, Gudrun made a lunge for Khotan-Kha.

Hobbled as she was, however, she did not get far. One of the acolytes arrested her, slamming her flat onto the floor with almost contemptuous ease.

Khotan-Kha brushed his hands together imperturbably.

"Well," he said, addressing all three of the humans, "I think we have tarried enough. I have satisfied your curiosity. You have yet to satisfy mine, but as it happens, I no longer care very much to learn how you made it here alive through the Rotlands. Suffice it that you did, and that here is where you are now going to die. You cannot be allowed to potentially ruin things for us. You have already caused an upset, and I both commend and condemn you for that. But it is time—well past time, indeed—that you were taken away for execution."

"So it's the headsman's axe for us?" Conan asked.

"Nothing nearly so crude," replied the Hierophant.

"Then fatal exposure to the light is to be our doom."

"You are unworthy of being in proximity to the light again," said Khotan-Kha loftily. "Your presence would profane it. No, the three of you are going to be escorted to the highest tower in Ghuht and thrown from its top. You enjoy irony, Conan of Cimmeria. What more ironic demise could there be for those who can fly to inflict upon those who cannot?"

Just as Khotan-Kha was delivering this grimly sardonic pronouncement, elsewhere in the city Bjørn was again languishing in his cell.

The commotion at the crater had calmed down some while earlier. He could no longer hear distant wails and moans—the aftermath of conflict—through his tiny, unreachable window.

He wondered how Zevia's brother X'aan had fared. He surely could not have come alone, else the tumult would not have lasted as long as it had. One man against so many lizard-people? Bjørn had seen firsthand how Folk of the Featherless Wing could fight. The battle would have been over in moments.

No, X'aan had had allies. Could those allies have included his parents, and perhaps Conan too?

But Bjørn chose not to torment himself with such tantalizing thoughts. Besides, if X'aan had been part of a many-handed rescue effort, it did not appear to have gone well. The resounding silence outside was testament to that. He could only assume that the lizard-people had been victorious and that his own situation was therefore unlikely to change, at least not in the immediate future.

A key turned in the lock, the door opened, and in walked Krraa-Bhaak, Bjørn's erstwhile abductor and transporter. Bjørn felt surprised and oddly pleased to see him. His was a familiar face at least, if not necessarily a friendly one.

"Greetings, Bjørn Hunwulfson," said Krraa-Bhaak, closing the door behind him. "I have something for you."

He produced Bjørn's whittling knife and held it out, handle first. Tentatively, fearing some trick, Bjørn took it.

"What's this for?" he asked.

Krraa-Bhaak hesitated, then said, "I leave that for you to decide. Tonight, you and the other youngsters are due to undergo an experience which may prove unpleasant. I would not wish for you, Bjørn, to face it undefended. Alternatively, I am giving you the option of not having to face it at all."

Bjørn took a moment to digest his implication. "Kill myself?"

"It might be kinder. Whichever option you choose, know that I am uncomfortable with our Hierophant's actions. He is my ruler, and my faith is strong, and it is not my place to oppose his judgment. But that does not mean I have to like it."

"I... I thank you, Krraa-Bhaak."

The lizard-man did one of those slow, crisscrossing double blinks. "Just be glad I have given you your knife and not that stubby little hammer of yours. I saw your barbarian friend Conan teaching you how to throw knives and you becoming quite skilled at the art."

"You were watching us at the stables?"

"I told you I had been keeping a close eye on you in Eruk ever since I first encountered you. One like me, who has access to high vantage points, could easily remain unobserved. You may wish to use that knife similarly tonight, as Conan showed you how. I am not sure it will be of advantage to you, however. On balance, I think you will be better off using it on yourself."

"Who else knows you've given it to me?"

"No one. I have done this of my own recognizance and would surely be in dire straits were it discovered. I simply felt I should listen to the dictates of my conscience." Krraa-Bhaak turned to go, but then said, almost as an afterthought, "You should know, too, that your parents are here in Ghuht, as is the barbarian, Conan."

Bjørn felt a thrill of elation. "They have come! I knew it!" He could not help doing a little caper.

"But," the lizard-man added, "they are now captives of Khotan-Kha, and he is going to have them put to death. That may well have happened already."

From a peak of joy, Bjørn was plunged into a slough of despondency.

"I was in two minds whether to mention it at all," said Krraa-Bhaak, "but I felt you should be told. The three of them, along with another ally, were responsible for the fracas at the Temple of the Light just now. The ally—some Kushite boy—is dead, I believe. Your parents and Conan put up an impressive resistance and slew many Folk of the Featherless Wing before being overpowered and incapacitated. I am sorry to be the bearer of bad tidings, Bjørn."

"No..." Bjørn said numbly, disbelievingly.

Krraa-Bhaak motioned at the knife which dangled loosely from Bjørn's hand. "Perhaps what I have just said may help you make up your mind one way or the other."

"Perhaps."

The lizard-man reached out awkwardly and patted the Æsir boy's shoulder. "You are valiant. You are stout-hearted. I do not believe you deserve what's coming. Our Hierophant is doing what he believes is right, and maybe he is, who can say? But he is not infallible, and I fear that in his drive to save his people, he has lost sight of morality. Fare you well, Bjørn Hunwulfson. I am glad to have met you."

The door shut. Krraa-Bhaak was gone, leaving Bjørn alone with the knife and his thoughts.

Just briefly he entertained the notion of heeding the lizard-man's suggestion and ending himself.

But that was not he. That was not the son Hunwulf Ivarson

and Gudrun Ingensdóttir had raised. His parents would not want him to take the coward's way out. They would want him to fight to the bitter end, as it seemed they themselves had at the Temple of the Light.

Bjørn slipped the knife inside his sleeve. Whatever might happen tonight, he would not go quietly. He owed it to his parents and to Conan of Cimmeria. He, Bjørn Hunwulfson, would die on his feet, fighting, as any good Æsir should.

One was never too young to be welcomed into Valhalla.

21

Providential Newcomer

When the acolytes had retied Conan's bonds, they had taken up the tiny amount of slack he had managed to generate. Since then, while Khotan-Kha had been busy preaching to them at the Granite Orrery, Conan had renewed his efforts at loosening the ropes, but to scant avail.

Now, as he, Hunwulf and Gudrun were being marched through Ghuht to their place of execution, he tried once more to free up his wrists just a little bit. It was futile, however. It only made the rope around his neck more of a garotte.

But all was not lost. Conan had another plan. It was one that bore a marked chance of failure, but it was a plan nonetheless.

A nine-strong contingent of acolytes were escorting the three captives, and none of the lizard-people bore arms; but then, with their talons, their wings and their distinctly greater physical strength, they had every advantage over a trio of bound, hobbled, weaponless humans. It was the talons Conan was focused on— those razor-sharp claws on their hands and feet. What if he could turn his foemen's greatest asset against them?

On a couple of occasions, as the group trudged along their route of doom, they passed other Folk of the Featherless Wing, who treated the humans to jeers and booing; a few even flung stones. Conan and the Æsir couple had not endeared themselves to the lizard-people by disrupting their ceremony and killing a considerable number of their race.

Then, ahead, a tall tower appeared against the twilight-empurpled sky, its sheared-off upper stories lending it the likeness of a sharpened quill.

The procession veered towards this, and Conan understood that here was where the execution would occur. He had little time left to act. It was now or never. There were no other lizard-people around.

All he needed was a diversion, a moment of distraction. He could pretend to stumble, perhaps, or strike up a bogus argument with Hunwulf or Gudrun, something that would oblige the acolytes to get directly involved.

Crom might not answer prayers, but nonetheless some divine entity seemed to have been mindful of Conan's desires—or else it was just a happy coincidence. For as they entered the shadow of the tower, a figure darted out from a gap between two buildings, screaming like a banshee. It was wielding a dagger, and it hurled itself at one of the acolytes so that the two of them went rolling to the ground in a thrashing tangle of robes and limbs.

Instantly Conan recognized this providential newcomer to be X'aan, and a split second of startlement was followed by the imperative urge to act, which superseded all else.

While the acolytes were overcoming their surprise and marshaling themselves to respond, Conan barged the one nearest him with his shoulder. The lizard-man retaliated instinctively, lashing out with his talons.

Conan had foreseen such a response—indeed was counting on it—and raised his wrists into the arc of the acolyte's swing. The maneuver demanded precision and perfect timing, otherwise he stood to lose fingers or even a whole hand.

Instead, as hoped, he lost his wrist bindings. The talons slashed through them as though they were made of gossamer, and as the ropes parted, the pressure on Conan's throat went too.

He seized the acolyte by his robes and yanked him forward, and while the lizard-man was off-balance the Cimmerian let go of his clothing and drove both thumbs deep into his eyes. The acolyte screeched as Conan twisted his thumbs and hooked out two jellied orbs. Blind and blubbering in pain, the lizard-man reeled away. His enucleated eyes dangled from their sockets on strands of optic nerve. Conan grabbed him roughly, hoisted him high and slammed him chest first onto the ground with enough force to drive his sternum into his heart.

Immediately he spun round to meet another acolyte who was making a beeline for him. His feat with the wrist bindings had been difficult enough, but what he aspired to do next was nigh-on impossible. Yet it had to succeed, otherwise this fight would be over before it had truly begun.

The acolyte came at him with bellicose speed. Conan ducked under his lunge and kicked with both feet, sweeping his legs from under him. Thanks to the rope between his ankles, he himself fell, but that was all part of the plan.

His legs were alongside the acolyte's. He drew them up sharply either side of the lizard-man's taloned foot. That lower set of claws split the hobbling rope in twain, and all of a sudden Conan's legs were as free as his arms.

He rolled behind the acolyte, gripping him around the midriff with his thighs in a scissor hold. Seizing his head with both hands, he wrenched it sideways with all his might. There was the dry-twig crackle of vertebrae snapping, and the acolyte, head lolling loosely on neck, emitted a dying gargle.

Conan was on his feet in an instant. He registered that X'aan was still grappling with the lizard-man he had attacked. He saw also that Hunwulf and Gudrun had taken their cue from him. Hunwulf had somehow managed to get his still-bound wrists around the neck of an acolyte from the rear and was doing his best to strangle him, while Gudrun was fending off another of the acolytes, a lizard-woman, who was bearing down on her with all her might.

Above all else, Conan needed a weapon. That was the thing that could tip this battle in his and his allies' favor. The lizard-people would surely prevail otherwise.

He hastened over to where X'aan and his adversary were tussling on the ground. The Kushite boy was struggling to bring the dagger blade down into the acolyte's chest, but the acolyte was holding it at bay.

Conan stamped on the unsuspecting lizard-man's head, a skull-splintering, brain-crushing blow that sent blood and teeth flying from his lipless reptilian mouth.

Then he snatched the dagger from X'aan's grasp. It was his very own poniard, last seen buried in the back of the lizard-man who had flown off with X'aan.

"Mine, methinks," Conan said.

X'aan, panting hard, nodded. "I am pleased to restore it to its rightful owner."

Conan sped over to Gudrun and, in two deft strokes, severed her ropes before inflicting a crippling injury on her opponent. He did the same for Hunwulf, enabling both Æsir to carry on their respective fights unencumbered against sorely wounded enemies.

Three of the acolytes had now been permanently disposed of, the humans' numbers were augmented by one, and Conan had a dagger. Everything had changed. The battle was no longer so unequal.

Like a whirling dervish, Conan moved among the remaining acolytes, never pausing, a blur of action. He slashed one's throat brutally. He slit open another's belly. A third he wrestled to the ground and stabbed between the shoulder blades.

That left just three lizard-people alive. Two were still engaged separately with Hunwulf and Gudrun, and losing. The third was looking perplexed and perturbed, caught in that timeworn dilemma of discretion versus valor. Flee, or stay and fight?

He opted for the former and took to the air.

Conan could not let him get away and raise the alarm. He broke into a sprint and, with a mighty springing effort of leg sinews and muscles, propelled himself onto the acolyte's back.

He seized one of his wings by the root and hacked through it with the poniard, severing tendons at the joint. The lizard-man dropped like a stone, headfirst, with the Cimmerian clinging on, still clutching the amputated wing.

They hit the earth hard. Conan rolled off the acolyte, who lay groaning pitifully, multiple bones shattered. Blood gushed from his wing stump. Conan crawled over to him and ended his misery.

He looked up to see that Hunwulf and Gudrun had between them polished off the last two acolytes. Both of the Æsir couple had sustained fresh cuts and grazes during the fray, while a fair few of Conan's wounds from the battle at the Temple of the Light, which had barely had time to close, had been reopened thanks to his exertions. All three were a bloodied, tattered mess; but the light of triumph blazed in their eyes, like a kind of madness, making such things as pain and blood loss feel trivial.

Conan, sheathing his poniard, turned to X'aan. "You live, boy," quoth he. "Wonders will never cease."

X'aan was on his feet but looking ashen-faced and unsteady. "I am in poor shape," he said. "I believe I have a broken rib or two. It hurts to breathe. But yes, to my surprise as much as yours, I live."

"Your arrival was timely. We three were being taken to our execution."

"By luck, I spied you being marched through the city, and I tailed you until we came to this spot where there were no other lizard-people present and the odds were slightly more in our favor. I knew that if I was to strike, it must be then. I… I was not sure whether it would help or if I would simply wind up being killed, but it had to be done."

"You did the right thing and did it well, X'aan." Conan was about to clap the Kushite boy heartily on the back but remembered in time about the broken ribs. Instead, he ruffled his close-cropped hair. "But how did you survive falling from the sky in that dying lizard-man's embrace?"

"We landed with me on top, much as you did just now with that lizard-man there, albeit from a far greater height. The lizard-man's body absorbed the brunt of the impact. I pulled your dagger from his back and staggered away. All was pandemonium at the time, so the other lizard-people did not notice me sneaking off. I have been in hiding ever since, moving from one place of concealment to another. I have had no goal other than to avoid the Folk of the Featherless Wing and if possible discover where Zevia is being kept. When I saw you three, I could scarcely believe my eyes. I was certain you were dead."

"Not dead," said Hunwulf. "Very much alive, and for that, you are in large part responsible, X'aan. You have more than redeemed yourself after the debacle at the crater."

"I hoped as much."

"And now we have our lives and our liberty back," said Conan, divesting himself of the scraps of rope still attached to him. "Not only that, we have a chance to save Bjørn, Zevia and the other children."

"How?" said X'aan. "We are only four, the lizard-people are many, and aside from your dagger we have no weapons."

"We could retrieve our equipment from the throne room," Gudrun suggested.

"Too risky," Conan said. "Besides, time is growing short. Look."

He pointed skywards. Darkness was falling, and a bright moon was rising over the horizon. Its features were sharply delineated except at the top edge, which was obscured by a blurry-edged shadow.

"The lunar eclipse has already begun," he said. "Khotan-Kha's so-called Obsidian Moon is nigh. We must get to the Temple of the Light. That's where the children will be."

"And when we get there?" said Hunwulf. "What then? X'aan is right. We are hopelessly outnumbered and have nothing to fight with apart from one dagger and our bare hands."

"I am no clairvoyant like you, Hunwulf Ivarson," Conan said, "but still I can foresee a way of achieving our aims."

"Then you are either hopelessly optimistic or hopelessly insane, Cimmerian."

Conan grinned wolfishly. "Trust me, I am neither. All I know is that what has already been toppled may be toppled further."

And with this somewhat cryptic comment, which he could not be drawn to clarify, Conan set off at a brisk pace towards the Temple of the Light; and his three companions, nonplussed but willing to give him the benefit of the doubt, fell in tow behind him.

Lizard-people acolytes came for the children in their cells. The children were made to line up and then file out towards the long tunnel that led to the temple, with the acolytes chivvying them along.

Bjørn wondered if he alone among the youngsters had any idea of what awaited them when they got where they were going. "Unpleasant," Krraa-Bhaak had said. Probably he *was* the only one, but the other children nonetheless were apprehensive, sensing the mood of the occasion from the acolytes' febrile intensity, and also no doubt recalling the last time they had made this journey and how it had ended in panic and chaos. Some of them whimpered, one or two wailed, while most were subdued, casting sullen, anxious looks around them.

Bjørn spied Zevia ahead, and he sidled forward until he was alongside her. She bestowed a cautious nod of greeting on him.

"Zevia, listen," he said in low tones. "We're being led to what may be our deaths."

The Kushite girl looked appalled but somehow unsurprised too. "I feared as much."

"What do you think about putting up a resistance?"

"How?"

"You!" yelled one of the acolytes. "What are you doing? Stop talking."

"I'm just comforting her, sire," Bjørn said. "That's allowed, isn't it? She's scared, and you want us calm, don't you? So that things go nice and smoothly for you."

The lizard-man shook his head irritably. "Very well."

Lowering his voice again, Bjørn said to Zevia, "You know I was only telling him what he needed to hear."

"I am quite scared," Zevia admitted. "And now you're talking about resisting the lizard-people, which doesn't help."

"I'm going to fight, and I'm ready to die if it need be. Anything rather than let the Folk of the Featherless Wing do to us whatever it is they're going to do. What I want to know is if you'll join me."

Zevia deliberated. "My brother came for me here. If he is still alive, I'll do anything to see him again. If he isn't, I'll do anything to pay these fiends back for his death."

"I hoped you'd say that."

Bjørn cast a surreptitious glance at the acolyte who had berated him a moment ago. He was currently not paying close attention.

Bjørn briefly, covertly showed Zevia the whittling knife secreted up his sleeve.

"It isn't much," he said, "but it's something."

"Back home," she said, "I'm known for communicating with spirits. They visit me in my mind and whisper secrets and truths. Since I got to Ghuht they've been silent. I think it's because they do not belong here. They are the spirits of my land, of the elements, of the earth and water and trees and sky; and this place, lying in the heart of the Rotlands, is alien to them. It repels them. I miss their voices. I feel lonely without them. If they were here, they'd tell me whether I should help you. They'd know if it was futile or not. Without them, only my heart can tell me what to do."

"And what does your heart say?"

"It says, Bjørn Hunwulfson, that you're foolish," Zevia said, "and maybe crazy."

"But?"

"But then I must be too, because I'm in. I will help you."

"Good," said Bjørn. "Then pass the message along to the others, any way you can. I will too. Don't make it obvious. Be subtle. Tell them to follow my lead. They may not all want to join in, but if even a few do, mayhap we can—"

"Enough!" The acolyte reached out and smacked Bjørn round the back of the head. "If the girl's nerves are not settled by now, they never will be. Everyone just keep walking. It isn't far to go."

Bjørn set his jaw and lowered his head. His task, and Zevia's, in the little time they had, was to ignite a spark of rebellion among their fellow children and fan it into a flame. He hoped that, once it caught, it would blaze.

In his heart of hearts, however, he suspected it was more likely to be snuffed out.

22

Night of the Obsidian Moon

The Folk of the Featherless Wing had regathered, and they were excited.

The Temple of the Light was now lit with torches, and in the tiered seats around it rows of lizard-people jostled and chattered, while above, in a sky as deep blue as lapis lazuli, the moon glided slowly and serenely upward to its empyrean height. A quarter of its face had succumbed to shadow, and with every degree it climbed further, this penumbra spread.

As the moon's glow dimmed, so the intensity of the lizard-people's mood grew, going from festive to feverish. This was the night long promised, not just the night when a lunar eclipse coincided with a particular stellar conjunction but the night when their race's fortunes changed for the better and for good.

So their Hierophant Khotan-Kha had told them, and who were they to disbelieve him? Under the Obsidian Moon the light would blossom to its fullest extent and the human children would be converted by it, becoming lizard-people too but with inherent fertility.

Then, in the years to come, a new generation would emerge, and they in turn would produce offspring of their own, and the Folk of the Featherless Wing would continue in perpetuity rather than die out.

Truly Khotan-Kha was the greatest Hierophant of them all, a visionary who had confronted a crisis and furnished a solution.

The lizard-people did not believe it possible that Khotan-Kha might be wrong and his plan doomed to failure, as previous Hierophants' plans had been. They did not dare. They themselves had too much invested in its success. The light would do what it had to. The light would banish the gloom of their race's predicament. The light would be their saving grace. This they told one another repeatedly as they waited for Khotan-Kha to appear and the moon to darken all over.

When at last their Hierophant emerged in his ornate priestly regalia, there was a vast, collective outpouring of approval.

Striding onto the dais, Khotan-Kha greeted the ovation with his hands held high, basking in it like a cat in sunlight for as long as it lasted. Then, minutes later, when the fervor had died down, he launched into a lengthy speech which recapitulated much of what he had said earlier that evening. Amidst the religious rhetoric and the self-aggrandizement there were the customary prayers and invocations, which his followers echoed with more than usual vigor.

"And remember," said he, "how a band of outsiders interrupted our worship earlier today? Remember that? They attacked us, some would say without provocation, and in the ensuing skirmish many of our brethren and sistren lost their lives. But we Folk of the Featherless Wing prevailed, and I have seen to it that those interfering humans will be duly punished. Even now I am awaiting word from my acolytes that the sentence—death, of course—has been carried out."

This was met with a roar of bloodthirsty delight.

"But there is a lesson to be drawn here," Khotan-Kha went on.

"It is that nothing can stand in our way. It is that we, as a race, are destined to surmount all obstacles. Even this greatest obstacle of all which we currently face, this potentially terminal catastrophe, the lack of births, may be overcome. You can see for yourselves that the moon is now more than halfway occluded. The stars around it are in their ordained places. The Obsidian Moon is almost upon us. Let us rejoice. Let us give thanks. The end was nigh, and now it is not."

The Folk of the Featherless Wing did as bidden. They made merry, they heaped praise upon Khotan-Kha, they sang songs extolling the glory and majesty of the light, and all the while the moon gradually ascended and blackened.

Such was the volume of the celebrations at the Temple of the Light, and so lost were the Folk of the Featherless Wing in their votive duties and their adulation, that there was hardly any need for stealth. Conan, Hunwulf, Gudrun and X'aan might as well have strolled boldly along the crater's rim, in plain view of all, shouting to one another at the top of their voices.

But, sensibly, they crept, and conversed in whispers. Discovery, even if unlikely, would have put them in grave jeopardy.

At last they reached a spot Conan had identified during their previous visit to this location. Here stood a single stone column some twenty feet high and six across, perhaps once support for a statue, now leaning precariously, the narrow plinth at its base angled out of the ground.

He halted and turned to his companions. "This is what I propose: we tip the column."

"And?" said Gudrun. "We draw attention to ourselves, the lizard-people spot us, and then what? We are killed? That is the plan?"

"Nay. See below." Conan pointed downwards. "First there are a further pair of columns, then the wreckage of a house, then what remains of, I think, a courthouse or meeting hall. Each is lined up neatly, one after the other in a row. Each, too, is fragile and clings to the crater's incline, its foundations loose, barely holding on. You Æsir hail from wintry, mountainous climes."

"Not I," said Hunwulf. "I was born and raised in the lowlands, remember."

"I likewise," said Gudrun. "I have no memories of Vanaheim."

"Regardless," said Conan, "you understand how avalanches occur. Snow breaks off and slithers downhill. It gathers speed and more snow until it becomes an unstoppable tide, sweeping all before it."

"'What has already been toppled may be toppled further,'" said X'aan, quoting Conan's earlier remark. "You mean to create a kind of landslide with these broken buildings."

Conan nodded. "One that'll travel all the way down into the Temple of the Light, crushing the lizard-people there. Thus we can kill the great majority of them and they'll no longer have such an advantage of numbers."

"And if it doesn't work? If we cannot shift the first column?"

"We can but try. Do you have a better suggestion, youngling?"

"The children have not been brought out again yet," Gudrun said, "but I can only imagine they will be soon. They too will be in the path of your avalanche, Conan."

"I suspect that Khotan-Kha won't produce them until the last minute, once the moon is in full eclipse. That way, his acolytes won't have to wrangle them in public for long, just as before with that 'brief foretaste' of his earlier, that moment of glory which we ruined. It also fits in with his sense of the dramatic. Still, the sooner we get to work, the better. Any further objections?"

The other three exchanged glances, and then shrugs. Gudrun's reservations were writ large upon her face, and her husband clearly had mixed feelings too. They understood, however, that the Cimmerian was set upon his course of action and would attempt to implement it with or without their help, whether they liked it or not.

Conan put his back to the column. Hunwulf joined him on one side, X'aan and Gudrun on the other.

The Kushite boy pointed out that, owing to his broken ribs, his contributions would be limited, but he would do what he could.

"Just push," Conan said. "We need only tilt the column slightly. Its own weight will do the rest."

So they began. They shoved, they strained, they heaved: they put everything they had into it, Conan most of all. His tendons stood proud beneath his blood-caked skin like taut wires. His muscles were bulging, corded masses. His forehead was furrowed, his mouth frozen in a rictus of effort.

Minute after minute the foursome applied themselves to the column, to no effect, until finally Conan called for a rest.

"It has not budged," X'aan commented between rasping gasps for breath.

"Not yet," Conan replied.

Hunwulf mopped sweat from his brow. "This is hopeless."

"It's only hopeless if we give up," Conan said. "Back to work."

Once more they pushed. This time Conan faced the column, his legs braced, his shoulder pressed against its stone. He refused to believe the column would not fall. This was as much an act of willpower as a feat of strength. Nothing, he felt, could withstand a determination like his.

His companions seemed to pick up on his sense of self-conviction and were heartened. The task might seem bootless, but if the Cimmerian was not prepared to quit, neither would they.

All at once the column gave slightly. It was just the tiniest amount, a mere fraction of an inch; but it had inarguably moved.

They redoubled their efforts. That which had yielded a little could yield completely. Out of the four of them, Conan continued to supply the greatest motive force. He was unrelenting. He did not relax for even a second.

When X'aan broke off because his ribs were hurting too much, Conan of Cimmeria persevered.

When Hunwulf collapsed in exhaustion, Conan of Cimmeria persevered.

When Gudrun staggered away, her limbs trembling because her muscles were so sorely overtaxed, Conan of Cimmeria persevered.

The column moved farther, and farther still. It was starting to lean at an acute angle. Its plinth was tearing free from the ground.

Above, three quarters of the moon was now obscured. Below, the Folk of the Featherless Wing continued their revels, whipped up by regular oratorical proclamations from Khotan-Kha.

Conan alone wrestled with the column, shunting it farther over a little at a time—and suddenly a tipping point was reached, and the column fell.

Conan stumbled backwards, losing his footing and himself falling. He sat with arms and legs akimbo and watched as the stack of chiseled stone performed a slow, almost graceful dive, breaking in half as it hit the ground.

The two parts of the column started to slide and roll in a manner that was both heavy and leisurely. Gaining speed, they rammed into the two close-set columns directly downslope. These crumpled and collapsed, joining in their comrade's descent and striking the ruined house that was next in line. There was a spectacular, crunching impact, and the house dissolved into fragments. The chunks of it, bouncing and spinning end over end, mingled with the column sections on their remorseless downward trajectory, with hundreds of torn-up clods of earth adding themselves to the mixture. All were traveling fast as they hit the third stop on the itinerary, the damaged civic edifice. That building exploded into countless pieces, and now the process triggered by the impetus of the first falling column had become a broad, thundering cascade of debris – and it was heading straight for the Temple of the Light.

Conan's face split into a grimace of gloating satisfaction. He had told Khotan-Kha he would destroy Ghuht and everyone in it. This was not quite that, but by Crom, it was close enough.

Initially, the Folk of the Featherless Wing were too absorbed in their celebrations and too focused on their revered Hierophant's pronouncements to notice what was coming their way. Their massed hubbub drowned out the rumble of tumbling masonry at their backs.

Not until the deadly cataract was almost upon them did they realize the danger, and by then it was too late.

A torrent of broken stone poured over the tiered seats, engulfing the lizard-people, crushing some outright and driving others helplessly before it like a hand sweeping chess pieces off a board. Not one of them had time to take flight and escape the onrush.

The semicircular shape of the amphitheatrical temple funneled the debris inward towards the epicenter, where Khotan-Kha stood, frozen in stunned disbelief. The cascade's velocity was petering out by this stage, and it expended the last of its momentum as it hit the temple floor. The assorted lumps and hunks of stone rolled to a halt like an ocean wave expiring on a beach.

There was still enough force in the avalanche, however, to sweep the Hierophant off his feet. He went down flailing, becoming lost amid the rubble.

A great cloud of dust arose from the jumbled wreckage, amongst which countless reptilian bodies lay. Here an arm pointed forlornly upwards, there a face stared sightlessly at the sky. The billowing powdery haze quickly hid the temple from sight, even as echoes of the manmade landslide's roar faded away. An eerie hush fell.

Overhead, meanwhile, only a sliver of moon remained visible, canted at an angle, like a shining, perverse smile.

At the crater's rim, Conan of Cimmeria got stiffly to his feet, planted fists on hips, and gazed down upon his handiwork.

"That went even better than I hoped," said he. "The children aren't here. Only lizard-people have fallen, and I think Khotan-Kha perished with them."

X'aan beheld the scene below with frank awe. "Remind me never to get on your wrong side, Conan," he quipped.

"Few who cross me live to tell the tale," the Cimmerian replied bluntly.

"We should get down there," Gudrun said. "There is an entrance to the side of the temple through which the children were brought out last time. That is liable to take us to where they are being kept."

She set off down the slope, tracing the furrowed, detritus-strewn wake of the cascade. Hunwulf followed in swift succession, then Conan and X'aan.

Not long before Conan visited untold calamity upon the Folk of the Featherless Wing, Bjørn and the other children were being held in a subterranean vestibule adjacent to the Temple of the

Light, a kind of waiting area connected to the temple itself by a short passageway.

Bjørn moved among the huddled youngsters from one to another, as did Zevia, ostensibly offering comfort and succor but actually giving quiet hints about the possibility of concerted action should an opportune moment arise.

All the while the two of them kept an eye on their lizard-people guardians, who were concentrating less on their youthful charges and more on the rousing words of their Hierophant and the cheers of his audience which filtered through to them along the passageway.

Bjørn found himself next to a Stygian girl whose name, he discovered, was Layla. As they spoke, he noticed that her eye kept being drawn to the wall sconces in which torches burned.

"Layla," he said, "I have this theory that all of us here have some kind of special gift."

It was talking to Zevia that had first got Bjørn thinking this way, and it accorded with something Krraa-Bhaak had said about having selected him for kidnap because of the way he had tamed the dog Wolfblood. He had been mentioning it to the other children and found they boasted a range of unusual abilities.

"Do you have one," he asked Layla now, "and if so, what is it?"

The Stygian girl nodded. "Fire," she said softly. "I am a friend to fire, and fire to me." Again she looked at the torches, and Bjørn saw attraction in her gaze, a kind of longing.

"You know how to control it?" He tried to mask a surge of excitement. The last thing he wanted was for the lizard-people acolytes to notice him behaving oddly and tumble to his scheme.

"I can," Layla replied. "But I have to be careful. Sometimes it can get out of hand. Flames don't want to be contained or directed. They don't like it. They resist. All they want to do is spread and consume and make more of themselves. Myself, I would rather just play with them."

"Could you play with the torch flames so that they attack those lizard-people over there?"

"I think so."

"I'm not asking you to kill them," Bjørn said, adding, "unless you want to, that is. But you could maybe singe them—hurt them so they can't hurt us."

A secretive smile came over Layla's face. "I think I could do that. Will it gain us our freedom?"

"I can't promise that. But it could be just what we need."

He caught Zevia's eye and indicated to her, with a twitch of the head and a quick jab of the forefinger, that Layla had something very useful to offer. The gestures were subtle but alas not sufficiently so.

"Boy!" One of the acolytes seized Bjørn by the scruff of the neck. "I saw you. You were signaling to that girl. What message were you conveying to her? Tell me!"

"Nothing. I was just telling her that this girl"—he meant Layla—"needs consoling."

"Lies! Something is going on between you two. I can tell." The acolyte hauled on Bjørn's collar, lifting his feet off the ground. His breath, gusting in the Æsir boy's face, was fetid. "You are conspiring together."

"To do what?" Bjørn said, resisting the urge to gag. "What can we possibly do? We're just children. Frightened children, too."

"You yourself do not look frightened, boy."

"Perhaps I hide it well."

"Or perhaps, as I surmise, you have something up your sleeve." The lizard-man did not know how close to the truth he was with this figure of speech. "You have a cunning air about you. I dislike it." He gave Bjørn a shake. "Out with it. What intrigue are you concocting?"

Bjørn understood that matters were coming to a head. He understood, too, that if he and the other children were going to

CONAN: CULT OF THE OBSIDIAN MOON

launch an assault on their captors, it must be now, and he must spearhead it. He might never have an opportunity like this again.

He reached into his sleeve, fingers closing around the handle of the whittling knife. The knife might not be big but it was sharp. This close to the acolyte, there was every chance he could deliver a good, solid stab. All he had to do was hit just the right spot, with just the right amount of thrust.

He prayed Ymir would guide his hand, and he thought of his mother and father and how proud they would be of him for striking this blow. He knew he might likely die tonight, but he was at peace with that. He would be seeing his parents soon, he was sure, reuniting with them in Valhalla.

All at once, every torch in the chamber flared strongly and brightly. The flame on each swelled to three times its size and extruded a portion of itself like a fiery tentacle.

These tentacles lashed out at the acolytes, touching them and igniting their robes.

Clothing alight, the lizard-people panicked—including the one holding Bjørn. He dropped him and started beating frantically at the flames that were licking up his robe, his face grimacing in atavistic fear.

His fellows did likewise, but the fires somehow refused to go out. Rather, they coursed eagerly through the fabric, scorching the wearers.

The acolytes began stripping naked. One rolled around on the floor, hoping this might put out the blaze. Most of them were screaming, but while their cries carried along the passageway, they were subsumed by the crowd noise outside and went unheard and unheeded.

Bjørn did not hesitate. He pounced on the acolyte who moments earlier had been trying to intimidate him. The whittling knife rose and fell, again and again, its blade becoming bloodier and bloodier.

As the lizard-man sank to the floor, Bjørn rushed over to another and repeated the action.

Other children, emboldened by his example, swarmed over the remaining few acolytes.

Layla stood apart. Her eyes were wide and had a vacant look. Her hands were extended, her fingers playing in the air as though strumming the strings of an invisible lyre.

The acolytes, still burning, fell before the onslaught of their erstwhile prisoners.

These youngsters had been wrenched away from their families and homes and held captive. They had been bullied, browbeaten, fed meager rations, deprived of sunlight, and otherwise been victims of neglect and abuse. The weeks—in some instances, months—of maltreatment they had endured spilled out in a massed surge of rage, against which the lizard-people, though each was larger and stronger than any of their assailants, could not prevail.

The children did not think what they were doing was wrong. They thought it only right and proper.

While it was happening, Layla made sure that the flames stayed clear of her fellow humans, and when it was all over, she snuffed them out with a wave of the hand. Smoke rose into the air, along with the smell of charred reptilian flesh. Blood pooled on the floor.

Bjørn looked over at Zevia, and she nodded to him and mouthed the words, "We did it."

That was when the earth started to quake.

From without there came a tremendous, deafening rumble. The vestibule floor shuddered and dust sifted down from the ceiling. Several of the children shrieked, and some clung to others. Bjørn feared that the chamber was about to collapse on their heads.

The tremor lasted a quarter of a minute, and then, as swiftly as it had begun, ended. Thick billows of dust purled in along the passageway, setting the children to choking and spluttering.

Several of them looked expectantly at Bjørn, and he realized they were seeking his guidance. Without meaning to, he had become their leader.

The logical course of action would be to retreat back along the tunnel that led to their cells. Whatever had occurred outside in the Temple of the Light was clearly catastrophic and might not be over yet. Safety lay in the opposite direction.

Still, Bjørn could not curb his curiosity. He had to know what it was that had quelled events outside so suddenly and absolutely.

As the dust cloud thinned, he crept along the short passageway and peered out.

What he beheld was utter devastation. The temple was now half buried in debris, and he traced a trail of destruction all the way up the crater's slope to the very top. He could see lizard-people bodies partly buried in the rubble, and a section of the temple floor had cracked and given way under the weight of wreckage.

From within this crevice an uncanny light shone forth, shedding a flickering, shifting nimbus of illumination all around.

Bjørn had never seen a light like it, and its coloration—shades of purple and pink mixed in with other hues he could not put a name to—both fascinated and repelled him. The same curiosity that had driven him to leave the vestibule now drove him to venture out towards the light in order to examine it more closely.

He had gone just a few paces when he heard a voice urgently calling out his name.

His heart leapt. He could scarcely believe his ears.

The voice called out again, and was joined by another.

"Bjørn! Bjørn!"

He turned to see his parents bounding down the slope towards the temple. Their faces were alight with joy, and Bjørn himself felt such happiness he could barely speak.

"Mother? Father?" he croaked.

Next thing he knew, he was being swept up in his mother's arms and held in the fiercest hug he had ever felt. A moment later, his father was hugging them both, weeping with relief and exhilaration.

Bjørn did not know how his parents were still alive, nor did he care to know. It was enough that they were, and that they were holding him, and that he and they were together once more.

23

Questions of Faith and Fealty

Conan and X'aan stood back as the three Æsir embraced. Neither wished to intrude upon their moment of happiness.

Then the Cimmerian nudged X'aan's arm. "Look. Over there." He had spied a face peeking timorously out from the entrance to the side of the temple. "Is that not someone you know?"

X'aan's and Zevia's gazes met simultaneously. Each let out an exultant shout and ran to the other. Zevia flung her arms tight around her brother, and he yelped in pain. She let go and stepped back concernedly.

"What is the matter?"

"Nothing, little sister," said X'aan. "Hug me again. Just somewhat more gently this time, if you please."

Behind Zevia, more children began to emerge from the entrance. Dust-coated, some of them bloodstained, they looked around in amazement. Several peered at Conan, and their expressions were puzzled and not a little perturbed.

"What?" Conan challenged. "Why do you stare at me like that?"

"I don't think they've ever seen anyone as large as you, Conan," said X'aan, "nor as covered in wounds."

The Cimmerian grunted. "Well then, keep looking, younglings. This is a Cimmerian in all his battle-scarred glory."

The family reunion between Hunwulf, Gudrun and Bjørn broke up.

"I know you must have questions for us," Gudrun said to her son, "and we have many for you. Now is not the time, though. We need to move away from this place." She waved an arm at the crack in the ground and the shafts of light stabbing upward from it. "I don't think it is safe. Would you not agree, Conan?"

Conan glanced up at the moon, which was now almost entirely obscured, the merest rind of brightness remaining. He returned his gaze to the light. It was stronger than he remembered from the last time, and not merely because he was standing much closer to it now. It was unmistakably brighter, with those nameless, indefinable colors swirling ever more fiercely, ever more repulsively, amid its effulgence. It seemed as though the light was eager to escape the confines of the fissure, striving to spill out into the world. Just watching it made the Cimmerian feel queasy.

As he looked, a winged insect—a moth of some kind—fluttered into the light's radiance. Almost instantly, the moth grew in size. Its wings darkened to a waxy blackness, while its abdomen became a grotesque, pendulous bulb as big as a man's fist and its compound eyes swelled into redly glowing orbs. The mutated creature flapped away into the night, emitting a weird, eerie chittering as it went.

Conan's eye then fell on a tangle of roots protruding from beneath the cracked floor right at the fissure's edge. Like the moth, this vegetation was also altered by the light. It was becoming abnormally gnarled and twisted and sprouting ugly, bruise-colored tuberous growths.

Gudrun was right. It was unwise for them to linger in proximity to the light's unearthly glow, especially with the Obsidian Moon in full swing and exerting a cosmic influence upon it. Indeed, the light might already have begun working its sinister magic upon them.

"I agree," Conan said. "We must leave. Children, get moving."

The youngsters hesitated. They still did not know what to make of this huge, wound-bedecked barbarian, and the way he had growled the order at them was more than a little intimidating.

Bjørn turned to them. "Everyone, do as Conan says," he said. "Head up the slope, that way. Quick about it."

"Follow me," Zevia said. "By the sound of it, we are not out of danger yet."

"I shall come with you," X'aan said to his sister. "I'm not letting you out of my sight again."

As the children—all save Bjørn—started traipsing up the incline of the crater behind X'aan and Zevia, a loud groan caught Conan's ear.

The groan originated from the dais where Khotan-Kha had been standing; and sure enough, its source was the Hierophant himself.

Conan watched Khotan-Kha totter woozily to his feet from amid a scattering of broken masonry, hand clutching head. He could only assume the lizard-man had been knocked out by some hurtling chunk of stone. He looked otherwise unhurt.

Immediately the Cimmerian steeled himself. Khotan-Kha may have been fortunate enough to survive the avalanche Conan had created, but now he was about to face the man himself. The two of them must surely have to engage in combat, and it was an encounter Conan would not and could not let Khotan-Kha win.

"You," the Hierophant snarled, his eye falling on Conan. "My acolytes failed to kill you, did they?"

"Aye, me and my Æsir friends too. You need to find yourself better executioners, Khotan-Kha. As for the ones you had, they themselves have been executed."

"Curse you, human. Curse you all." Khotan-Kha's gaze roved around the half-destroyed temple and the slew of rubble studded with his dead kinfolk. "What have you done?" he lamented. "You have ruined everything."

"I have done what any sane man would do," Conan said. "I could not let you go through with the atrocity you had planned." He beckoned. "Now, fight me."

Khotan-Kha swiftly doffed his robes, leaving himself naked except for a loincloth. He shook out his wings and canted his head from side to side, a gesture of acknowledgment and preparedness.

"And you without a sword, human," he said. "This should not take long, and then I will slay the other adults and drag the children back here to be exposed to the light. This is not over."

"No," said someone. "It is."

The voice came from an unexpected quarter. Another lizard-man shambled into view, limned by the eldritch glow of the light. He was in a sorry state: battered, his clothes torn, dragging one leg, with one arm hanging loosely by his side, obviously broken. Conan could only infer that he had just pulled himself out of the rubble, having narrowly escaped death.

"Krraa-Bhaak?" said Bjørn. "Is that you?"

"It is I, Bjørn," the lizard-man replied wanly, "more or less."

"You know him by name?" Hunwulf said to his son.

"He's the one who kidnapped me. But he's decent enough, kinder than the others."

"Krraa-Bhaak," said Khotan-Kha icily. "You have the temerity to say no to me?"

"This has gone far enough, o Hierophant," said Krraa-Bhaak. "Accept that you have been defeated and your scheme lies in tatters. More killing, more harming of humans—what good will it do? It will change nothing."

"I believe it will change everything," the other lizard-man retorted. "The Obsidian Moon will last several minutes more. Our race may yet live on. Assist me in disposing of these infidel wretches and then regather the children. We can do this together, you and I."

Krraa-Bhaak clambered up onto the dais. "No, Khotan-Kha. I shan't help you. I shall, instead, do my utmost to stop you."

"You would side with humans over your own kind?" the Hierophant said. "Where is your faith? Your fealty?"

"Fading, perhaps lost altogether; both of them," said Krraa-Bhaak mournfully, "dispelled by the realization that our leader is a deranged, deluded madman. The sad fact is, the Folk of the Featherless Wing are fated to die out. It cannot be avoided. It cannot be remedied. Why can you not accept that?"

"I refuse to. What is a Hierophant for if not to promote his followers' best interests and bring them hope? Our race does not have to end. We can be resurrected."

The two lizard-men were now standing face to face. Krraa-Bhaak looked weak and weary. Khotan-Kha was as imperious as ever.

"You say you will stop me," the Hierophant said. "How, Krraa-Bhaak? You have a broken arm and you can barely stand."

"I said I would do my utmost. I would rather try and fail than not try at all."

"A shame." Khotan-Kha shot out both arms, seizing Krraa-Bhaak's neck in a vicelike grip. "You will die first. The humans will follow shortly."

Krraa-Bhaak clawed at the Hierophant's hands with his one good hand. Rasping, gurgling sounds escaped his throat as

Khotan-Kha applied greater pressure. Directly behind them, the light spilling out from the fissure in the ground was reaching new heights of luminosity. Its lustrous, multihued shimmer was dazzling; the way its beams danced and wavered, mesmerizing but also nauseating. As for the moon, it had disappeared entirely. There was just an empty circle amid the stars, as black as the volcanic glass which lent the moon its descriptor on this particular night.

Conan reached for his poniard.

Then, out of the corner of his eye, he saw Bjørn produce a knife. The Æsir boy held it by the blade and adopted a throwing stance. He took aim at Khotan-Kha.

Conan elected to give him his chance. If Bjørn missed, he himself would step up. He willed the boy to remember his lessons: keep the grip on the knife loose, rest your weight on your back foot, shift that weight forward as you throw, arm out straight as you release.

He felt pride and pleasure as Bjørn hurled the knife straight and true.

It thudded into Khotan-Kha's flank, all the way to the hilt, and the Hierophant recoiled, relinquishing his grip on Krraa-Bhaak. He took a couple of lurching steps backward, staring down at the knife's deer antler handle in disbelief, then over at Bjørn with something akin to indignation. He was now on the brink of the fissure.

Krraa-Bhaak summoned his last scraps of energy and lunged at him. They collided, and Khotan-Kha fell. He plunged into the light with a scream of alarm.

The light absorbed him into its incandescence, cutting his scream short. Conan half expected there to be a greater disturbance in the glow, as a pond's surface will ripple when a stone is thrown in, but its turbulent surface showed no trace of Khotan-Kha's entry.

Whether the light had melted Khotan-Kha, or had drowned him, or was holding him suspended within its depths, was unclear. All Conan could be sure of was that the Hierophant was gone. He had disappeared into the fissure and, Crom willing, was never coming back.

Bjørn hastened over to Krraa-Bhaak on the dais. The lizard-man had sunk to his knees. His head was bowed, his wings drooped, and everything about him suggested he was hanging on to life by a thread.

"Get up, Krraa-Bhaak," Bjørn said. "Let's move you to somewhere where we can tend to your wounds."

"I think... it is too late for me... young human," the lizard-man gasped. "I have... nothing left."

"Don't talk nonsense. You had the strength to shove Khotan-Kha."

"Only just. I am... broken."

Krraa-Bhaak slumped to the floor. Bjørn knelt beside him and looked over at his parents. "Can't we do something?"

"I don't think so," said Gudrun.

"I don't like you being so near the light, Bjørn," Hunwulf added. "Leave him."

"Yes," said Krraa-Bhaak. "Do... as your father... says, Bjørn. The longer you spend... beside the light... the more likely it is... to harm you."

"I'm sorry, Krraa-Bhaak," Bjørn said.

"Don't be. This is... how it has to be. I am... probably the last... of my kind. With me... die the Folk of the... Featherless Wing."

"If so, then they died well."

"Thank you, youngster. That is..."

Krraa-Bhaak did not finish the sentence. He lay still.

Bjørn got up and returned to his parents' side, and the Æsir family moved off tiredly together, climbing the temple's tiered seating side by side.

Conan followed. Already he was thinking ahead and planning for contingencies. There were thirty-some children needing to be escorted out of the Rotlands. That was going to be no easy task. First, the weapons in the throne room would have to be retrieved. Then supplies would have to be gathered, food mainly. Then Hunwulf would have to be coaxed into performing his clairvoyance trick in order to smooth their passage through the deadly jungle.

All in all, the next couple of days were going to be a taxing ordeal.

Nonetheless, Conan thought, victory was theirs. The children had been rescued. Khotan-Kha had been dispatched. The Folk of the Featherless Wing had been eliminated. The worst was over.

He could not have been more wrong.

Conan was halfway to the rim of the crater when something—some primal, hackle-raising instinct—made him turn.

A huge arm was reaching out of the light-filled fissure, groping around. Its hand found purchase on the dais. Then a second arm emerged and did the same. Like the other, it was as long as a man was tall, and it was covered in thick, brown-green scales, and its fingers were tipped with talons big as sword blades.

Both arms levered downwards, and now a head rose clear of the light's embrace. Its features were more reptilian than humanoid but still recognizably those of Khotan-Kha. It was as though the Hierophant's face had become distended like a reflection in a warped mirror, the nose projecting farther forward, the brow ridges deeper, the skull flatter.

The more of the giant Khotan-Kha that crawled out from the light, the more Conan perceived that the lizard part of "lizard-man" now far outweighed the man part. Somehow, as well as growing to thrice his former size, the Hierophant had regressed through several evolutionary stages to become a more purely saurian version of himself.

As the transformed Khotan-Kha stepped clear of the fissure, he let out a roar of sheer, bestial rage.

"Humans!" this fearsome apparition thundered. "All humans must die!"

24

The Meaninglessness of Things

"There you are," Khotan-Kha boomed, espying the Æsir family and Conan. "Did you think you'd seen the last of me?"

"It was our fondest wish," Conan shouted back.

"I am glad to disappoint you. It felt as though I was absent for eons, but I see now that it has been only moments, for you have not gone far and the Night of the Obsidian Moon is still upon us. But during that time, those swift-passing eons, what I have seen! What I have learned!"

The mammoth Khotan-Kha looked down at the dead Krraa-Bhaak at his feet. Then, flicking the corpse aside contemptuously with one foot, he took wing. Within seconds he had landed in front of Conan, looming over him.

Dwarfed, the Cimmerian nonetheless stood his ground. He fixed the Hierophant with a steely glare, refusing to be cowed.

"Let me tell you where I was, Conan of Cimmeria," Khotan-Kha said. "I was in the heart of the light, and there I encountered something I can scarcely comprehend, something as terrible as it is magnificent. There are worlds beyond worlds beyond worlds, and spaces between those worlds, and what lives in those spaces defies description. It is power, and it is malevolence, and it is wonder. I now know what the eye represents. It represents a void at the center of all creation. It is hopelessness and inanity and tragedy and the slow decay of everything. It gazes at us without compassion but also without judgment. It tells us that all we believe to be significant, is not. All that we strive for in our pitifully short lives is a waste of time. All we hold dear, an illusion. Nothing has meaning, meaning is nothing. We are..."

He groped for words.

"We are dust," he said at last. "Infinitesimal. We have no purpose in the cosmos. And to know this is to be liberated. How joyous it is to be free of consequences, free of obligations, free of scruples."

"Isn't that how you were anyway, Khotan-Kha?" Conan retorted. He was damned if he was going to show this hulking saurian monstrosity an ounce of fear.

"Whatever I was, I am far more so now. The Rupture, by chance, opened up a conduit between this world and the dimensional planes beyond, allowing the light to leak through. The light is just a tiny fraction of a power that exists over there, and I myself have now been imbued with an even tinier fraction of that power. It is mighty nevertheless. It is power not just to swat my enemies like the gnats they are; it is power to rove across the entire world, laying waste to human civilization wherever I go, until your race is obliterated just as mine has been."

"Enough talk, Khotan-Kha." Conan snatched up a hunk of brickwork as big as his own head and hurled it at the twenty-foot-tall saurian. It hit him smack in the face. Khotan-Kha, taken wholly by surprise, fell onto his backside.

He sprang upright and lashed out with one hand in retaliation. Conan was too nimble for him, however, ducking under the sweep of his arm.

"Not mighty enough," the Cimmerian jeered.

Khotan-Kha leapt into the air, his wingbeats loud as thunderclaps. His eyes shone with pure malevolence as he flattened his wings vertically and descended upon Conan, feet talons outspread.

With a desperate lunge, Conan dove out of the way. Khotan-Kha struck nothing but bare earth.

Conan scrambled to his feet, only to catch a sidelong slap from the Hierophant's wingtip. It sent him tumbling head over heels down the slope.

He fetched up in a heap of limbs, and as he gathered himself and rose again, he saw Khotan-Kha come running towards him, making the ground shake with his thumping footfalls. He evaded the charge just in time, but nonetheless caught a glancing blow from his adversary's leg. Once more he went flying, sliding headlong onto the earth.

In his heart of hearts, Conan knew the fight was futile. Here was as formidable an enemy as he had ever faced, and he did not even have a sword to defend himself with, nor any kind of weapon save his poniard—and he doubted the effectiveness of that against something as huge as this creature. Khotan-Kha's hide now looked much too thick for its blade to penetrate.

That left Conan with only his wits, his speed, and his strength to rely on, and these, for all that they were considerable, were not equal to this particular challenge. Khotan-Kha would wear him down and would eventually win. There seemed no other conceivable outcome. It was just a question of how long he could hold out.

The Cimmerian picked himself up, dusted himself off, and turned towards Khotan-Kha. "Is that truly the best you can do?"

"Why persist with these taunts, Conan?" said the giant testily. "They are pointless and only defer the inevitable."

"If they irk you, then they are not pointless."

Khotan-Kha laughed hollowly. "Did I not just explain to you the meaninglessness of things? I care naught for your petty satisfactions.

Slaying you is not to appease some sense of vengeance on my part. All I am doing is ridding myself of an impediment."

Conan glimpsed movement nearby. Hunwulf and Gudrun were sending Bjørn sprinting up to the crater's rim. He assumed they wanted him away from immediate danger, and he approved of the decision. He similarly wanted Bjørn gone, if only so that the lad would not have to see him being annihilated by Khotan-Kha. A Cimmerian had his dignity.

The Æsir couple, their son now out of harm's way, ran in the opposite direction, downslope. Conan could see they were coming to his aid and was grateful—for all the difference it would make.

"Impediment, am I?" he said to Khotan-Kha. "So be it. But impediments can hurt. I have proved that already, and shall prove it again."

He grabbed a fresh chunk of masonry and flung it at the Hierophant, then another, and another. A handy byproduct of his avalanche was that it had made plenty such ammunition available, and he used these makeshift projectiles to harry his opponent, bombarding him relentlessly, at the same time darting hither and yon constantly so as not to offer a stationary target.

Hunwulf and Gudrun picked up on his example and copied it. Whichever way Khotan-Kha turned, pieces of stone whizzed at him. Some he deflected with an arm or wing; the rest glanced harmlessly off his hide. Only a rare few seemed to cause him any pain.

"You understand that all we're doing is annoying him?" Conan said to his two allies. "A worthwhile goal, but we cannot keep it up forever."

"We do not have to," Hunwulf replied. "We just have to keep him occupied."

"Ah, a delaying tactic. We're buying time for Bjørn and the other children to get well away from here."

Hunwulf shook his head and shot Conan a meaningful look that Khotan-Kha did not see. Its import was quite evident. Some stratagem was in play, devised by him and Gudrun, and the Hierophant was not meant to learn its nature.

With a grim smile of acknowledgment, Conan renewed his efforts. He would not let up. He would give Khotan-Kha no quarter. He would carry on pelting him until his arms wore out.

The giant lizard-man elected to take flight, just as a well-aimed throw from Conan caught him on the side of the head. Gudrun moved in close so as to follow up Conan's accurate strike with one of her own, shying a small but sharp rock straight into the Hierophant's eye and arresting his flight.

"Witch! Harlot! Whore!" Khotan-Kha boomed. "That hurt!"

Gudrun's only response was to snatch up another rock.

Before she could launch it, however, a swipe from one of Khotan-Kha's wings fetched her a powerful blow to the shoulder. Gudrun staggered and collapsed.

Hunwulf let out a cry of alarm and hurried over to his wife's side. Before he could reach her, Khotan-Kha struck him down too with the same wing. Both Æsir lay sprawled on the ground, stunned.

Khotan-Kha prowled over to them. "I shall flatten you," he said, blood trickling down his face. The eye Gudrun had hit was damaged but still functional. "I shall make mincemeat of you all."

"No," Conan said. He punctuated the remark by flinging a particularly large morsel of building material at the Hierophant.

Khotan-Kha deftly caught the missile in midair and, just as deftly, sent it hurtling back whence it came.

Conan, for all his pantherish reflexes, was a fraction too slow in twisting aside. The piece of masonry made contact with his temple, a glancing blow but still enough to stagger. He went down on his knees, and for a while the world pitched and yawed sickeningly around him. He could not rise. His limbs refused to work as they ought.

In the meantime, Khotan-Kha made good on his promise of a moment ago. He leaned over the stricken Hunwulf and booted him heftily in the ribs. The impact sent the Æsir man spinning through the air like a ragdoll. He landed hard, limbs flailing. Prone on the ground, face in the dirt, he groaned.

Then Khotan-Kha bent down and plucked Gudrun up with both hands. He held her aloft, pinning her arms against her sides, bringing her face to face with him. The Æsir woman writhed and kicked in his grasp, to no avail.

"The boy who lobbed a knife into me earlier," the Hierophant said, "that was your son, was it not?"

"No mother could be prouder," Gudrun replied, gasping through pain.

Khotan-Kha shook her violently. Gudrun's head snapped this way and that.

"You will not break me," she said, after he relented.

"I think that is precisely what I shall do," came the reply. "Break you, bone by bone."

Suiting word to deed, Khotan-Kha tightened his grip on her, forcing a scream from her throat.

That was when Conan barged into him from behind.

The Cimmerian, though still woozy from the blow to the head, had forced himself to rise to his feet and run at their adversary. He rammed into Khotan-Kha at speed, planting his shoulder in the meat of the other's thigh. Khotan-Kha's leg crumpled under him, and he sagged to one knee.

Conan reared back to avoid a retaliatory strike from one of the Hierophant's wings. He circled round, seeking a fresh angle of approach.

In response, Khotan-Kha tossed Gudrun aside, realizing he had a more pressing matter to attend to.

Abruptly, Conan lunged at the giant lizard-man.

His head had not yet fully cleared, however, and his coordination was somewhat off. Not only that, Khotan-Kha had a far greater reach than he.

The result was that the Hierophant met the Cimmerian's sortie with a solid punch to the chest, halting him in his tracks.

The blow was such that it would have caved in the ribcage of a lesser man. As it was, Conan reeled, the wind knocked out of him.

Khotan-Kha came in to deliver a follow-up strike. Conan recovered just in time to catch his wrist in both hands.

The saurian giant bore down on the Cimmerian with all his might. Conan resisted, digging his heels in and shoving back.

The two of them stood locked together, Khotan-Kha towering over the barbarian. The Hierophant could have used his free hand to hit Conan, but it seemed he would rather engage in this kind of tussle for now, pitting his strength directly against the human's.

"I am going to crush you," he declared. "It is inevitable. How long do you think you can endure?"

Conan did not reply. All his energies were devoted to holding his own against the Hierophant. He could feel his legs beginning to buckle. His whole body was trembling, every muscle strained to its utmost, every sinew at breaking point. Khotan-Kha's strength had already been great, but now, with him newly enlarged, it was tremendous, far outstripping Conan's own. It was clear to anyone that there could be only one outcome to this test of might. Yet Conan was not prepared to go down without giving his all, right to the very end.

The Æsir couple, both still suffering after the severe mistreatment they had received at Khotan-Kha's hands, looked on dazedly from where he had deposited them. They were willing the Cimmerian to win this pitched struggle, even though they knew he could not.

Further, and further still, did Khotan-Kha bear down on Conan. Yet Conan withstood, the veins in his neck standing proud like whipcords, his teeth clenched together so hard they seemed fit to splinter.

Khotan-Kha, brow starting to furrow, brought his other hand into play, placing it atop the hand whose wrist Conan was grasping. Now the strength of both his arms was acting upon the Cimmerian, and Khotan-Kha put all his weight into it. Conan was bent almost double beneath the pressure. The Hierophant began chortling triumphantly. It seemed Conan might snap in twain.

At that moment, memories of Bêlit entered Conan's head, unbidden. He thought of the winged beast that had slain her. He thought of his failure to save her from its depredations. Fury filled him then, sending molten lava coursing through his veins, lending his sorely pressed muscles renewed vigor.

These Crom-damned lizard-people! A pox on them! He had killed countless Folk of the Featherless Wing, and now he was determined to finish the job.

This, if no other reason, must be why fate had sent a whole race of winged monstrosities his way: destroying them was not going to bring Bêlit back, but it might at least serve to exorcize his sorrow and expunge his guilt once and for all.

With his strength augmented by rage and hatred, Conan pushed back against Khotan-Kha ever harder.

The Hierophant's arms began to rise. All at once, his expression went from jubilation to disbelief.

Conan was levering Khotan-Kha's arms up. His body was straightening. A guttural roar of sheer brute defiance escaped his grimacing lips. With a last, maddened thrust he shoved Khotan-Kha away, letting go of that inches-thick wrist.

Khotan-Kha tottered backwards. He shook his head, scarce able to believe that this barbarian—a mere human, a creature one third his size—had managed to repel him.

"So," he said in surly fashion, "it would appear that yet greater might is called for. Very well. I know how to remedy that."

So saying, he turned and flew towards the Temple of the Light.

"Have we seen him off?" Hunwulf wondered, sounding more hopeful than convinced.

"Doubtful," said Conan, panting hard, soaked in sweat. His rage was abating, but simmered still. "If I don't miss my guess, he has gone to bathe in the light again."

And so it was. Khotan-Kha landed beside the fissure, knelt, and spread out his arms. He uttered an invocation to the light, inviting it to lend him more of its power.

The glow responded as though a living thing, reaching out and enfolding him. He was surrounded in a purplish-pink corona, reminiscent of the queer blue fire Conan had once seen dance across the mast and yards of the *Tigress* during a tropical thunderstorm. To his thinking, the light and Khotan-Kha had become inextricably linked since the Hierophant's immersion in it. The one was drawn to the other, like seeking like.

Conan and the Æsir couple looked on in astonishment and dismay as Khotan-Kha increased yet further in size. At the same time, the Hierophant became even less humanoid than before. Jagged dorsal plates sprouted all along his spine. His brow ridges extended to either side until they resembled horns. His wings grew to gargantuan proportions, while sentience all but vanished from his face, to be replaced by a brutish, animalistic leer.

By the time this second transformation was complete, lizard-man had become almost fully lizard. He was also nigh-on sixty feet tall.

The saurian behemoth reared away from the fissure. Peering up at the eclipsed moon, he beat his breast and uttered an ear-splitting roar, as if paying tribute to the celestial alignment that had made this extraordinary metamorphosis possible.

Then, head lowered, his narrowed gaze sought out the three humans.

"Ymir preserve us," breathed Gudrun.

"We are doomed," said Hunwulf.

"Spare me your prayers and your defeatism," Conan rumbled, "and prepare to fight."

He could not deny, however, that all seemed lost. Whereas before Khotan-Kha had been a daunting proposition, he was now patently unbeatable.

Nothing could save them—and after they fell, the whole world would follow.

25

The Poisoned Well

Nothing could save them, no.

But the snow-haired boy running down the slope with a broadsword in his clutches might at least help tip the scales ever so slightly their way; as might the handful of other children who came after him, each carrying a weapon too. Another of the children, a Stygian girl, bore a flaming torch.

Minutes earlier, Hunwulf and Gudrun had given Bjørn directions to Khotan-Kha's throne room and instructed him to take a group of his peers with him to fetch their armaments thence. Bjørn had gone as fast as his legs could carry him, accompanied by Zevia, X'aan, and a couple of the others.

Returning, they understandably balked at the sight of the towering saurian whose monstrous form now dominated the Temple of the Light. Yet they scarcely missed a step.

"Conan!" Bjørn cried breathlessly, brandishing the sword. "Yours!"

"Ho!" the Cimmerian replied. "Toss it here, boy!"

He caught it by the hilt and brandished it with satisfaction.

The titanic thing at the temple began lumbering up the rows of seating, whose carven stones crumbled under its massive tread.

Gudrun shooed the children back to the crater's rim, telling them to find refuge in a building. Bjørn protested, but his mother was in no mood to brook any argument.

"We can help," Bjørn said. "Layla can especially." He gestured at the girl with the torch. "She found that torch in the throne room. She can control fire."

"The daughter of Abrax and Aminah," said Gudrun, understanding. "Can you exercise your power at a distance, Layla?"

Layla nodded. "I think so."

"Very well. If you spy an opportunity to burn that monster, do so. But do it from a place of safety, understand?"

"Yes," said Layla.

"Then go. All of you. Now."

As the youths retreated up the slope, Gudrun selected a sword from the weapons they had retrieved, while Hunwulf picked up his trusty double-headed axe. Husband glanced at wife, wife at husband, and a look passed between them that spoke of love and trust and mutual understanding.

Conan, seeing this, found himself almost envying them their bond. It had held them together during their years of exile and peripatetic hardship, and it was holding them together now, granting them strength and courage as they faced certain doom. He had known such a bond himself—but the Queen of the Black Coast was dead.

He looked back at Khotan-Kha. Now that he had his broadsword again, all at once things seemed marginally less bleak. It was wondrous strange how without a sword he felt bereft, and with one he felt whole.

"I might yet die today," Conan muttered to himself, "but it is better to die armed than unarmed."

Khotan-Kha loomed close.

Then Conan, somewhat to his surprise, saw him stumble. Khotan-Kha's left-hand wing suddenly grew, becoming swollen and misshapen. Now twice the size of its counterpart on the right, it dragged along the ground as the saurian monster resumed walking. The wing had lost its leathery smoothness and seemed too heavy, too lumpen, to work anymore.

A moment later, Khotan-Kha stumbled again, and this time one side of his face bulged outward as though blighted by a host of sudden-grown tumors. The disfigurements of wing and face left him not only asymmetrical but looking even more grotesque.

"What is happening to him?" Hunwulf said.

"I know not," Conan replied. "But I wonder..."

He left the thought unexpressed, for once more Khotan-Kha was making his way resolutely up the slope.

Conan, Hunwulf and Gudrun girded themselves, and then battle was joined.

It was the equivalent of three minnows besetting a shark. Yet these minnows had teeth. Conan and the Æsir couple struck at Khotan-Kha's legs. They hacked at his feet and ankles, leaving slits in his hide which, though minor by his standards, still bled.

In return, Khotan-Kha bent low and swung at them with his hands. Any one of these swats, had it connected, would have pulverized its intended victim. His prodigious size, however, meant his movements were commensurately slow.

He tried stamping on the humans, too, with a similar lack of efficacy. As long as his opponents kept their wits about them, they could see his attacks coming in good time and take avoiding action.

"Yes!" Conan yelled to his allies. "That's it! Keep up the pressure on him!"

Hunwulf shot the Cimmerian a look that clearly asked if he was mad. The minuscule weals their weapons were inflicting on Khotan-Kha were pointless. Sooner or later his blows would land, and the three of them would be reduced to two, and eventually one, and then none.

Abruptly Khotan-Kha changed tactics. He snatched up a stone pillar that lay on the ground and wielded this like a gigantic cudgel. The pillar swept sideways through the air with a tremendous, low whooshing sound, sending his three adversaries diving for cover beneath its arc of swing. Raising it aloft, Khotan-Kha hammered it downward where they lay.

Conan sprang out of its path, avoiding the pillar by a hair's breadth as it crashed to earth. He saw Hunwulf and Gudrun scrambling away, unharmed, as Khotan-Kha lofted his stone cudgel once more.

All at once, Khotan-Kha's vast form stiffened and shuddered. There came a mighty creaking and rending sound as his right hand bloated, each finger becoming like some vast, fat slug. Unable to hold the pillar anymore, he dropped it. It plunged through the air and landed with a massive thump, breaking in half.

The great behemoth that was Khotan-Kha reeled on the spot, staring at his distended hand and bellowing as though in agony.

"It's as I thought. His growth is out of control," said Conan.

"Yes, I see that," said Gudrun. "He is losing integrity."

"He has been greedy. His body cannot contain the light's power. If this goes on, it'll leave him crippled, unable to move."

"Then we should not be fighting him. We should just turn tail and leave him to his own devices."

"No. Fighting him will encourage him."

"And that is a good idea?"

"Yes, because he'll become ever more bent on killing us and will want yet more power to help him accomplish that," said

Conan. "He will go back to the poisoned well and drink deeply from it again."

"Which will, through sheer surfeit, destroy him," said Gudrun.

"That is my guess."

"Might your guess be wrong?" Hunwulf asked.

"It might," the Cimmerian allowed.

With that, Conan swung his broadsword at Khotan-Kha's leg once again, and the Æsir couple likewise renewed their own slashing, smiting assault.

From the saurian behemoth's perspective, it must have been tormentingly frustrating. The tiny beings at his feet were inflicting constant pain on him, and he, for all his colossal size and might, could not seem to get rid of them. They scurried out of the way whenever he pawed at them. They were infuriatingly quick and agile, and he was hopelessly cumbersome by comparison.

Even as he rained down blows on his enemies, Khotan-Kha's gaze kept straying to the Temple of the Light. In those slitted reptilian eyes Conan could see need and avarice writ large. The light was calling to him, offering the promise of yet greater power. Khotan-Kha must have realized that this same power was deforming and disabling him, but nonetheless he craved it, craved *more*.

As for Conan, he was starting to tire. The constant harrying attacks on Khotan-Kha's legs, interspersed with the necessary evasive maneuvers, were taking their toll. His lungs were heaving. His limbs felt leaden. He could tell that the Æsir couple were likewise succumbing to exhaustion. He did not know how much longer any of them could carry on.

As he went in for one more assault on Khotan-Kha, the Hierophant's good hand swooped upon him, fingers outstretched. Conan swerved aside, but alas, too slow. Next thing he knew, he had been scooped up in that vast scaly paw and was being borne rapidly aloft.

Khotan-Kha gripped him around the torso with enough force to squeeze the breath from his lungs. Conan did not pause, however. His sword arm remained free, and he hacked and hewed savagely at the fingers that held him. Khotan-Kha was crushing the life out of him, yet the Cimmerian still fought back as best he could, slicing into the dense leathery hide of the saurian behemoth's hand—for all the difference it made.

He could feel his bones creaking under the pressure being exerted on them. His vision began to dim. Consciousness was slipping away from him.

That was when a tongue of flame several yards long shot through the air, striking Khotan-Kha in the face.

The flame originated from the crater's rim. It was born from the torch in Layla's hand, and she sent it hurtling like a dart, straight and true, from her to Khotan-Kha.

It blasted into the Hierophant, flattening against his thickly ridged brow and billowing outwards, scorching several square feet of his visage before it dissipated.

His roar of pain was volcanically loud. Reflexively, he let go of Conan.

The Cimmerian fell.

As it happened, Khotan-Kha had been holding Conan close to the side of his body at the time, not far from his left wing—the one that was misshapen and limply drooping.

Conan acted on pure instinct. He twisted in midair and struck out with his sword, plunging it into the wing. Grasping the hilt with both hands, he hung on as his weight carried him downwards, the blade ripping through the appendage's membranous flesh.

Thus was the rate of his descent slowed, the resistance of wing meat against sword acting as a brake, until all at once he reached the bottom of the wing and was tumbling through empty space again.

But it was a distance of no more than twenty feet from there to the ground. Conan landed hard, his knees bent to soften the impact. He rolled over and over, ending up in a ball some dozen yards from where he had come down.

Getting back to his feet demanded an almost superhuman effort. Every part of him hurt. Yet the pain, perversely, was comforting. It meant he was still alive, at least.

Hunwulf came rushing over to him, Gudrun following.

"Conan!" the Æsir man cried. "How in the name of all the gods did you manage that? If I hadn't seen it, I wouldn't have believed it."

"Never mind me," Conan replied, teetering on unsteady legs. "What about him?"

He peered up at Khotan-Kha. The saurian behemoth looked to be in a parlous state. His face was disfigured not just by those tumor-like growths but now by a large patch of flame-seared skin as well, while his bad wing had a jagged tear in it from top to bottom that was bleeding profusely.

Even as he looked on, Conan saw resolve enter Khotan-Kha's eyes.

He grinned, reckoning that this augured well.

"Khotan-Kha is stymied, and in pain, and he hates it," he said to Hunwulf and Gudrun. "He can think of only one thing to do."

As if proving the Cimmerian's point, Khotan-Kha turned and strode purposefully back down to the Temple of the Light. He stooped beside the fissure, his eyes gleaming avidly, and the light responded to his presence by shimmering upwards and flowing over him, embracing him like a lover. Tendrils of lambency writhed around his scaly flesh.

"Now to learn if I am right," Conan said, "or if I'm an addle-pated clodpoll who has made the greatest blunder of his life—and the last."

Khotan-Kha reveled in the light. He imbibed it like a drunkard supping on a chalice of fine wine. He let it crawl all over him. As it took effect, he began to enlarge further, in fits and bursts, and he emitted a raucous bellow of triumph.

This turned into a howl of distress as the growth continued unchecked, wildly, past the point of desirability. Helplessly, haplessly, Khotan-Kha bent; he twisted; he ballooned. His figure lost definition, becoming neither humanoid nor saurian, and his hide went the sickly color of gangrene. Limbs fused together. Torso and head merged into one. Wings became wedded to back.

The power of the light was too much for him, and he was devolving even as he expanded, degenerating into an enormous, undifferentiated, protoplasmic mass.

The horror of understanding dawned in his eyes. He had overreached. He had wanted more than he could hope to handle. The light was not his friend, nor had it ever been. The light belonged to something unfeeling, indifferent, something that tainted everything it touched. Its corruption had met his own, and now it was feeding him to the point of excess, and thus destroying him—and there was nothing he could do to stop it.

The enormous, shapeless entity that had once been Khotan-Kha flailed and churned and roiled. His mouth was open but no sounds emerged anymore. Beneath the rocking of his unfathomably immense bulk, the floor of the temple was smashed to smithereens. The fissure lay fully exposed, and the light poured out, untrammeled.

Conan had been watching Khotan-Kha's ghastly mutation with fascination. That turned to concern as he detected a distinct shift in the light's behavior. It was darkening and becoming agitated.

Strange energies began to fill the air. He felt the hair rise on his scalp and his skin break out in gooseflesh.

"I like this not," Conan murmured.

"Me neither," said Hunwulf.

The ground underfoot started quivering. Khotan-Kha's amorphous form was pulsing and throbbing, the light around him likewise. A reaction was building. Some critical point was being reached.

"I propose we withdraw," Conan said.

"I second that," said the Æsir man.

Gudrun, perhaps sensibler than both, was already on the move. The two men followed her upslope.

Behind them, Khotan-Kha was shuddering tumultuously, and the light around him was a maddened, kaleidoscopic blaze. It lit up the broken cityscape of Ghuht in all manner of awful, indefinable hues, while the shadows it cast were a thousand shades of gray, the color of cobwebs in nightmares.

Reaching the crater's rim, Gudrun called out to the children who were gathered there, her son among them. "We need to leave this place at once."

Bjørn relayed the instruction to the other youngsters, and in no time they were moving along, ushered by him, his mother, and the Kushite siblings, X'aan and Zevia.

"Stay close to one another," Gudrun urged, taking the lead, "but keep going, quick as you can. Stop for nothing."

Conan and Hunwulf fell in behind the group, there to help keep everyone together and chase any stragglers along, like sheepdogs with a flock.

The Cimmerian dared a last look back.

Down in the bowl of the crater, Khotan-Kha and the light had amalgamated into a single gigantic sphere. Crackles of purplish-pink incandescence shot across this orb's greasy green surface, like veins in marble.

Briefly, terrifyingly, these bands of light coalesced into the shape of an eye.

And not just any eye, but that from which the eye sigil was derived. Conan knew this without knowing how he knew it.

The eye gazed upon him, and for several moments the Cimmerian was rooted to the spot. He had never beheld anything so empty, so soulless, so redolent of the universe's vast, implacable aloofness. Nor had he ever felt so insignificant. In that eye's gaze he was not a grain of sand, not even a mote of dust. He was truly nothing.

It chilled him to the core, this awesome cosmic apathy. He did not feel hated or spurned. He just knew that nothing he did mattered. The battles he had fought—irrelevant. The money he had gained and spent—immaterial. The friends he had made and lost—unimportant. The love he had known with Bêlit—inconsequential.

He realized that this awareness would haunt him for the rest of his days, wherever he went, whatever he did. He might conquer a nation, become a king, accumulate more wealth than a man could ever wish for, and still it would all ring hollow.

Then, in a flash, the eye was gone, and the sphere collapsed in upon itself. There was an almighty silence, the opposite of a bang, the non-sound of implosion. The thing that had been Khotan-Kha vanished, and all that remained was the light.

But the light was dissatisfied. That was the only word Conan could think of to describe it. The light—or whatever animated the light—had taken its power back from Khotan-Kha, but this was not enough for it.

As he watched, slabs of shattered flagstone skittered towards the fissure and tipped over into it. What else remained of the Temple of the Light was also drawn in. The dais, the amphitheatrical seating, all broke up and went tumbling and rolling into the fissure, along with the debris from the landslide. The light, like a disgruntled investor clawing back his money, was recouping everything it had doled out, with added interest.

Conan feared that this process would not stop until the whole of Ghuht had been gathered into the light's bosom, and the whole of the Rotlands too. It was not happening fast but it was steady and inexorable. He found the sight weirdly mesmerizing to watch, but knew he could not linger. The light, as it undid all that it had created over the centuries, would surely think nothing of sucking him in, and the people with him, if they happened to be within its remit.

Their only option was to keep on fleeing; and perhaps, just perhaps, they could reach a place of safety before the light's work of violent reclamation was done.

26

That Dreadful Calculation

Out of Ghuht, into the Rotlands they went, and behind them, at their heels, all was demolition and destruction—an unpicking, a disassembling, a retrieving.

The jungle itself was succumbing to the light's remorseless draw. Trees disintegrated, becoming splinters and flinders that slid along the ground in a bristling, rolling tide. Insects were whisked along like iron filings attracted by a magnet. Larger animals were stripped of their flesh, crumbling into skeletal fragments.

Everything the light had ever touched and transformed was being unraveled, and the pieces were all heading in the same direction, converging on the fissure. Only Conan and those with him were going the other way.

It was like swimming against the pull of an undertow. The very air seemed against them, tugging at their limbs, resisting. The forces at play set the earth trembling. Every step was an effort.

Then there was the fact that the majority of the people striving to escape the light were children. Several of them were keening and gibbering in fright. They had to be coaxed, goaded, sometimes manhandled. Conan scooped up two of the very smallest and carried them along, one upon each shoulder.

They labored onward through the maelstrom, out of the valley that had been home to Ghuht for hundreds of years. The eclipse was passing and the moon's light returning, giving them a scintilla of illumination to see by.

Gudrun remained at the vanguard, and Conan called out to her, voice raised above the surrounding tumult. "Keep going south," he said.

"That is what I am doing," she replied.

"I thought so."

They had both had the same idea. Due south lay the river—the broad, turbulent river whose current flowed much faster than they were presently traveling. The river could bear along those who could stay afloat in it. The river could take them swiftly out of the Rotlands.

The one saving grace of all the light-induced chaos was that the Rotlands themselves were no longer dangerous. Flora and fauna that were falling apart could not do harm.

Still, it was tough going, and many of the children were getting tired and fractious, and Conan began to doubt they would all make it to the river. The idea of abandoning any of the youngsters was hard to stomach, but he wondered whether he might at some point be forced to make that dreadful calculation: sacrificing a few in order to save the majority.

Eventually, through the assiduous efforts of the adults—and with help from Bjørn, X'aan and Zevia—the entire party arrived at the beach by the river bend, where the rapids swept ceaselessly across the barrage of boulders. The children were footsore, filthy, and woebegone, and most of them looked as though they could not go another step. That was fine, though. As long as they could swim, they had a way out.

It transpired that not all of them *could* swim. A quick poll revealed, through a show of hands, that a dozen of them had never acquired the skill.

Conan's heart sank. To have got the youngsters this far through the foundering Rotlands, only to learn that roughly a third of them could not take advantage of their surest route to safety...

Again he pondered on that dreadful calculation. Could he do it? And could he live with himself afterwards if he did?

"You have a choice," he told them all. "Enter the water and take your chances, or stay here and perish. You know as well as I do that it is no choice at all. Swimming isn't so difficult. Just keep moving your arms and legs, and hold your head above the surface. The rest of us who can swim will try to support you. Now hurry. There's no time to waste."

He stepped into the moonlight-glittering shallows, reasoning that juveniles needed to be led by example. As he did so, he was greeted by a familiar but unwelcome sight.

"Oh, by Crom," he sighed, reaching for his sword.

The giant turtle that had proved such a hindrance earlier that day was back.

It must be the selfsame one, for its head was above water and Conan could see the neck wounds he had dealt; they were raggedly raw-looking but appeared to have closed.

Presumably this stretch of river was the turtle's territory, and Conan knew from experience that the beast did not take kindly to trespassers. He wondered why it was not succumbing to the light's decohering influence like everything else around it. He supposed that being immersed in the river, whose waters must surely originate outside the Rotlands and therefore remain untainted, was somehow insulating it from the light's effects, for now.

As the turtle swam towards him, a thought flashed into his brain, and he relaxed his grip on the sword hilt and retreated back up the beach. He beckoned to Bjørn.

"This is where you take over."

"You want me to kill that thing?" Bjørn said. "You can't be serious, Conan. That's a job for you, not me."

"Not kill it. I said take over. Control it."

"Control...?" Bjørn surveyed the huge outline of the turtle, finning ever closer through the night-black waters.

"Tame. Befriend. Whatever you did with that dog in Eruk, do the same here. Bring it under your command."

"But it's so much bigger than a dog, so much—"

"Just do as I say," Conan interrupted. "Now! We don't have much time."

The Æsir boy looked to his parents for affirmation. Gudrun said, "If Conan has in mind what I think he has in mind, then it is our best chance," while Hunwulf shrugged, uncritically deferring to his wife's judgment.

Bjørn stepped warily forwards. The turtle swam straight up to him, its huge beaky maw agape. Conan kept his hand on his sword hilt, poised to jump in at any second should Bjørn fail to dominate the creature. He would be able to behead it with one well-placed lop, he thought.

Bjørn squatted down on his haunches and held out a hand. The turtle halted in the shallows and peered at him with cold, chelonian appraisal.

For a short span of time, boy and beast regarded each other, and Conan, despite the tension in his body and the urgency of the moment, was fascinated to see how the turtle's demeanor clearly softened. Having looked as though it was going to attack Bjørn and make him its meal, now it was eyeing him inquisitively. Some unspoken communication was passing between the two of them and an accord was being reached.

"She's frightened," Bjørn remarked. "She can feel something happening to her. Something is dragging at her, eating at her from within."

"It is the light wresting its power back."

"She also says you hurt her, Conan."

"She tried to kill me. I was defending myself."

"She understands that. She doesn't hold it against you. It's just the way of nature."

"Do you have the thing under your command, Bjørn?" his mother asked.

"She and I have an understanding."

"Then let her know we need her help. If I am right, Conan wishes her to carry the children who can't swim."

"They can sit on her back," Conan said. "There should be room. The rest of us can go alongside, holding on to her if necessary."

Bjørn engaged in silent mental intercourse with the turtle, then nodded. "She consents."

Gudrun turned to the children. "Anyone who can't swim, climb onto the turtle's back. Don't be afraid. She won't harm you. Bjørn is her master now, and she is docile and will do his bidding."

"Think of her as a boat," Conan said, "and Bjørn the captain."

Tentatively the youngsters filed forward and clambered onto the turtle. Bjørn himself took up position at the front of the creature's shell, sitting with his legs astride her neck.

The turtle drew away from the beach with leisurely sweeps of her fins, moving from the shallows to deeper water.

"The rest of you," Gudrun said, "get into the river. Let the current carry you, but stay as close to the turtle as you can. If you tire, cling on to her for a while."

"Quick now," Conan said. The jungle on either side of the river was fast disappearing, as though being swept up by a huge, invisible broom.

Soon everyone was in the water, clustered around the giant turtle. The current caught them and they glided along. The children perched on the turtle's back looked anxious to begin with, but they relaxed as the beast, under Bjørn's stewardship, sedately bore them downstream. A couple of them even smiled.

Of those swimming, Conan made sure that the weaker, less capable ones kept hold of the skirts of the turtle's shell, and whenever somebody looked in danger of floating away from the group, he swam over and steered the stray back.

Initially the current was strong, but once they had put the rapids behind them, it mellowed to a gentler, more even flow. For an hour or so the river ferried them through the Rotlands, then past the narrow barren zone at the perimeter, after which the jungle on both banks reverted to ordinary forest. Gone was the Rotlands reek, and gone, too, was the sense of things falling apart around them.

Shortly afterwards, Bjørn announced that the turtle could not continue much farther.

"She's weakening," he said. "I think she may be dying."

"We can pull in to shore over there," Conan said, "by that clearing."

The children on the turtle's back disembarked onto dry land. The swimmers trudged out and sank down exhausted.

Conan stood beside Bjørn and the two of them watched the turtle cleave dumbly away through the water, heading back upstream.

"She knows she doesn't have long," the Æsir boy said with a tinge of sorrow. "She's returning where she belongs, knowing it is going to be her grave. She wasn't a bad animal, Conan. No animal is really bad. They just are what they are. They accept themselves, without shame or judgment."

"That," the Cimmerian avowed, "is something I can sympathize with."

The group made camp in the clearing on the riverbank and waited for dawn. The children were soon fast asleep, wrung out after their strenuous endeavors.

Hunwulf and Gudrun sat with Bjørn between them, keeping watch over him as he slumbered. Conan wondered if they would ever willingly let their son out of their sight again.

X'aan and Zevia, lying side by side, chatted together awhile before tiredness overtook them as it did their peers.

Soon the Æsir couple nodded off as well, leaving only Conan awake. He gazed up at the moon as the last of the eclipse's shadow retreated and it returned to being a simple bright disc, charting its slow course amongst the constellations.

As day broke, he looked upriver and saw, a quarter of a mile distant, the outermost edge of what was once the Rotlands. Where there had been a hideous parody of jungle, now there was nothing but scraped-raw earth. He pictured thousands upon thousands of acres of such barrenness extending in a rough circle around where Ghuht once stood, and reckoned that, in time, the land would return to normality. Plants would grow, animals would return. Nature would restore itself.

Alternatively, it might not, the soil too contaminated for such a revival; then here, for all time, would lie a desolate plain where few dared tread, a forbidden region like a scar upon the face of the earth.

Conan hoped for the former outcome but feared the latter.

A Stygian girl nervously approached, intruding upon his thoughts. "I want to thank you for leading us to freedom," she said.

"You're welcome. But answer me this. When Bjørn led you out of the tunnel at the Temple of the Light, many of you youngsters had blood on you, obviously not your own. How come?"

"We fought the lizard-people who were minding us. We..." She hesitated. "We had to kill them."

"I thought that might be it," Conan said.

"The girl who masters fire—Layla—she did the most, but we all joined in, even me, though I was loath to."

"You should feel no shame about it, lass. Your lives were at stake. You all did a brave thing together."

She shrugged, as though she would rather not talk about it any further. "You are hurt." She indicated Conan's numerous cuts and scrapes. "I can do something about that if you'll let me. I am a healer."

Conan grasped that this must be the girl whose mother had been persecuted by the people of their town as the murderer of her daughter—the widow woman Heqet, whom he himself had slain in order to spare her a long, agonizing death at their hands.

He did not have the heart to tell the child she was an orphan now. He was unsure how you broke such news to one of her tender years, and he hoped the responsibility would fall to somebody else, perhaps Gudrun.

All he said was, "I'm fine. I have had worse and will get well of my own accord. If you wish to fix someone, the Kushite lad X'aan has a broken rib or two."

The Stygian girl obligingly headed over to X'aan and ministered to him. Laying hands on his chest, she closed her eyes and murmured to herself, an invocation to some goddess. Visible relief passed over X'aan's face as her healing power took effect, and shortly he was prancing around and turning cartwheels to show that he was fully fit again.

Conan contemplated the many flesh wounds he had sustained this past day. All were smarting but had begun to scab over and heal. In addition, the river water had rinsed them clean, meaning infection was less likely.

A sudden insight struck him. The fissure whose arrival had partly destroyed Ghuht might itself be likened to a wound, a rift in the skin of this world that revealed another place within; and by the same token, the light that shone forth from it was comparable to blood oozing out. For five centuries the wound had remained open, and whatever the light belonged to had somehow not noticed the slow, incremental leaking of its lifestuff, perhaps because, to it, the loss was relatively trivial.

That was until Khotan-Kha had demanded too much from it, whereupon the injury had at last been noticed. The reclamation of the Rotlands, therefore, had been a kind of sealing-up process, cauterizing the wound. By that logic, the fissure should now be closed and, all being well, would remain so indefinitely.

It was a comforting thought.

Later that morning, Gudrun returned from a hunting expedition with a large, freshly slain warthog slung across her shoulders. She bled, skinned and gutted it, and in no time the carcass was skewered on a spit over a fire. Several of the children, drawn by the delicious aroma of roasting pork, sat watching the warthog cook, hunger in their eyes. Others of their number were playing together, or in huddles chatting.

Conan, seated on a rock at the edge of the clearing, marveled at how normally they were behaving.

The Æsir couple wandered over to him. "What are you thinking, Cimmerian?" Gudrun inquired.

"I always knew how resilient children are," Conan replied. "These ones here prove it. They have endured great trials and hardship, but to look at them now, you'd hardly know it. But we have a problem. What are we to do with thirty-odd displaced younglings? They must all be returned to their homes." Those that still have them, he added inwardly, thinking of the now-parentless Stygian girl.

"As it happens," said Hunwulf, "Gudrun and I have just been discussing that very thing."

"Now that we no longer need worry about Ragnar pursuing us," Gudrun said, "we are free to do as we please. We have agreed we will dedicate ourselves to escorting each and every one of the children back where they came from."

"A worthy enterprise," Conan said.

"I have no notion how long it will take—many weeks, I suspect— but we shan't rest until it is done. After that, who knows? It feels strange to think that we are no longer going to have to live on the run. We can settle down somewhere, anywhere we like."

"Except Eruk," Conan said. "The arrest warrant for Hunwulf remains in force there. The city watch are firmly in Baron Caliphar's pocket, and I'll wager he is unlikely to forgive and forget any time soon."

"Except there," Gudrun acknowledged, "and by extension the whole of Shem. Anywhere else, however, we can put down roots. Bjørn can have a normal life at last."

Conan cast a glance over at the snow-haired boy. He was using a stick to demonstrate the finer points of knife-throwing to some of the other children, while at the same time bragging about how through his mastery of this art he had helped end the menace of Khotan-Kha.

"You are lucky, both of you, to have a son like him," said the Cimmerian, "and to have each other."

"Is that yearning I hear?" Gudrun said in that deadpan teasing way of hers. "The sound of a man contemplating marriage and fatherhood?"

"No. Mayhap one day I shall take a wife and have offspring of my own. When, however, is another matter. For now, I like my freedom. That being said, were I ever to sire a son, I should want him to be like yours."

"We are lucky to have him," Gudrun said.

"Seconded," said Hunwulf, slipping an arm around his wife's waist and drawing her close. "Whatever miseries I may have in life—and there are a few—I always know that I am blessed with my family."

"Well, now you know what we have planned for ourselves, Conan," Gudrun said. "But what about you? What do you propose to do next?"

Conan had not given the matter much thought, but then he seldom did.

"No idea," he said with a shrug. "Just move on, see what awaits me."

"I foresee peril and adventure in your future," Hunwulf said.

"Your incarnations have told you that?"

"No," the Æsir man replied with a chuckle. "Anyone who has met you would be able to predict as much. You are the sort of man who roams incessantly, seeking whatever lies over the horizon. You go where fate or fancy leads you, and you take whatever comes your way, be it good or bad. The more that events test and challenge you, the more you relish them, and as long as there is food, and ale, and perhaps a supple, compliant maiden at the end of each day, you are content. All said and done, it is not a bad way to live."

"Aye," Conan agreed, and somewhere, distantly, he heard a lusty, approving laugh that he knew to be Bêlit's. "When you put it like that, it's not a bad way to live at all."

James Allison
Lost Knob, Texas

October 1935

Halston Knox
Anomalous Adventures
Chicago, Illinois

Dear Mr. Knox,

Thank you for your reply, and the contract that
came with it. I'm delighted you've agreed to take
the story, and I appreciate you congratulating
me on its merits. I hereby return the contract,
signed, and look forward to seeing my work in
print in your magazine.

I would be grateful if you could let me know
when the issue featuring the first instalment
is due to appear on the newsstands. I would also
be grateful if payment came promptly. I mean
no disrespect, but in the past the checks from
Anomalous Adventures have arrived sometimes
weeks or even months later than they ought. In
fact, I believe I am still owed money by you.

But that is all by the by. I note with
interest the comment in your letter about the
dark mystery at the heart of my tale. I wish
I could explain the nature of the light which
is the focus of the Folk of the Featherless
Wing's worship and the source of our heroes'
travails. I cannot wholly account for it
myself, and similarly I cannot wholly account
for what the eye sigil portends. I know only
that these things denote a great arcane evil.
I am as sure of that as I am of anything. It
is ancient and timeless, and its reach extends
through the eons, all the way to the present
day. I know that it bodes ill for humanity,
and every time I think about it I am gripped
with an abiding and fathomless dread.

I wish I could tell you, Mr. Knox, that this evil exists solely in the realm of fiction, but you know, for I have told you, that <u>Cult of the Obsidian Moon</u> is drawn from life. It is an account of events that did happen, back in the mists of prehistory, and I swear that the echoes of those events are still rippling through to the present day.

Sometimes, of late, I go out at night and look up at the moon, and I think of that same moon shining down in Hyborian times, and I think of how all times are one time, all eras one era, and of how I am alive in most of them as one of my previous selves, an embattled warrior forging a bloody path through his world. To me, what happened then happens now. There is little dividing past from present.

The eye sigil is likewise eternal, and its sinister import still lingers here in the twentieth century, our age of scientific wonders and ever accelerating progress. It threatens us, as it did the barbarian Conan and my alter ego Hunwulf and all those with them. It is, I fear, a harbinger of doom.

By all means dismiss this as the ramblings of a crazy author. We writers are renowned, perhaps justly, as an oversensitive, often mentally unbalanced lot. You'll have had plenty of experience of that in your role as editor. I would not blame you for thinking me quite mad.

All I can say is, I wish I were, Mr. Knox. I wish I were.

Yours faithfully,
James Allison

AFTERWORD

When I was eleven years old, my grandmother gave me a book token which I promptly blew on the first six volumes of the Sphere paperbacks reprinting Conan's adventures. These were the UK equivalent of the Lancer editions in the US, with those ravishing, irresistibly dynamic cover paintings by Frank Frazetta.

I already knew about the character, having read several of the Marvel Comics adaptations by Roy Thomas and Barry Windsor-Smith. I liked those well enough, but the original prose stories by Robert E. Howard himself were even more enthralling. It was like starting out with decaf coffee and then going on to the fully caffeinated version. My eyeballs popped. My brain zinged. I couldn't get enough of this brawny barbarian who approached everything in life lustily, from vanquishing devious villains to slaying foul monsters to wooing ample females.

I had become a confirmed Howardite, and it was the start of a lifelong passion. I have read the vast majority of his works, written during that extraordinary decade-long burst of creativity that ended prematurely only because his life ended prematurely. I have constantly drawn from and been inspired by his stories during my own writing career. His mastery of pace and language are, in my view, second to none. Though often ghettoized—and dismissed—as just a pulp-fiction fantasy author, Howard is truly one of the all-time greats.

So when I was offered the opportunity to write some Conan of my own, I jumped at the chance. (I would say jumped at it with pantherish speed and litheness, but I am a middle-aged Englishman, not a battle-born, sword-toting Cimmerian in the prime of life.) I could hardly believe my luck, and this book, *Cult of the Obsidian Moon*, came out of me at an astonishing rate, like a dam bursting. It was as though it had been lying latent within me for over forty years and could not wait to see the light of day.

I'm indebted to George Sandison and Daquan Cadogan at Titan Books for giving me this chance, and to everyone at license holder Heroic Signatures—including Chris Butera, Jay Zetterberg and Fredrik Malmberg—for trusting me to do the job.

I'm also grateful to super-scribe Jim Zub and his adept artistic collaborators for allowing me to add to their excellent Black Stone series of Conan comics, also published by Titan. This novel can be read by those who don't have any knowledge of the comics but contains some references and Easter eggs that will give it added spice for those who do.

The eleven-year-old me, if he could see me now, author of my own Conan adventure, would be running around in circles and dancing with joy. The modern-day me—much older and nowhere near as fit and agile—is content to do a sedate little shimmy on the spot.

And as for my grandmother, now long deceased... I hope, wherever she is, she'll be thinking, "That was money well spent."

—J.M.H.L

ABOUT THE AUTHOR

James Lovegrove is the *New York Times* bestselling author of *The Age of Odin*. He has been shortlisted for many awards including the Arthur C. Clarke Award, the John W. Campbell Memorial Award, and the Scribe Award. He won the Seiun Award for Best Foreign Language Short Story in 2011, and the Dragon Award in 2020 for *Firefly: The Ghost Machine*. He has written many acclaimed Sherlock Holmes novels, including *Sherlock Holmes and the Christmas Demon*. As well as writing books, he reviews fiction for the *Financial Times*. He lives in Eastbourne in the UK.

THE HEROIC LEGENDS SERIES!

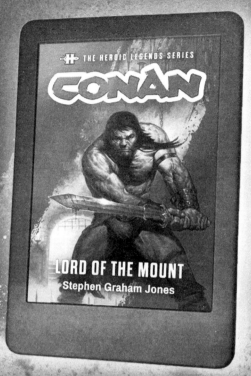

THE HEROIC LEGENDS SERIES

CONAN

LORD OF THE MOUNT
Stephen Graham Jones

Also available now:

CONAN:
BLACK STARLIGHT

JOHN C. HOCKING

SOLOMON KANE:
THE HOUND OF GOD

JONATHAN MABERRY

CONAN:
THE CHILD

BRIAN D. ANDERSON

CONAN: THE SHADOW
OF VENGEANCE

SCOTT ODEN

BÉLIT:
SHIPWRECKED

V. CASTRO

BRAN MAK MORN:
RED WAVES OF SLAUGHTER

STEVEN L. SHREWSBURY

CONAN: TERROR
FROM THE ABYSS

HENRY HERZ

CONAN: LETHAL
CONSIGNMENT

SHAUN HAMILL

SOLOMON KANE:
THE BANQUET OF SOULS

STEVEN SAVILE

BÉLIT:
BONE WHISPERS

MICHAEL STACKPOLE

CONAN: THE HALLS OF
IMMORTAL DARKNESS

LAIRD BARRON

EL BORAK: THE SIEGE
OF LAMAKAN

JAMES LOVEGROVE

CONAN

CITY OF THE DEAD

By JOHN C. HOCKING

TWO EPICS IN ONE HARDCOVER!

The long-awaited follow-up to *Conan and the Emerald Lotus*
brings John C. Hocking back to the sagas of the Cimmerian.

In *Conan and the Emerald Lotus*, the seeds of a deadly,
addictive plant grant sorcerers immense power, but
turn its users into inhuman killers.

In the exclusive, long-awaited sequel *Conan and the Living
Plague*, a Shemite wizard seeks to create a serum to use as
a lethal weapon. Instead he unleashes a hideous monster
on the city of Dulcine. Hired to loot the city of its treasures,
Conan and his fellows in the mercenary troop find themselves
trapped in the depths of the city's keep. To escape, they must
defeat the creature, its plague-wracked undead followers,
then face Lovecraftian horrors beyond mortal comprehension.

TITANBOOKS.COM

CONAN

BLOOD OF THE SERPENT

By S. M. STIRLING

Mercenary, thief, soldier, usurper... CONAN OF CIMMERIA

Conan finds himself in Sukhmet, aka "the arse-end of Stygia."
Serving as a sword for hire, he fights alongside soldiers
of fortune from Zingara, Koth, Shem, and other lands—
a hard-handed band of killers loyal to anyone
who pays them well.

In a tavern he encounters Valeria of the Red Brotherhood,
a deadly swordswoman. When she runs afoul of an exiled
Stygian noble, things take a deadly turn, embroiling her and
Conan in the schemes of a priest of the serpent god Set.

The first new Conan novel in over a decade, *Blood of the
Serpent* leads directly into one of Robert E. Howard's most
famous stories, "Red Nails." As a bonus feature that
story is included in this volume.

TITANBOOKS.COM

CONAN THE BARBARIAN

THE OFFICIAL MOTION PICTURE ADAPTATION

By L. SPRAGUE DE CAMP AND LIN CARTER

In 1982, Robert E. Howard's iconic literary antihero, CONAN, slashed his way from page to screen after a perilous decades-long journey. With its potent mix of epic vistas and bloody battles, CONAN THE BARBARIAN thrilled moviegoers around the world and launched the film career of Arnold Schwarzenegger.

To mark the occasion, CONAN authors and editors L. Sprague de Camp and Lin Carter were tasked with translating the visions of filmmakers John Milius and Oliver Stone back to the printed page in this rollicking novelization of the original screenplay.

Heroic Signatures is proud to bring this sublime work of sword and sorcery back into print!

TITANBOOKS.COM

For more fantastic fiction, author events,
exclusive excerpts, competitions, limited editions and more

VISIT OUR WEBSITE
titanbooks.com

LIKE US ON FACEBOOK
facebook.com/titanbooks

FOLLOW US ON TWITTER AND INSTAGRAM
@TitanBooks

EMAIL US
readerfeedback@titanemail.com

FOR EVERYTHING CONAN RELATED
conan.com